Love Covers

Center Point
Large Print

**This Large Print Book carries the
Seal of Approval of N.A.V.H.**

Love Covers

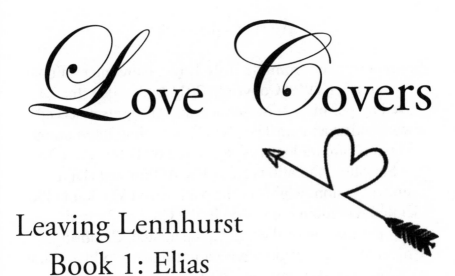

Leaving Lennhurst
Book 1: Elias

JULIA DAVID

CENTER POINT LARGE PRINT
THORNDIKE, MAINE

The text of this Large Print edition is unabridged. In other aspects, this book may vary from the original edition. Printed in the United States of America on permanent paper. Set in 16-point Times New Roman type.

ISBN: 978-1-64358-397-6

The Library of Congress has cataloged this record under Library of Congress Control Number: 2019946824

I dedicate this novel to all those who give their lives to help children reach their potential. Besides parents, step, grand, birth, foster and adoptive, I'm honored to know many teachers, church volunteers, social workers and the like.

Without your smiles, touch, prayers, words of hope and direction. Where would our world be?

Astounding Holly Caldwell, *you better know I'm talking about you.*

Above all, love each other deeply, because love covers over a multitude of sins. Offer hospitality to one another without grumbling. 1 Peter 4:8-9 NIV

Chapter 1

Greenlock, Ohio
1866

L AUREN CAMPBELL BLEW out the single flicker of light and darkness enveloped her small upstairs room. Thankfully, death had given her the day off.

Resting her cheek on her cool pillow, she massaged her neck, trying to remove the knots and kinks with her dry and cracked hands. She yawned. After working all week on Mrs. Wiggin's funeral, her hands were paying the price of the harsh embalming solutions.

Today had brought some needed diversion. At least a day without funeral work enabled her to start the sweater for her father. The pattern wasn't too difficult, and knitting relaxed her, removing her mind and nose from the smell and sight of death. She pulled the covers close and rolled to her other side having memorized the late night sounds from Main Street, Greenlock by heart. Even on the second story of her father's funeral home, she could hear the jangling sounds of poor piano playing coming from the bar down the street. Occasionally, a good argument broke out.

Such simple entertainment—listening to people who had had too much to drink.

She flipped to her back and pulled her thick curly hair to the side, as she heard a wagon with two, maybe three horses.

Please just keep rolling by, please, oh please, she thought. "It's late, and I'm tired," she moaned softly, flipping to face the wall and pulling the covers tightly under her chin. She closed her tired eyes, and snuggled in.

The wagon slowly creaked and rattled closer, but then no one ever rushed to pull up to a funeral home; nothing much ever happened in Greenlock, Ohio. She pulled the covers tighter. *I hope they just lost a dog or need the doctor.*

The wagon stopped outside. Lauren rose up on one elbow, listening. Men's voices, maybe two of them, floated up from the street.

They pounded on the front door.

She threw her legs out from under the warm covers, her feet hitting the cold floor. She rose to lean over her night table and pulled the curtain back. "What in the world? We are closed," she muttered to the window, grinding her teeth.

Her father had started drinking by midafternoon. He'd barely touched his dinner of barley soup. He would be in no condition to take a business call. She peered through the shadowy night and saw what looked like three bodies in the back of the wagon.

"Please go away, please . . . they'll still be dead in the morning, then my father can help," she whined, rubbing her face. The large man at the door took out his pistol and banged its handle against the door.

"Mr. Campbell. It's Sheriff Dodd. Can you open up?" He rapped on the door again. Another man cupped his hands, peering in their parlor window. Looking up, he unexpectedly saw her. Gasping, she clutched her gown's collar and pulled back out of sight.

"For heavens sakes, this has to beat all." She flipped her nightgown up and over her head and threw it on her bed. Finding her corset under the chair, she pulled it on jerking the strings into a bow. "Ouch." She tried to adjust it, so it didn't cut off the circulation in her chest. Fingering an opening in her stockings, she fed her toes in then attached her stockings above her knee. Seeing her petticoats rumpled in the corner, she rolled her eyes. Her brown dress and heavy apron would suffice.

"Laurie," her father's voice echoed up the short hallway. "Can you come down and help me?"

"I'm coming." She called, shoving her toes into her shoes. Grabbing her thick, curly hair, she pulled and twisted it up on top of her head, shoving a few clips here and there.

"Laurie!"

"I said, I'm *coming*." She called, jogging down

the stairs, tying the apron on around her waist.

Stopping in a huff at the parlor entrance, she noticed the sheriff, his deputy, and her father all looking at her.

"Miss Campbell." The sheriff nodded. "Sorry for the late hour."

Lauren looked down, not making eye contact with any of them.

"I was just telling your father we caught a lucky break tonight. We've been tracking this gang for months. These three lowlifes have been involved in selling illegal ammunition after they escaped from prison. They're deserters from the Union forces."

"Can you bring the wagon around the back alley?" Lauren motioned to them. Who cares who they were or what they had done, they're dead now. She turned to go down the basement stairs, and the sheriff kept recalling the night of guns and glory as if her father would remember any of this in the morning.

She lit the lanterns in the morgue area, then jerked the heavy doors open so the wagon could fit down the ramp and unload the bodies. The sheriff and her father came down the basement stairs.

"Let's put them on the ice table." *So I can try to get back to bed.* She signaled to the wagon driver to stop. "Father, can you help me with the ice?" She glared at him, waiting for him to acknowledge her, but his bloodshot eyes already conveyed his answer.

He pulled his old brown robe together at his chest. "I haven't been feeling well." He glanced at the sheriff.

"Forget it. I can do it." She pulled the lid off a large thick steel box, letting it thud onto the dirt floor.

"Give me a minute, miss, and I can help ya." The sheriff had already grabbed one of the men by the boots as the other lawman carried him under the arms. Lauren grabbed her thick gloves—her hands had seen enough today, and now this. She took the pick and stabbed at the large chunk of ice as chips pecked her in the face. She stopped and grabbed the broken ice and slid it onto the tray under the table. Three stinking outlaws. This would take all night. She bit her bottom lip hard.

The younger deputy took the pick from her. "Here, I can do this." Without looking at him, she flung the heavy gloves off.

Walking around the ice table, over to the desk, she grabbed her tablet and pencil. Dropping her chin, she shook her head. The sheriff was back telling her father detail by detail of the excitement of the night. Well, for Greenlock, it's probably the excitement of the year.

"Excuse me—time of death?" She interrupted.

"Can you go ahead and pronounce them,

Laurie?" Her father peeked around the animated sheriff's large bulk.

Lauren pulled the clock up to the lantern light. She moved around the deputy who was helping load the ice chunks under the table. Glancing at the three bodies, she laid two fingers against the first one's neck. "Eleven-forty." Quickly she pressed her fingers against the second one's blood-caked beard. "Eleven-forty-one." She moved around to the other side of the table and stopped.

She'd seen him before. What—two, three months ago? That crazy hair, and fuzzy nest for a beard, how could she forget? Long twisted locks of hair were pulled back with a leather strap. Half man, half animal. She could tell he was trouble. *Good riddance.* "Eleven-forty-two." She refused to touch him. This night, their blood-soaked, bullet-riddled bodies were fast burning away her good graces.

"I need their names to file the death certificate." Lauren waited, but the sheriff still rambled on.

"I can get them for you," the other lawman said.

"The filing is five cents." She scribbled on her tablet.

"Okay." He nodded.

"Plain pine coffins?" She never looked up. "Those are a dollar."

"Fine."

14

"Gravediggers for three will cost ya about two dollars."

"The county will pay."

"Headstone or plain wood cross?"

"I suppose plain."

Still scribbling notes, she asked, "Expect anyone is coming for the deceased? Or just bury them in the pauper cemetery?"

"Ahh . . ."

"These clothes or new?"

"Ahh . . . Sheriff?" The skinny young deputy frowned.

The sheriff finally turned and joined the conversation. "Yeah, just bury them in the indigent area behind the Catholic church. The priest can do some last rites or whatever."

"Those are *before* you are dead," Lauren grumbled into her tablet.

"Wait." The sheriff stepped toward her. "I want them photographed."

Lauren wilted. "There are two camera boxes in town," she pointed out. "The Land Improvement Office has one, but I understand it's always out. And Mr. and Mrs. Waxner have the other one."

"I know the Waxners." The sheriff nodded. "I'll ask them tomorrow."

"We'll have the coffins ready, the diggers digging, and I will check with the priest. Without new clothes that comes to six dollars."

"Send the bill to the county."

"And you will have Mr. Waxner here tomorrow. They need to be in the ground by day two." Lauren handed the sheriff her tablet. "Please sign here."

The sheriff signed and gestured to the other man to quit chipping the ice and get the wagon out. He turned and patted her father on the back. "So sorry to hear you are under the weather, Mr. Campbell. Good thing your girl knows this mortuary job. She's a rare one." He nodded to Lauren as they climbed the basement stairs.

Lauren clenched her jaw, pursuing her lips in a line. *Rare one? Hardly. More like abnormal one.* She came up behind them and opened the parlor door for the sheriff. She knew she should be polite and thank him for protecting the little town of Greenlock. Maybe bid him a restful evening. But no matter how she tried, goodwill would not rise past her anger. It was late, and she was tired. Mrs. Wiggin's family had insisted on everything under the sky and now this.

The sheriff let himself out and reached up to jump up on the bench of the blood-soaked wagon. She let out a long sigh and closed the door. Her father started up the stairs, shoulders slumped, his robe belt trailing loose behind him.

"Can you catch the lanterns in the basement, Laurie? Oh, and we forgot to ask if they'd already gathered their valuables. That too, huh?" He didn't turn to see the daggers in her eyes as he closed the door to his room.

16

Chapter 2

LAUREN SAT UP in bed rubbing her face, dreading another bleak day at March's end. Blowing out a sigh, she rehearsed ideas and plans to gather her mother's things and find a way to join her in Denver City. It had been over a month since she had received a letter from her mother or her sister, Cammi. Neither had ever invited her to join them—she frowned out a huff. She had wanted to ask her father a hundred times how parents that could no longer live together could split the family in two. But she already knew, she was the oldest and had the constitution to help her father in the business. He couldn't run this place without her. What a lot in life.

She pulled herself out of bed and froze. Smacking herself on the forehead, she dropped her chin to her chest. Being so tired after washing her cracked hands last night, she never returned to the basement to turn the lamps down. *So what, it's just oil. Who really cares?* Her father would never know. He certainly wouldn't check. She yanked her skirt hook closed.

Two years ago, her mother had left. Her father's melancholy had gone downhill fast. Sadness is one thing, but he'd given up on life, failing to find the energy or spur for much of anything beyond liquor, forcing her to do his job and hers.

Entering the small kitchen, she started the fire in the stove and made the coffee. A rare one the sheriff called her last night. Maybe he didn't mean it, but it felt like an insult. Everyone in this town knew she was the mortician's daughter. How could she ever have a real life here? It didn't take more than a half a brain to realize she handled dead bodies. She dressed them, fixed their hair, added some rouge, and posed them. Yes, she listened to everyone tell the wonderful stories of their loved ones. She would nod and masquerade a compassionate smile but living the lie that she could shoulder all this was crushing her.

As much as she sympathized for their loss, no one yet had given a second thought to getting to know her, the real Lauren. They hugged and held each other, but no one would ever touch her. She was contaminated, and she didn't blame them. She'd never be invited to their table, sharing polite conversation on salting the dead. No decent folk in this town would ever introduce their son to her.

Waiting for the water to heat, she walked by the mirror in the parlor. Her reflection glared back at her. The tiredness in her eyes probably aged her past her twenty years. Looking closer, she patted her pale cheeks. She stretched her lips apart, teeth straight. Her teacher in primary school had told her to cheer up after the children teased her about living with dead people.

"Girl as pretty as you doesn't need to be sad," the teacher had said. It stopped her tears that day, but her sense of seldom belonging never went away. That was years ago. She walked back to the kitchen to pour her coffee. None of that mattered now.

The oil still burned as she went to her desk in the basement to look over her list. Her father could sleep till ten, then he would need to get to work on the coffins. She glanced over where the three men lay shoulder to shoulder on the ice bed. The first two were of average height, but the third beast was big. It wasn't her problem; her father could make the adjustments.

She looked back at her tablet. Better meet with Father Michael within the hour. He would need time to find some young men looking for work to dig the graves. Mr. Soure had the crosses in stock at his woodshop. It was Friday, but she should be able to get the certificates to the courthouse if the sheriff returned with their names. She let out a tired sigh. Her father had asked her to check for valuables. If the sheriff wasn't so enamored with his tale of blazing guns, he could have done it himself last night.

She walked to the first body and pulled his

pants pockets inside out, nothing. Grimacing, she pushed his stiff body onto his side and reached into his back pants pocket. A pouch of nasty snuff. She left it. Unbuttoning the bottom of his bloody crusted shirt, she found a leather billfold tucked in his waistband. She flipped it open, a few dollars and an old, faded, creased photo of a little boy. "My, my." *Another fatherless child,* she sighed. Glancing over her shoulder, she flung it on the desk.

The second man had a large hole in his shoulder, arm dangling loose over his blood-soaked chest. *Probably shot at close range and bled to death,* she sighed. His body was wedged between the other two, and she couldn't really move him. Her father could do it. She sneered at the third body. Months ago, she had been minding her own business while paying for some penny nails at the hardware store—another thing she'd taken over for her father. This criminal had stepped too close to her in line. His rogue smile underneath that rat's nest beard was highly inappropriate, and he even had the nerve to say *"nice"* while looking her over like a stock mare for breeding.

The public mocking scalded her. Maybe worse than any of the others, the only person who ever looked at her like she was a woman had to be a troublemaking barbarian. Spinning on her heel and walking away that day seemed like too little recourse for such rudeness. "If you live by the sword, looks like you die by the sword," she mused aloud, and as she reached in and pulled his pants pockets inside out, a small item in a wrapper fell out.

"Is hell always this—cold?" someone asked from the table.

Lauren squealed and flew back as if invisible hands had pushed her. She landed with a splat into the mud puddle the melting ice had created on the floor, and the wrapper and whatever was in it flew into the air. Her skirt was soaked, but she quickly scrabbled backward digging in with her heels until her back hit the big double doors.

Did that corpse just talk?

She gripped her neck to hold her heart from beating out of her throat. Suddenly feeling the cold water soaking through to her drawers, she stood up quickly. "Did you just speak?" She panted, arms looking for support against the heavy wooden doors.

He slowly raised his hand, a thumb in the air.

"Good heavens!" She nervously scanned the muddy basement. Why didn't she check . . . last night? He wasn't supposed to be here. The sheriff should have—

"Can I ask a favor?"

"No! Of course not." She pressed her back harder against the doors, trying to steady herself.

"I looked around last night . . ." His words were clipped, stuck between small groans. "Just one

21

blanket . . . would be nice. I hate being cold."

Lauren let out a constricted grunt. "Oh, really?" She couldn't believe she was conversing with a dead man—well presumed dead. "As soon as I get the sheriff here for you, you can ask *him* for a blanket." Her words got caught in her irregular breaths.

"Could you please—put that—wrapper back—in my pocket, then?" He still didn't move, just a little movement from his beard. "It's important to me. I'd do it myself, but I can't seem to move. I have no strength."

Lauren leaned forward on her toes. His voice seemed weak and gentle, and his eyes had yet to open. The blood soaked into his shirt was real. Maybe he was dying. What if she ran to the sheriff and by the time she got back he was dead? She would look ridiculous. The wrapper laid between the legs of outlaw two and the one who was supposed to be a dead man.

As long as his eyes were closed, she braved the four silent steps forward and reached for the wrapper. His hand shot up and grabbed her wrist. She sucked in a loud gasp and tried unsuccessfully to break his hold. "Let go!" she growled. Her weight held taut against the cold table. Straining, she pulled at his fingers with her other hand. Unmoving, he held her fast.

"You were so sneaky. I thought you were going to steal it." His eyes started to break open.

"Sir, I said, let go!" She could drop a quick elbow where blood soaked his shirt—it would probably kill him straight away.

"Wrapper—pocket." His eyes rolled back, he swallowed hard and squinted, glossy-eyed at her.

She took the old wrapper and shoved it in his pants pocket, now more humiliated that she had been touching the pants of a real man—a live one anyway.

He let go so quickly, she staggered back and clutched her wrist. "I wish my father had seen that. He would save the sheriff the trouble of hanging you. One more bullet should do you in for good."

"Mmm hmm." His eyes fell back closed. "Going to hell twice."

"You know you are not in hell." She glared at him. "Not yet, anyway."

"What's your name?" He let out a low moan. "You look familiar?"

"That's none of your business." She needed her father to wake up and watch him while she went for the sheriff.

"*I have no strength,* he says," she mumbled, mimicking his exaggeration while rubbing her wrist. "Healthy, he could probably bend nails." *What a liar the man was.*

If she opened the big double doors, he might try to get out. Her wrist still stung from his grip. If she headed up the stairs to the parlor, he might follow her and attack her father unaware.

"I've never had a sweetheart. Can I call you sweetheart before I die and go to hell?"

"Stop being ridiculous!" She rubbed her forehead. "I think you landed on your head after that gunshot knocked you off your feet."

"Humph." He frowned. "I'm Elias Browne; I am twenty-six. I think. I grew up at Lennhurst Asylum Hospital. . . ."

"That explains a lot." Lauren took another look at his hair. Those long, fuzzy ropes were probably full of lice and . . . Her lips curled and nose wrinkled.

"I have a sister named Anna."

"How does one grow up in a hospital?" She knew something was wrong with him.

"My mother was crazy," he whispered.

Lauren shook her head, why was she even having this conversation? Another absurd moment in her absurd life. She needed to stop this and go for the sheriff herself. Searching around the damp basement, she needed to find something to tie him up with. Maybe his leg to the ice bed, or his wrist to dead man number two.

"I won't call you sweetheart if you do me just one favor?" He still hadn't moved an inch.

"Get you a blanket?" Sarcasm, though unusual from her, spewed from her mouth. This time she wouldn't be tricked.

"Nope. Will you help me stay dead?"

Chapter 3

HELP YOU STAY dead?" she shot back. "I told you, you are alive, barely, but alive."

"Just listen to me for one more minute, Miss . . ." His tone strained and airy with his question hanging between them.

"Lauren." She slapped her palm on her forehead. Dang nab it, she fell right into that one, like she was having a conversation with a proper civilized person. His head finally shifted toward her; his eyes were puffy slits with watery blue behind them.

"Miss Lauren, I want to stay dead. Just not in a box—underground."

His pale cheeks wrinkled, he looked much older than twenty-six. He tried to look at her. Uneasy in body and spirit, she didn't want to see his pain-filled eyes, so she looked to the ground.

"Help me," he pleaded.

Fresh resolve flooded her senses. "So when the photographer shows up to take your picture and my father goes to put you in the coffin, from where you will be lowered into a deep hole and covered with packed dirt, I'm supposed to help you? How?" She shook her head. "Don't bother to answer that, because I wouldn't help you in a million years."

"Tell me what you want. I have money."

"I also have money, sir. I work for a living. Unlike those who steal and kill their way through their *very short life.*"

"Ouch." His eyes squeezed shut. "Now my feelings can suffer along with my external suffering."

Lauren chewed on her bottom lip, full of her own pain and self-doubt of late, although, she rarely attacked others. "You know me from the hardware store. I was in line, and you came up behind me. You were rude to me, mocking my appearance."

"Yes, that's right." He glanced over at her. "How did I mock you?"

"You said, 'nice.'" Why was she telling him this? Could she be this starved for conversation?

"Telling a woman that she looks nice is offensive?"

"That's not what you meant. You looked me over, your eyes belittling me."

He slowly raised his hand to rub his brows, a low groan escaping. "I assure you, Lauren, you are lovely, beautiful in face and body. I was admiring you."

For a split moment, she wished she could believe him. He was probably just trying to gain assistance from her. But a criminal? How

26

gullible could she be? She glared at him, eyes narrowing. "It was an inappropriate thing to say to a stranger," she turned her nose up as she delicately sniffed.

"For that, you may prosecute me as guilty."

Someone pounded on the large double doors, and Lauren jumped. Thank God, the sheriff had come.

"Miss Campbell?" A man called outside the doors.

Lauren took a deep breath and pushed the large door open, wincing at the bright light.

A short man in a brown suit tipped his derby looking past her. "I'm Mr. Waxner, I-I—" He kept looking over her shoulder and Lauren looked over his shoulder, not seeing the sheriff or his assistant anywhere.

"I brought my camera and stand. I usually don't do well in small spaces. The mortuary is a bit difficult for me. I did pound on your front door. No one answered."

Lauren hid her impatience and bit her bottom lip. "Did the sheriff say anything about coming this morning?"

"No, no. He said he was having breakfast at his mother's." He swallowed, crinkling his nose. "Are they going to smell?"

"Not yet." Lauren tried to push the door back farther. Certainly, the other lawman should be coming with the names. She stretched out to look left and right down the alley. It was empty. *Where are they?* Feeling a headache coming on, she helped Mr. Waxner set up his equipment. Watching the stillness of the three bodies, she stepped away from Mr. Waxner. "I need to go see to my father. He hasn't been feeling well. Will you be okay?"

"Oh, no, Miss. I-I—can't be alone here. You need to stay. Trust me, I will not be long."

Lauren pursed her lips. Should she tell him the man with the light brown rope hair was alive, so he was not alone with the dead? She imagined the story getting out on the front page of the Greenlock Gazette. Oh, the ridicule. She would leave town for sure.

"I think the sheriff wanted them in the coffins, but I'm guessing they aren't ready yet." He set down his step stool and climbed it to pull the camera to its height.

"That's right." She dropped her fist on her hip. What if this Elias Browne moved or sneezed? Poor Mr. Waxner would plummet clear off his perch. Her hand reached back and met with a soggy skirt. Looking to her backside, the wet mud ran from the tips of her loose curls to her ankles. Mr. Browne said he had money. He could pay for new fabric.

"I guess we don't need to ask anyone to hold still for the count." Mr. Waxner chuckled at her over his shoulder.

Lauren rolled her eyes after he had turned back to the camera. "I hope not."

"Well now, give me about three more minutes and I can wrap this up. Mrs. Waxner didn't want me to come. She doesn't like us using our belongings for these type of things, you understand." He closed the camera lid and carefully came down his step stool. "I'll get this off to the sheriff. But I think we all have our duty to help the community." He nodded, brows creased. "I'm sure you understand." He paused when she agreed. Disdain crept into his expression as he gazed at her and continued, "Helping your father here wouldn't be something anyone would ever choose." He collapsed the camera stand.

What choice? Lauren growled inside. Staring him down with rounded eyes, she thought right about now would be a good time for Mr. Browne to come off that ice table. She jerked on the large door as Mr. Waxner scurried to exit.

"I will get these off to the sheriff," Mr. Waxner said as she pulled the doors closed. Was she going to despise everybody who disapproved of her vocation? Dropping the metal bar over the door, she huffed at the ridiculous irony of never locking the doors. No one ever wanted in here. But someone wanted out. She glanced at Elias Browne from the Lennhurst Asylum or Hospital. Was any of that even true? A sister named Anna—unlikely.

"Miss Lauren—uh, Miss Campbell."

Lauren stepped closer but out of his reach. Now he knew her last name.

"So the photo is over." He clutched his side, wincing. "But I realize without using some sandbags in my place, the rest of the burial cannot happen."

"You guessed right." She rubbed her throbbing head, sneaking a glance at him as he watched her. Turning away quickly, she blew out a breath. The other two bodies were starting to smell. "My father and some local young men help load the bodies," she said. "They aren't going to load any sandbags. You might as well stay in jail. It will prolong your life a bit."

"I don't think so," he whispered.

"What? What are you saying?" A twinge of undeserved empathy rolled around her gut.

"I've been to prison. I didn't like it. It's the cold. I just don't like it," he said, his voice like gravel.

"But you got out. How did you get out?"

"Got drafted to the Union Army. I was a blasting agent." He stared at the ceiling with wells of pain in his eyes. "Don't have any family or future, so I set explosives. Half of us blow ourselves up in the process. No loss, ya know."

Lauren watched him trying to block the softening response rising within her. The war had broken as many good people as bad.

"So, I have an idea, lovely Lauren."

She squinted at him.

"I do have money, and I want you to have it. You don't have to tell me what you want, but I can see it in your eyes. Something wanting, a desire behind those green beauties. So whatever it is—"

To get to Denver City, almost slipped from her mouth.

"—it's all yours. I can't take it to the grave with me, but you use it to make your heart free."

Why did his voice have such a calm lilt to it, like they were just two friends sitting on a park bench?

"Go get a piece of paper and write this down."

Chapter 4

LAUREN HUFFED, BEWILDERED that she was even writing down these directions. Certainly, he was taking her for a circus ride. The pond he spoke of was real, even the frayed rope that still hung from the tree was there. She remembered how the schoolboys would run and jump on it during the summer. The one thick branch he described matched her memory. How could it hurt? Even if it was a hoax, what was she out?

"Is it a trap waiting to explode on me?" She stopped writing.

"I like how smart you are." He released a short moan and held his side. "I would never hurt anyone as *nice* as you."

She couldn't help but catch his reference. She cast him a sidelong glance. "I would imagine your charm has gotten you far."

"Not far enough to get a blanket."

The desk clock revealed how quickly time had gone. Nine-forty-five. "I need to awaken my father, and the sheriff should be here any moment." She looked around. What could it hurt to grab an extra blanket just right up the stairs?

"I understand the dilemma." His eyes narrowed. "How did the dead man get a blanket? Forget it. I think I will try to get up when he gets here. You need to scream like you didn't know," he said, his voice breathy. "He will shoot me, and it will all be—over."

Lauren stilled. Pulling her hair out of her band, she glanced at him and nervously fingered her hair back into a bun. "Please, just let him take you to jail. Please. Do your time and then come find me. If the money is really there, I'll save it for you. I don't need to go. I'll be fine."

He slowly shook his head.

"Please, I promise I will find wherever they take you. I will bring you a blanket." She stepped closer, manufacturing a grin. "I will."

He grinned back at her, their eyes locking for the first time. "Where do you want to go?" he whispered.

"What?" A strange heat ran up the back of her arms.

"You said you didn't have to go."

"Oh, to Denver City. My mother and sister live there. I have this crazy notion to join a wagon train and make the trip."

"You could take the train and stage. The money in the tin box will get you there and back many times."

"It's complicated. I have some of my mother's dishes and her harpsichord."

"Okay." He nodded. "A wagon train it is. Promise me that you'll take the money and go to Denver City." His watery eyes widened, waiting for her promise. She noticed softness flicker in their blue hues.

"I don't—know." She tilted her head. Why, after this harrowing morning, wasn't her heart nervous anymore? "I-I have to get going. I need to change and get over to the church and courthouse. This is all too strange, but your friends are still dead and need to be buried." She walked over and grabbed her tablet. "Tell me where your sister lives, I'll make sure she gets your money."

"I have no idea. We lost track of each other years ago. That's why I want you to have it. You remind me of her."

Lauren shook her head. It was all likely a swindle. "Mr. Elias Browne, this has to beat all."

"Help me stay dead. You want to go to Denver City, and I want to go to California. I hear it's warm there almost every day."

She rubbed the tension in her neck from this ludicrous morning and looked around again. There was nothing to tie him to the table with. And when she got back someone would ask why she had done it. This had to be the worst dilemma. Why hadn't she asked Mr. Waxman to bring the sheriff?

"Listen, Mr. Browne, you are not going in the ground, and you are not going to be killed again in my basement," she stopped, confused by her own words. "Anyway, you *are* going to jail. I'm sorry. I have to go." She ran up the stairs and into the parlor. The blanket on the back of the settee glared at her, she growled and went up and knocked on her father's door. "Father, I need you to get up." She knocked again. "Father, please!"

"Laurie, I'm just under the weather today. Mr. Soure has the wood cut. Can you ask him for whatever you need?"

Lauren pounded a fist twice against his door. "I can't do this. I don't run this business, you do. There are three bodies to be processed."

"I know. I'm sorry, honey. I've got the chills and fever today." His weak voice far away and muffled by the door.

Lauren dropped her head against his door with a thud. After a moment, she leaned back, raised her chin, and willed a real scream to come out of her open mouth. Not even a squeak came out. Dropping her head back against the door again, she whined. "I can't do this anymore." Back and forth, she rolled her forehead, willing this to all go away. With one last weak pound on his door, she waited. Nothing.

Slowly, she found her room and closed the door. It was the only sanctuary where she could drop her wet clothes and stare at the wall. Something inside her was sinking faster than usual. Why did she want to crawl into bed and weep? She touched her wrist where the should-be-dead man grabbed her.

Elias and his money. Hadn't she just been in a pitiful place believing no one would ever touch her? With his grizzly beard and face it seemed like no one would dare touch him. Maybe they had something in common. She pulled an old Christmas wrapped box out from under her bed and sat down. Inside was the entire five dollars she had to her name. Enough to get to Cincinnati but not Denver City. She scanned the old newspaper ad about the wagon trains leaving from Independence, Missouri. Her five dollars couldn't even get her there. And was she just hoping to catch a ride with a stranger? Wouldn't she have to have her own wagon for the harpsichord and the dishes? She slammed the lid on the box. How dare that criminal read her thoughts? Seeing something in her eyes . . . What a bunch of horse manure. The sooner she could get those bodies out of her home, the better. This was making Mrs. Wiggin's funeral look like a school cake walk.

LAUREN TOOK A deep breath and opened the door to the sheriff's office. The younger lawman jumped up. "I was hoping you'd be by for this." He handed her an envelope. "The sheriff headed out to his mom's this morning. I guess she had a list of chores for him a mile long." Someone yelled obscenities from down the hallway. "I gotta go, Miss Campbell, someone's been causing problems all morning." He walked away as Lauren held her mouth open. She hadn't even had a chance to form the words that she knew would sound ridiculous. "Can you send the sheriff down as soon as he's free?" she called down the hallway.

"Will do," a voice called back.

Lauren walked the three blocks down to the Catholic Church and caught Father Michael cutting bread in the church kitchen.

"Hello, Lauren." He looked up. "I bet you're here about some grave sites."

"Yes, Father, I need two or . . ."

He looked up, waiting for her to finish. "Three, I heard." He smiled, creasing his worn olive skin. "Word travels fast in Greenlock. Interesting, not your common horse thiev'n and bank robb'n." Lauren watched him as he kept cutting bread. "Explosive runners. Who would think that something that dangerous could get into the wrong hands?" He looked up at her. "Are you feeling okay, Miss Lauren?"

"Hmm? Yes, I'm fine." Remembering Elias's story, his calm voice seemed to swirl around her. Maybe he wasn't as ruthless as she supposed?

"Well, I had some young men here earlier looking for work, so I already got them digging. I got this bread and soup for them."

"You're a good father," slipped out from Lauren's thoughts.

"Oh, well, that is kind of you to say. I have also admired your help in the passing from life to eternity. Not everyone can prepare the deceased with the care and strength that you do."

Lauren scanned the warm kitchen. Father Michael was old enough to be her father. Did he realize he was her only true friend? "I'm off to Mr. Soure. If we can't get them in the ground tonight, it will be at first light tomorrow."

"Right-toh, and I'll pay the diggers tonight. So whatever you charged the County, we can put in the offering plate."

Lauren breathed in the aroma of the warm soup and his generous heart.

"And Lauren," she heard him call after her. "Get some rest; you look plumb wore out."

ELIAS TOOK A deep breath and tried to find the strength to pull himself up. His side screamed like white-hot switchblades cutting him over and over. He gritted his teeth; fresh blood soaked into his stiff shirt. He grunted with clenched teeth as he sat up. Trying to focus as things went spotty-black, a wooden shelf with cloths seemed close—maybe? He slid off the cold metal table, trying his weight on his feet. Sight fading, he gripped his gang member's dirty britches and steadied himself to the shelf. Grabbing what looked like a clean cloth, he pulled up his shirt tails and pushed it against his wound. Holding it tight with his elbow, he slouched over, his breath locked in his throat.

The room started to spin. He gulped some air, then doggedly tried to find a large enough piece of cloth to wrap around his middle. His breathing grew labored, and sweat had begun to form on his forehead when he finally found one. Unsure if his knees would hold him, he leaned heavily against the shelf as he wrapped the long cloth around his ribs. The heavy bar over the large wood doors loomed impossible—not only so far away, but too heavy as well. He felt as weak as a kitten, but the sound of a door slamming upstairs awakened his failing senses. Was he passing out, or were the lights flickering?

Chapter 5

A BOLT OF panic struck Lauren as she crossed the threshold of her home and father's business. *Why,* she thought, *would slamming the door scare anyone wanting to jump out to get me? That makes no sense.* She looked around her simple home. No fires had been lit. The blanket was still in place along with her cup, the only one on the kitchen table. Her father must be abed.

And Elias Browne? He may even be dead by now. The only person with a heart racing was her. She licked her lips, took a deep breath, and started down the basement stairs. At the bottom, it appeared pitch black. *The oil lamps! Empty! How stupid can I be!* A small whimper escaped as she tiptoed down to the last step. The light from the top wasn't enough to see into the middle of the damp morgue. She could go back up, but it was only two steps to the matches. She swallowed hard and stepped forward. Stupid shelves, the matches were always right here. She moved her hand back and forth across the wood. One more step and her foot collided with something very large.

"Ahhh!" Her hands flailed forward as her foot missed a place to land. Hands suddenly grasped her arms. She squealed as the warm hands held her suspended in air.

"You're going to wake the dead, girl. Please." Elias's arms gave way. She tumbled onto him and quickly pushed herself over to the dirt floor. She could smell the blood and grime on him. He was panting and moaning at the same time.

"What are you doing?" She sat up, brushing her dress free of his touch.

"Keeping you from stepping on my bullet hole. It's a bit sore today."

She reached over him deducing he must be flat on his back.

He gently found her hands. "Please don't touch me, everything—hurts." His words were labored like he couldn't get a breath. A strange, clammy heat came through his hands.

"Put my hand on your forehead." A moment later, the heat and sweat seared her fingers. His skin was like touching a hot stove. "You're burning up. An infection has set in."

"I was going to tell you—to—skip—the blanket, but then I started to shiver."

Lauren rose up and reached for the shelves. She found the matches and struck one against the box. He lay at her feet, eyes closed, face beet red and shivering. She stepped away, grabbed for the oil and refilled the lamp. "You were trying to escape?"

"No, I just wanted something to cover this hole in my side. I think it was causing a draft through—my—insides." His teeth chattered.

"I'm going to fetch the doctor. He can give you something."

"No." He reached his hand toward her. "I need to stay dead. Please help me stay dead."

She carefully reached out and found his hand. At her gentle urging, he pulled against it trying to stand.

"Help me back to the dead bed." He groaned under the pain.

Even bent over, Lauren could tell he was a strong man. The strange rope hair was hanging off the center of his back. "Let me get the doctor. Who knows when the sheriff will call for him? Just let me go see if he's available." She held his arm as he lay back down.

"I beg you, do not. But I have little ability to stop you." He closed his eyes. His pain was obviously intense, but she hesitated then questioned her wavering.

Finally, she moved to the bucket of water and dipped a cup in. "Here, try some water." She put her hand under his head and brought the cup to his lips. He drank it all. "Can I ask you about your hair?" It felt so strange against her palm.

His head laid back, and a small smile broke

across his face. "Yes. What do you want to know?"

"Did it always grow that way?"

"No."

"You do that to it on purpose?"

"Yes."

"Is there a reason?"

"Umm, I was a Nazarite."

With his eyes closed, Lauren took a curious look at him. "Like in the Bible?" She couldn't tell if he was joking. She'd never heard that anywhere else.

"Mmm," he moaned. "Don't cut their hair or touch the dead. But that's broken now." He elbowed the dead man next to him.

Lauren glanced wide-eyed at his two table mates. "So you think if you cut your hair, you will be without your strength? Like Samson?"

"Cut it all," he whispered. "Let's find out."

"I'm not cutting your hair." She shook her head. "But let me take a look at that wound." Carefully lifting his shirt, revealing the strips of cloth wrapped around his waist, she lifted the pad and frowned at the angry red skin underneath.

"This is not good," she said. His hand suddenly grabbed her wrist. How many times had he touched her? Today alone, more than anyone in years. She stared at him; he was too far gone to know better. His grip was firm but not demanding.

"Please, help me." He let her go.

"I can't." She exhaled. "I don't know how."

"When we are all loaded in the coffins," his voice tremored. "Find an excuse. Ask everyone to leave." He licked his chapped lips. "I will get out, and we'll put something heavy inside and nail the lid."

"You're just going to jump out?" she squeaked. "While I try to lift sandbags, rocks, and whatever myself?" Turning away from the table, she pulled her hair loose from the band. "Then," she yanked her fingers through the curls, then made a knot at the back of her head, "I'm going to be guilty of helping you escape." She didn't want to turn around. Something unexplainable was drawing her to his calm and steady voice. She turned to the stairs, hearing something from above. "I think I hear my father." Grabbing the folds of her skirt, she ran up the stairs. Gripping the stair banister, she could hear his faint voice.

"Laurie," he called.

"Coming." She bound up the steps to the second floor.

He cracked the door, and the wave of horrid alcohol-breath hit her face. "Could you grab me some food. Anything will be fine."

She nodded and turned. He didn't ask for any coffee. No coffee, no effort to join the day. She stalked around the kitchen, eventually heating last night's barley soup and slicing some bread.

44

Reheating the cold coffee, she stood back staring at the prepared tray. If she told him about the criminal in the basement, would he get up? Should she sacrifice Elias to see her father care about something? Biting her bottom lip, she glanced at the basement stairs and then to the house staircase. She had no faith in her father. Not today, anyway. She took the tray up the stairs and stopped at his door. At the closed door, she released a sigh with her hands gripping the tray until her knuckles turned white.

A decision was rising along her backbone, and it felt powerful and reckless, rebellious and appropriate. The closed door in her face seemed to approve the insane decision brewing in her mind. She set the tray next to her father's closed door and knocked. He would have to take care of himself. She'd made a decision and by death or jail, at least it was hers, and she was willing to pay the price.

Chapter 6

ELIAS BROWNE COULDN'T stay awake. He willed his eyes to stay open one moment then faded into darkness the next. The nightmares were coming and going like slaps to the face. The worst ones were being held down back at the asylum. Knives at his throat, pillows over his head. Air—he needed air.

"Mr. Browne? Elias?"

It was Anna, his sister. The light sparkled in her eyes, her smile was gentle. She leaned close, comforting him with her soft voice. Someone dark came up behind her, grabbed her face and threw her to the ground; the brutal hand came quickly up, pinning his neck. No air! Air, he needed a breath. He tried to fight—

"Whoa!"

His eyes peeled open as Lauren Campbell gripped a wobbling cup above her head.

"You almost knocked this out of my hand." She brought her other hand around the cup to steady it. "It's not hot, just some soup. You must have had a bad dream. Can you lean up a bit?" Her hand pressed under his head.

Please let this be real. He felt her warm hand

and the soup placed against his lips. It tasted real, the pain in his side was still excruciating.

"I went to see the doctor and I told him it was for my father." He eyed her, and she quickly dipped her face. "I put the powder in the soup. It's supposed to help fight the infection. When you're done with the soup, I have a clean pad and poultice to apply."

"You are very kind," he said between sips. She still looked everywhere but at him. "What time of day is it? When is the burial?"

"It's late afternoon. As soon as the coffins get here, it'll take only a few minutes to load and then lower them into the ground. I have the sheets to wrap you all in. I was thinking I would wrap you like the others. Your face is bright red compared to theirs, but I think you'll be able to breathe fine." She glanced at him as he tried to focus on her words. "I will find an excuse to ask them to leave. I found some bricks on the side of the alley on the way back from the doctor. I've filled two pillowcases. I also have two full gallons of embalming solution, which is heavy. I will wrap some bedding around them. Hopefully, that will be enough weight."

How he prayed this wasn't another dream. Even in his disjointed mind, it sounded as if she was willing to help him. In his weakened condition, she was his only hope. He drained the last of the soup and watched her fill the cup with water and offer him some more. He took three more drinks, wondering what changed her mind. She was pretty and young, maybe twenty or so and altogether too trusting. Soft brownish-blonde hair tied in a loose knot, loose curls surrounded her face, and her green eyes were kind and soft. He would get away and still bring her the money he had promised.

"I want you to take your trip." He gazed sincerely into those soft green eyes. "I'm going to bring you the money I talked about. I'm telling the truth." He believed his own words, but she thought him a strange bandit, why should she believe him?

"I don't want your money," she whispered, cautiously lifting the old pad sticking to his wound.

He ground his teeth and tried not to grab her offered arm.

"I'm sorry, it's all stuck together." She slowly removed the old dressing. "I'm going to clean it before we add the new pad."

His eyes rolled back. If he lived through this scrape, it would be another miracle. So many times he should have died. If he hadn't run from the asylum, he would be dead and buried out back with all the other defective paupers. His first gang, running until they were beaten and robbed, had been so young and stupid. It happened too many times to count. In prison, he'd caught some lung disease and they left him for dead. Somehow he'd lived to see another day, only to fall into a new gang that taught him everything he knew about explosives. Then the war.

"Are you doing okay? I'm almost done."

A loud sound approached outside the basement doors.

"Oh no, I'm not ready." Lauren jumped and ran for the shelves. Someone banged on the doors. "Hold up. I'll be right there," she called.

He clutched the new bandage in place as it stung his side. She flung a sheet over him and tucked it around him. He struggled to get air and clenched his teeth to steady his chest from rising. It sounded like she removed the large bar and pushed the doors aside. The sounds of the wagon drew in closer.

"That's good," Lauren said.

Please, God, he begged for the first time today. The reality of being buried alive was choking him. He couldn't cough. *Be still, be still,* he rehearsed, a hair tickled his nose. *It's just a sheet. You can breathe.* He tried to distract his thinking. *Like in your hiding spot, open and easy to hide in, and easy to get out of.*

"Ok, this one's ready."

The cold table rocked with the removal of Norvell. *Steady, hold steady, will she come up with something? Will she wait till they have the coffin lid nailed on? Can she remove it?* He forced the panic down. Maybe he *was* the victim this time. Maybe she never intended to help him. Heightened instinct said to fling the sheet off and jump off the table. *No, no hold steady. Believe that she won't betray me. Remember those eyes, that matter of fact voice.* She is smart, but not evil. The pounding of the lid for coffin two rang loud in the damp basement. *She wants to see her mother and sister in Denver City, does that sound like someone who—*

Hands roughly jerked him off the table and strained to pull him up into the wagon bed. One more heave into the coffin, his head hit the end as his whole body broke out in a dizzying sweat. His boots stuck at the other end, knees bent upward. *Now, Lauren now! Something . . . before they . . .*

"He don't fit good," someone said above him.

He heard Lauren let out a long sigh. "I know what I have to do."

Taking off his boots would probably do the trick. *Good Lord, what is she thinking now?*

"I forgot to tell Mr. Soure to make this one bigger."

He heard her voice move to another area of the morgue. "Listen, I-I—have to do something that is—"

"You gonna' break his knees with that sledge-hammer. Then he'll fit," someone said above him.

"Yes—and I need you all to go stand by the tree behind the alley."

"He's already dead, just go ahead and knock those kneecaps out. I can do it if you want me to. I can—"

"I don't think I know you." Lauren cut him off, her voice coming closer. "Would you ever be interested in helping in the funeral parlor?"

"I'm Albert Fernandez, ma'am. I do whatever work I can get. Father Michael sent me today."

"Nice to meet you, Mr. Fernandez. For today, I'm going to *fit* this last guy in the box. It would help me if you could all wait over there."

"Come on, Al," another voice said, "I'm feelin' my gut coming up."

Elias expelled a held breath as the sheet came off his face. Lauren stood over him, pulling on his arm. A strength that he didn't know he could possess came over him as he stood up and stepped from the coffin. He gripped his side as he sat and slipped off the wagon. Lauren had already jumped down and pulled on the heavy brick-filled cases. They both grabbed the fabric and flung it in the coffin. One more at the other end of the pine box. The room spun as he gripped the heavy gallon jugs they hauled up and over into the box. One more and she jumped up on the wagon, shoving blankets around the glass. He stood back—black spots vied for his vision as she tucked his sheet around all the items.

"Laurie."

She gasped, wide-eyed, and panicked, as he stumbled back into the corner shelves where jugs had been. A man's voice floated down to the bottom of the stairs.

"I thought I heard the diggers doing a pickup. Do you need some help, honey?"

"No, I've got it." She reached for the lid and tried to pull it over his coffin. As she would get one side on, the other would slip crooked. Her face shown red, her lips drawn in a tight line, she finally pushed it in place.

"Need any help with the nails?" The man's voice seemed closer.

"I think I'll have the guys do it," she called back. Her chest rose and fell with strain.

Elias suddenly thought he should have never asked for her help. That voice was obviously her father, a caring father. Why should she risk all this for him?

"I'm going to have the guys pull the wagon forward. It's crowded with three boxes."

"Okay, honey." He let out a few small coughs. "Hopefully, I will feel better tomorrow." His voice trailed off.

Lauren flailed her arms out, fists waving wildly, shoulders shaking. If he were closer, she would certainly jump off that wagon and strangle him.

Stepping over the crowded coffins, she looked outside. "Mr. Fernandez, can you lead the team forward. I'll hold the lid steady until you can nail it."

The end of the wagon pulled out. The sound of the nails pounding brought a dizzying relief and Elias slid down the shelves and dropped his head back. He tried to swallow the bile in his throat as the large doors came together. Face and body drenched in sweat, he cracked his eyes open. She was leaning back against the large doors, hands over her face and shaking her head.

"Now what," he whispered.

Chapter 7

THIS MORNING HER father had decided to come down and sit at the square breakfast table. For three days Lauren had been able to take food back and forth through the kitchen pantry and into the broom closet. But Mr. Elias Browne's breakfast was to be late today. She tried to review her gratitude to God this morning as she poured her father a second cup of coffee. If Mr. Browne had taken a turn for the worse, she would be hard-pressed to order another coffin and grave for a man who was already dead. Even burying a drifter, Father Michael would want to see him to see if he could notify family. He was so close to being able to leave that she had allowed herself to daydream. What if she did take some of his money and go to Denver City?

"Father, I think I have someone to help you here at the funeral home."

His tired face looked up. "Why is that Laurie, you think we need help?"

"His name is Albert Fernandez. You could check with Father Michael for a recommendation." Might as well come right out with it. "I've decided to take a trip to Denver City, to see mother and Cammi."

"Oh, I see." The bags under his eyes seemed to darken. "How long would you be gone?"

"It's been two years. I miss them terribly. Maybe months, a year, maybe a little longer."

Her father dropped his head to the side and scratched his greasy hair. He sniffled as if he might cry. "I understand. I just need you here." He sighed. "And I don't think I have the money right now."

Lauren felt a bolt of resentment. Because it's all spent on liquor, she wanted to spew. "We should be getting the county check for the last three burials." She looked out the window. With all the commotion, had she turned in the bill?

"And, thankfully, that should get us through April." Her father rose and headed for the staircase. "We can talk about it later. I just don't think this is the right time."

Lauren dropped her cup on the hard table. The messy table mimicked her insides, and she dropped the plates together and tossed the silverware on top. "No, I don't need help. I've got this, too!" With a clatter, she dropped it all in the wash tub. She heard the click of his upstairs door closing. Another rod of determination shot through her spine.

ELIAS HEARD THE creak of the thin door, but it was the angry words he overheard coming from Lauren that woke him up. Sitting up, he leaned against the wall of the broom closet, striking a match to the oil lamp. The door opened further and, in his weakness, he remembered the days of not knowing if a meal was coming or a beating was coming. He shook it loose; it was just Lauren with a plate of biscuits and gravy. He reached up to take the plate, as she could barely walk in because his blanket-covered pallet took up the entire space. She handed it over but seemed to loom over him with arms crossed. "So is that money really real?" Her jaw rocked back and forth.

"Good morning, Lauren." He squinted at her. "Thank you for this." She looked away, as he took a warm bite. "Yes, it's real. Are you ready to go get it? Ready to go to Denver City?"

"Why, yes, I am." Her crossed arms switched into fists on her hips.

"Going on the wagon train, taking your mother's things?" He licked the gravy from the fork.

"Maybe I will. Is there enough for me to hire someone?"

He stabbed another bite of gravy-laden biscuit. "I will take you. For all you have done for me."

She dropped her defiant stance. "You would?"

"I'm going to California or Texas. I've heard they are both warm." He gave her a slight smile. "Denver City is cold, or I might consider it." Lauren dropped her head to the side. She had been generous with her food and doctoring, but mistrust marred her expression, and the fact that she would never look him in the eye. "When I was in the asylum, I never looked eye to eye at anyone older than me. I didn't trust anyone except my sister. Then, when I lived on the streets, I learned to look everyone in the eye. It was the only way to survive." He paused. "Why do you always look everywhere but at me?"

She met his gaze for a split second. "I don't know."

"Trust," he whispered. "Go get the money today. You'll see I've been truthful with you. And then I need you to help me tonight."

Wary of what she was getting herself into, she stared at him through thick eyelashes. "What kind of help?"

"Bring a razor." He handed her back the empty plate.

THE FRESH SMELLS and breezy sounds of spring somehow renewed her being. Living in a dark house, working in a dark basement all winter tried to drain her soul dry. She followed the bubbling creek that overflowed into the pond about two miles from town. Even if it was a wild goose chase, the fresh air had put a spring in her step.

What if the money was real? Could she allow Mr. Browne to help her get to Denver City? Does trouble follow him everywhere he goes? Truth be told, he was closer to being her only friend who was her age than she'd had in years. The distance between their lives was wide, but most often, he was interesting and engaging.

So many times she wanted to enjoy a conversation, look at another human being eye to eye. She had told herself long ago never to look at the dead. A thread of compassion would make her wonder how good a life the dead person had lived. If she never really looked at them, she could pretend they hadn't ever laughed and cried or hurt like everyone else. At least Mr. Browne appeared as strange as she was. Spotting the tree where the old rope, shredded with much use from years gone by, still hung, she grabbed Elias's instructions from the basket. He had told her to take a basket and cover the tin box with flowers. He seemed to have common sense in spades.

She counted off the steps and stopped. Looking around. Suddenly a shiver ran up her back. What if someone had followed her? Why didn't she ask common sense questions? Was the money stolen? What if someone grabbed her? For heaven's sake, he was a criminal! She paced around in a circle, nervously scanning the area where she was to dig—there. There was the large tree root just as he had described.

She hesitated. Was this the worst form of greed?

Would God forgive her for helping a criminal and now taking some of the money for her own gain? How had her life taken such a wicked turn? She didn't have to do this. The thought taunted her. She could send him on his way and go back to her life as it had always been—until he got arrested for something else and the law had a few questions for her.

She squeezed the basket handle until her knuckles turned white.

Dropping to her knees, she grabbed the garden spade from the bottom of the basket and began to dig. *I must be crazy. Mr. Browne is halfway across Common County right now having a good laugh at my expense.* She could just hear his thoughts *"That stupid, naïve girl."*

Something clunked hard against her shovel, and Lauren gasped. Digging wider she found the edges, and then she was able to pry the tin box free from the dirt. Quickly, she stashed it into the bottom of her basket then rose and looked around. It only took a moment to kick the dirt and leaves back as they had been. She brushed her skirt off and replaced the spade in the basket. Her heart was erratically pounding, and her breath came in nervous puffs as if she'd just awakened from a nightmare.

She was keenly aware of the black, rusty box. As she headed back across the pond trail toward town, she shook her head. *Alone, how ridiculous, no common sense.* She almost stepped on a group of wildflowers. Bending quickly, she grabbed the whole bunch. The tops hung in a perfect disguise over her basket.

She approached town telling herself to slow down, as her skirts whipped her legs rashly. *Just out gathering flowers.* She tried to breathe in and out slowly. Believable. A funeral director's daughter needed sweet flowers to cover the nasty smells of death.

She nodded to a few faces that passed her, her pace slowed even more, then her breathing evened. Finally, she was in front of her home, the funeral home. After stepping inside, she couldn't drop the basket on the table fast enough.

Her fingers tingled, as she tried to get the blood to flow from her tight grip. She pulled her hair ribbon loose, and a riot of curls fell into her face. The thick locks briefly swirled about as she rubbed her head. That felt better and was somewhat calming. She swiftly wound her hair back into a knot and tied the ribbon. She patted her hair, licked her lips, and took a calming, deep breath. Back to business.

She had no fortitude for this. *Never will I have the bravery to travel to Denver City, I can't make it to the pond and back without giving myself the vapors. What was I thinking?* She went back and locked the front door. Holding the knob, she dropped her forehead on the door, pounding it three or four times. *Oh, this is much better, since the criminal is already inside.*

"Laurie," her father called from his room. "Someone's at the door. Could you take care of it?"

"Yes." Rolling her eyes, she unlocked and opened the door. "Hello," she spoke to the fresh breeze. "Welcome to the craziest funeral home in Ohio. How can I help you?" She shook her head and closed the door.

"They were just selling something," she hollered up the stairs. "Oh, Lord." The basket on the table spooked her. Might as well see what rocks and paper lay within.

Chapter 8

ELIAS STOOD AND took some deep breaths. His whole body still wobbled like a newborn foal. He could hear Lauren and opened the pantry door. The house had been silent for over an hour. He took some steps into the kitchen and put his hands out to stop her from running into him.

"Oh, you're up. I didn't see you." She moved back as if his touch was painful. Glancing back toward the stairs, she hesitated. "I don't think my father will be down, but I never know," she whispered, looking at his feet.

"You found the box?" he said quietly.

"Yes, here it is." She pulled out the tin box spilling flowers and dirt on the floor. He took the box as she bent down and tried to sweep up the mess with her hands. Watching her, he frowned. Something upset him about her cleaning the floor at his feet. He pulled her up. "I'll do that."

Why did it rub him the wrong way? She wasn't an underling, but she didn't know better. He held her arm and gazed too long. Strange how hard it felt watching her look so worried. He sucked in a breath and let go. The deep breath almost pushed back the strange gut twist. He tried to focus. "Can you grab your tablet and pencil?" She nodded and quietly went down to the basement.

Elias rubbed the back of his neck watching her descend. She had on a light green skirt today, that soft curly hair escaping its pins and falling against her cream blouse. Why did she have to be so pretty? He'd always needed to stay hard, shrewd, and calculating. Look what had happened with his own turncoat gang? A gunshot to the side accidentally serving him well. He would not go soft for a woman. He set his jaw; he felt gratitude for her but nothing else. Lauren came back up the stairs. He twitched a grin as she handed him the tablet.

"Maybe we should go back to the broom closet so we can talk?" He nodded toward the pantry.

"I'll bring some coffee." She turned to the stove.

He held the items and walked back into the pantry. With the door open they both should fit. After he set the tin box down, he pushed his blanket into a pile and carefully lowered himself down.

She came in and handed him the coffee.

"Maybe you could pull that crate out and sit?" He felt like a donkey asking a mare to come for a visit. He held out his hand to hold her coffee. She handed it to him and pulled out the crate and sat. After their rocky start, now what was the strange rhythm that they shared? He handed her back the coffee. They were like two people who had known each other for years. He'd never just sat and visited with a woman before. Is this what normal people do? Talk over coffee? It was stirringly odd.

"I don't know if I've said thank you for the food and blankets." He smiled, and she smiled back. Suddenly the pantry space got smaller. "The medicine and the clothes, the soap. You have covered me with your care." He couldn't help but notice she held his eyes for more than a few seconds then sipped her coffee.

"No lock." He flipped the metal clips up and opened the lid.

"Is this money stolen?" Lauren blurted out as he lifted a thick stack of bills.

"No. I earned it."

Suspicion squinted from her eyes. "Not around here you didn't."

"No." He combed his fingers through his long beard. "You might not want to hear what men bought explosives for. The war may be over, but revenge still costs a few bills." He waited, and raised his eyebrows quickly. *"But what does it profit a man to gain the whole world, but lose his soul?"* he quoted. He showed her the empty tin then dropped the bills back into the box. "So since you helped me stay dead," he lifted his eyebrows, "I'm going to help you run away from home."

Startled, she jerked back a bit.

"Let's start with the big stuff. You'll need a wagon for this wagon train." He scribbled some things on the tablet. "A team of horses, or mules or oxen."

"A reputable driver for the wagon," she added.

His face shot up, and he held the pencil clutched to his chest. "That hurts, Lauren." When had he been given permission to use her first name? "You want someone else besides me? Someone more reputable?" Silence took up the space as she waggled her head looking at the floor.

"I-it's your money. I didn't know . . . if you were serious about—"

"I'm *dead* serious." He smiled. She finally looked up and smiled back.

"I'll get you to Denver City, with the harpsa-whatchacallit."

"Harpsichord and dishes," she piped in.

"Is it that long organ looking thing in the parlor?"

"You've been in the parlor?" she said, wide-eyed. "I knew there was a valid reason I couldn't sleep at night."

"I wasn't sneaking around your house. I just have to stretch now and then." *And debate going to get the money myself and get out of town. If I*

65

had the strength. "So the wagon has to hold that harpsichord. Is it heavy?"

"No, not really. Not like an organ."

"All right, so big stuff, and then food, bedding, pots, and pans."

"I watch the paper, often in the spring there's a group who travel together." Her eyes lit up.

"Good, can you check on that?"

"Yes." She sat straighter, and just as quickly her body drooped. "I don't know if I can do this. I don't even have an invitation from my mother to come."

"Do you need an invitation? From your own mother?" his soft voice questioned.

"I suppose not. I'm using the harpsichord and dishes like a calling card."

Elias wasn't sure what a calling card was, but could guess it gave her an excuse to show up.

"And then the travel," her brows creased. "I've never left Greenlock before."

"I've done a lot of traveling and living in different places." He stopped, would that help her or scare her off more? Her eyes seemed wider than usual; she was a sweet girl . . . maybe this wasn't so wise. "It's your decision, Lauren." He cleared his throat. "Remember, if you don't like Denver City, you can always come back."

"I want to go." She fearfully looked at him as something started to pool in her eyes. "But there's you and me," she said, looking quickly at her lap.

"What about you and me?" Did she already have some expectations set in her mind? Had he missed something?

"I can't just travel with you, eat with you. We certainly don't look like brother and sister." She sucked in a breath and shook her head. "People talk." Looking down, she swiped something from under her eye. "It won't work."

Elias scratched his neck, looking around the pantry. "I suppose your father won't take you."

She shook her head.

"Can you think of anything?"

She gave a slight nod. "We could say—just because people will never see us again—that we are married. But because we aren't, we can go our separate ways after we get there." She sighed, and her expression was troubled. "Oh, forget it." She rubbed her forehead. "I think I've fallen down the road of perdition too far."

"That will work." That lie was nothing on his list of infractions. A long moment of silence hovered. "But you need to know something about me." He scratched and pulled on his thick beard.

She swallowed, eyes down, and began to wring her hands. "You're already married," she whispered. "You have four little, rope-haired, small ones that need . . ."

"No." He gave a gruff chuckle. "I don't and I

won't." He tried to lean back; his side throbbed. "But *I am* very loyal. That's what you need to know about me."

She squinted, and her eyebrows drew tightly together looking adorable in her confusion.

"Those two dead guys I ran explosives with— one of them shot me in the back when the sheriff started shooting. My own guy is the reason I have a hole from back to front. I was already face down on the ground when the other two guys got shot. I would have defended them, though. We'd been tight for almost a year. Obviously, it isn't that way with everyone. Norvell and I had argued earlier, and he must have thought I went rogue. But I didn't. I don't know how the law got wind of us."

"What if he saved your life?"

His eyes narrowed, the blue hues deepening. "You, lovely Lauren, saved my life."

"No, I mean the sheriff's bullets were to the death. Norvell's wasn't." She shrugged.

"Something to think about I guess." He tried to sit forward and winced. "If you want to go forward with our plan, I will be loyal to you. To those who are very good to me, like you have been, I am very good to them." His mind flashed to the ice water at Lennhurst, someone pulling him out and covering him with a blanket. "For those who try to hurt me, *I will* hurt them." He paused. "Anna wasn't a blood sister, but she took care of me when I had no one. She taught me about loyalty. In my eyes, she is my sister. But there is a big difference between loyalty and love. Loyalty I give out fervently—love I do not and won't ever. I never will marry or have children. So we pretend, then go our separate ways?"

"Of course." She nodded quickly, looking down. "I think I understand."

Chapter 9

LAUREN BROUGHT HER father's tray down the stairs and started the water heating for dishes. Out of the corner of her eye, Elias peeked around the wall handing her his plate. "You're a good cook." He stayed half hidden but Lauren could feel his eyes on her as she moved about.

"When you're done, can you help me with my hair?"

She grabbed the warm water and a rag and began to work it over the dirty dishes. "Yes. These will take a few minutes." Something strange had been curling in her gut all evening. Like the idea of getting a wagon and heading out of town wasn't enough, his speech about being loyal had been unnerving. She loved her father but was about to be incredibly disloyal to him. Was Elias trying to make sure she never developed any feelings for him? Why waste his breath?

She had one goal—to get to Denver City—and had no intentions of falling for some jailbird. She had risked a lot to help him, and it sounded like he understood that. If he would help her and see it through, she would get what she wanted.

Lauren paused with the rag in one hand and

a plate in the other. *His childhood sounded horrible. What could he possibly know about love or commitments?*

"Let me dry." He grabbed a towel and took the plate from her.

Their fingers touched in the passing, and her stomach fluttered again. He stood next to her in her kitchen in the extra clothes she had found. He smelled clean, like vanilla soap, anything different than mortuary odors was refreshing. Looking down, she saw his wool stockings were only a few inches away from her feet. The familiarity of having a man help her with anything was dizzying, but those bootless feet were somehow so intimate.

"Your face is red, Miss Lauren."

She plunged the rag into the soapy water. "The water's hot."

"Do you have scissors or a razor?"

And what about his voice? It was masculine, yet calm. Aren't all criminals mean and nasty? His tone could almost convince her they could be friends. "Yes." She glanced at the staircase. "Do you want to sit here at the table?" She listened and didn't hear any movement upstairs. He dropped the towel on the table and sat. Blinking, she touched one of the strangely twisted locks of hair. "How does one cut these?"

"I guess with the scissors. Maybe . . ." He took off the leather strap holding them at the back of his neck. "You could just pull them out one at a time and cut like here."

"Like an inch or two from your scalp?"

"That's fine. I don't care."

She took a deep breath and grabbed one of the thick ropes of hair. Snipping it where he said, left her holding the rope hair. "Do you want to save one, it must have taken years . . ."

"No." He held out the dish towel. "Put them all in here, and I will bury them in the alley."

Lauren pursed her lips and snipped away. "How did you keep this hair in the Union Army?"

"I said it was my religion."

"Is it? Something about being a Nazarite?"

"No, I lied to keep it. They figured I'd blow myself up any day, so they let it go."

"Are you a religious man though? You know the Bible, I would guess."

"Humm, I would say I am not religious. I've never been to a church, but the asylum taught the Bible. Like anywhere, there were very few people there who treated the sinner with grace and many who despised them."

"You were there as a child. How could you be a sinner?" She snipped another lock of hair.

He turned to look at her. "We were all there because we were idiots or morally defective." He turned back.

"Oh." She had to think. "But you don't seem . . ."

"An imbecile?" His shoulders tightened. "My mother was mad."

"What about your father?" She carefully snipped around his ear.

"I never knew him—likely someone from the asylum. My last name is Browne with an e at the end. Lennhurst is in Brown Township. The workers named me and added the e." He pulled on his long beard. "My head feels cold."

"I can knit you a cap." The words escaped her lips, sounding embarrassingly overeager.

Setting the mound of brownish blonde hair on his chair, he stood and ran his fingers through her finished work. Walking slowly to the pan of water, he bent over and scrubbed his scalp and rinsed it with a cup of water. Squeezing the water off, he combed it back and forth with his fingers. "I haven't had a comb in years."

Lauren gaped wide-eyed, frozen by the shocking transformation.

"Now, the beard." He took the scissors in one hand and held his beard tight with the other. Two or three snips later it was gone. He gathered a bit of soap and rubbed it along his cheeks and chin. "Can I use that razor?"

Lauren was still staring as she handed him the sharp razor. "I have a small mirror in the washroom." She turned a corner and came back and held it in front of him.

"Can you turn up the light?"

Lauren rotated the oil lamp knob, noticing it was already black outside. She held the mirror up as he scraped his jaw and cheek up and down. Her breathing grew irregular. Without the hair, his shoulders were manly, thick and wide. Rinsing the razor in the dishpan, she held her breath as he placed it next to his neck again. *Breathe. Think of something else.* He scraped his skin up, and she noticed the scar across his jaw. "What happened there?" She pointed, hoping to break the strange nearness between them.

"Little sinners got to me." He scraped another section.

"I can't imagine what it would be like for a child to live—"

"It's all I'd ever known." Turning toward the basin, he splashed water on his face. He raised his arm and used his shirt sleeve to dry his chin. With only a flash of eye contact, he reached his hand out for the mirror, and she gave it to him. He brought it close to see if he'd missed anything and then with an outstretched arm he looked again. "Wow." He shook his head.

Lauren blinked and swallowed hard. A completely different person stood in her kitchen. He appeared at least five years younger. Even his voice matched this clean solid face. If she could compare him to the Greek gods they read about in school, he could be one. His light brown hair still messy but slicked back, his face chiseled

74

and strong. Something squeezed her chest. What was she thinking? When he'd looked like a wild animal, she easily kept a fearful distance. Now with the obvious massive shoulders and that smile with real lips and skin and— *Oh no,* she'd have even a harder time looking him in the eye. *My, oh my, he is handsome aplenty.*

"So you can knit?"

She nodded and snapped her open jaw closed, still speechless.

"And cook and run this place." He shook his head, wondering "What do you think? You seem tough and determined. You know we will be on the trail for weeks, months. Hot, dirty, bugs, blisters. No soft beds or stores, no bathtubs."

She drew a choppy breath. "I think so. I'll be honest, I'm sure there will be moments . . ." *like this one,* she grabbed the pan of dirty water, "where I might question everything I know." She headed for the back door, which he held open for her as she walked ahead. Stepping out, she slung the water into the alley, then stood still a moment, the cool air helping her relax. She heard him move outside with her and realized with the quiet, he seemed to need it, too.

The sun had settled behind the horizon, giving the stars a faded twinkle. They stood watching heavenward, the unknowns of this whole night diverting. He stepped away, still favoring his injury with every movement. His hand gently pulled over his top lip and hairless chin. They smiled awkwardly at each other and turned back toward the kitchen.

"Father!" Lauren gulped and froze. "What are you doing?" Her high pitched voice and shaking knees immediately betrayed her.

"I'm going to the outhouse." He stepped out. "The question is what are you doing?" Grabbing his robe tight, he glared at Elias. "And where are your shoes, young man?"

Chapter 10

LAUREN OPENED HER mouth to blurt out some kind of explanation when it hit her that her father did not recognize him—at all. He had only been in the basement a few times. But the hair, the hair was left sitting on the table. *Oh, no.*

"A lazy habit, sir." Elias smiled at her father as he lifted up his feet. "Was just taking a short stroll and didn't want to bother with my boots."

"I . . . I . . . was just emptying the dishwater." She giggled nervously. "Good thing I didn't get you wet with this water." She walked back toward the door. Elias nodded at them and walked on down the alleyway. Her father walked to the outhouse and closed the door. They turned back to each other and Lauren made a circle with her finger in the air and then pointed to the back door. He walked on holding his hip and stepping tender over the rough ground. Could he walk around the block? Running inside, she found the hair on the chair. He'd never taken more than a few steps. She shook her head and quickly hid the hair in the compost. Grabbing the scissors and razor, she shoved them in a drawer. Her father walked back through the kitchen, steadying himself by holding the wall. He stopped and glanced back at her.

"It's hard to hear you want to go see your mother. It would kill me to think of you all being together without me. I suppose I should have let go of the notion by now—that we could all be together again." His voice trailed off. "But at least having you here with me—at least someone cared about me." He slowly took the stairs up to his room.

Lauren stood with her mouth open. *Of course, I care for you.* She gaped at the empty stairs, her heart squeezing. How could she leave him? When she was angry, it all made sense. Now she felt like she was doing something cruel and heartless. What kind of child abandons her own father? Long, wet tears fell as she turned to the dried dishes and began to put them away. She couldn't go, not now anyway. He didn't just need help with the funeral home; he needed help to live. How could she leave him alone? He was obviously as downcast as one could get. She dried the dishpan and set it down. This entire home was depressing. She heard a small tap on the back door.

"Elias!" She wiped her face quickly, almost forgetting about him. "I'm so sorry," she said, opening the door. He walked in and sat carefully on the low window sill by the back door.

"Is your father near?"

"He's upstairs."

"You've been crying." He squinted.

She sucked in a long breath and looked back toward the empty parlor. "You spoke of loyalty, earlier," she whispered.

He nodded, holding his side.

"I can't go to Denver City. I can't join a wagon train. I-I have my father to think of. You saw him. He used to walk and stand upright. Now he's so downcast he just drinks and shuffles. It's a wonder he hasn't fallen head first down those stairs."

"I understand." He glanced up and carefully stood. Making his way into the pantry, he turned. "Can I ask you one question?"

"Yes." She lit the small lantern, illuminating his pallet in the broom closet.

"What will change for him, if you stay?"

She shrugged. "I-I will make sure he's fed and cared for."

Elias carefully lowered himself down and grabbed the blanket. "You've been doing that all along. What will change for *him?*" He wrapped the blanket around his shoulders.

"I don't understand what you're getting at?"

He nodded to the side. "Just seems you have been doing everything he needs you to do, yet he makes no effort to help himself."

Lauren's back straightened.

"You said he used to work and provide?"

"Yes."

"Why won't he do it now?"

"How should I know? He misses his family, his wife." She rolled her shoulder at him. "I don't think you could understand these things." The barb was out. She shouldn't have said it, but how dare he presume anything about family life—as if she had aided her father's choice to quit living. How absurd.

"You're right." He tightened his lips in a line. "I know nothing of families."

The air thickened with tension, she moved a few cans around on a shelf. "I'll let you rest then." She stared ahead.

"I suppose I can get out of your home tomorrow. With your help shearing me, I can go now." He rubbed his hands back and forth over his short hair.

"You do look completely different, but your voice . . ."

"My voice?"

"You have a calm, strong . . . I don't know, it may be something people will recognize."

He nodded and smiled as she turned to leave. "And Lauren, you're a good daughter. I admire your loyalty and your love for your father."

She turned back and held his gaze. "Thank you for saying that."

LAUREN EXTINGUISHED THE lights and locked the door. She went upstairs and could hear her father snoring as she passed his room. How could so much excitement die so fast? She sat on her bed and kicked off her boots. Her pile of knitting sat on her chair. She thought she would have to rush to finish her father's sweater, and now she would have no time limits—*not going anywhere.* She sighed. Only the next dead grandpa, dead wife or dead baby would take up her time. All the deadness made her sigh again.

She dropped her skirt and blouse and pulled her nightgown on. A weak puff blew out the flame, and she sat in the still darkness. How could she fault her father? The gloom was tangible, and hopelessness was flooding her soul. All those empty bottles that filled the back of the basement, maybe alcohol was the only way to survive this life. For some reason she pictured Father Michael, he never seemed weary of helping others. Maybe she got too caught up helping Elias.

No, that wasn't it. She pulled the covers over her body. She had been miserable before he came. All his crazy talk of money and how he would give it to her, just allowed her to dream for a moment. She wished she'd never met him. He was fine looking and fine sounding, but the sooner he left, the better for her. She reached for her little box and felt the paper advertisement for the wagon train. It tremored in her hand waiting to be wadded up and thrown away. She had dreamed for so long of a fresh start. Her eyes pooled with tears. Had she taken care of her father *too much?* Is that what Elias had been saying?

Chapter 11

THE NEXT MORNING Lauren wrapped one of her knitted shawls around her shoulders. It did little to provide any warmth or comfort as she set a match to the kindling, heating the stove and starting the coffee. She peeked into the pantry and jerked back. Elias stood tucking his shirt into his pants. He looked up and spun away from her. She slapped her hand over her face, and walked out. "Sorry."

"Is it clear for me to come out?" he said softly from the pantry.

"Yes." She pulled the frying pan off the shelf and set it on the stove. Taking a clean bowl, she grabbed the flour, salt, baking soda and mixed them together. Opening the icebox, she pulled out the milk then splashed some in the bowl.

"I want to ask you a favor, but you are so busy." He stood back, her arm jerking with the frantic whisking.

"Breakfast. I'm just doing what I do every morning. Ask away." She flung a chunk of lard into the hot pan.

"First, tell me what's wrong?" He stepped a bit closer.

Brave, she could give him that. "Just ask for what you want," she said, resigned. "I'm *sure* I can oblige." She bristled. That came out bitter. Reaching for the pan handle, she cried out, "Ouch!" While she shook her hand in the air, he caught her wrist and grabbed a towel to remove the smoking pan. He pulled her wrist in the air toward him leading her around the corner and into the pantry. Why was he always grabbing her wrists?

"I don't see any burns. Does it sting?"

"No, not really." She tried to pull it down, but he held it fast. "Go ahead, go ahead and ask." They were standing too close. She locked her eyes on the pantry shelves.

He lowered her arm slowly. "Would you help me with our list?" He finally let go.

Our list? "You are going to get a wagon? Get to Independence?" Her eyes got wider. "Join the wagon train?" *You're stealing my dream,* she wanted to spit. "Going to Denver City to see my mother, too?" She dropped her chin to her chest. "Forget I said that." She sucked in a few calming breaths. "Yes, I can order the things from the mercantile. The last advertisement said a group was passing through the last day of March. You seem to be healing fine. I suppose you will do well." Her voice trailed off. Why did a dagger just enter her chest? "I have to get to breakfast." She walked out, despising him.

• • •

ELIAS HAD KNOWN the feeling of not being wanted most of his life. At this moment standing in a broom closet was just like his past. She was done with him. Time was up. He had offered her a way out, but she didn't want it. He didn't want to leave with her scorning him, and he hadn't thought asking her for help would upset her. What was his other choice?

Standing alone with her, seeing the hurt in her eyes, either from a burn or her life's disappointment, weakened his resolve. Did she know how hard it was to not pull her wrist just another inch toward him, to place her warm hand on his naked neck? Warmth came up from his feet and squeezed his chest. To really look into those soft, round, green eyes. Bring her in close until her loneliness melted into his. If he had the strength, he'd wrap his arms around her, squeeze her, lift her off her feet and kiss her breathless. Energy he hadn't experienced since he'd been shot, pulsed through him. He grabbed some bills from the box and penciled a note on her tablet.

LAUREN KNOCKED ON her father's door asking him if he wanted to come down for some breakfast. He asked for a tray, and she slumped. Stiffly, she went back down the stairs. Grabbing a spoon, she plopped the eggs on a plate, the oatmeal in a bowl, and poured his coffee. Each movement was on automatic. She barely remembered walking upstairs to place the tray outside his door and then head back to the kitchen. Seeing the extra serving still on the stove, she made Elias a plate and bowl and took it back around the corner.

She stopped and stared at the pile of folded blankets. He was gone, and she knew instantly, he was gone for good. She had helped a common criminal escape. Willingly, she'd opened her heart to his needs and desires, and in the process, he'd stolen hers. *What did I expect to happen? I knew he was a thief. How stupid could I be?* Nothing had ever drained her like this. She turned back around the corner and dropped all the dishes and food into the waste barrel.

After dark, hunger brought her up out of bed. The small home was still. She stopped at her father's door. A low snore reassured her he was alive. She lit a lantern and went downstairs. Was it just this morning she had peeked in on Elias and found him dressing? It seemed like weeks ago. Was he always planning on leaving today? Most likely her hostile words this morning had driven him out. She stopped at the corner of the back kitchen wall. Clutching her hands behind her back, she wanted to look inside the pantry like a child stealing a treat. But her adult brain soured—there was no treat.

Exhaling, she turned and picked up the pitcher

of milk. The cold oats were stuck hard in the bottom of the pan. Glancing back towards the pantry, she waited for his voice, knowing it would never ask again if it was all clear. Finally splashing some milk on the oats and using her mixing spoon she took a bite of the lifeless breakfast from the cold pan.

She leaned her forehead on the heavy rim of the pan. She grieved his cap. Yes, she was still going to make him a warm brown cap. He hated being cold. Heaven forbid, he would be off on *her trip* with an uncovered, cold head. Maybe another sappy young woman desperate for companionship would take him in. That voice and soft blue eyes would woo any woman who could see. Loyalty.

As long as they did right by him, he would stay loyal. Dropping the big spoon with a clank, she rose up and took the lantern into the pantry. She reached to take the blankets and noticed a folded piece of paper on top. She grabbed it and felt the money tucked inside. Dropping the blankets, she came back around the corner and sat back down. Setting the bills aside, she pulled the light close to see his uneven handwriting.

Lovely Lauren,

I am sad that you won't join me on this addventure, but I think if I had a father to call my own, maybe I would not leave eether. I promised you money for your help, and I want to thank you for all you did for me. Please set some aside for your trip to Denver City. I have taken note of your adress and will keep it in my pocket with my other valable memento. It would mean a lot to me to hear how you are doing.

Corgually, Elias Browne

Lauren dropped her forehead on her palm; he had misspelled *"cordially,"* along with many other words, but it somehow touched her. A strange warmth came over her cold skin. No one, criminal or not, had ever written such sweet endearments to her.

Sad. He was *sad* she wouldn't be joining him. Interesting. Pushing the pan away, she set her arms flat on the table, the letter between them, she stared at the paper. He would keep her address next to the little wrapper in his pocket. What was the importance of that wrapper?

Funny how she had been hurt and weepy all day, and now a crazy contradiction rose in her. Truly, she would miss him. His eyes, the way his touch made her scared and safe at the same time. Companionship. The word sounded silly, but she would miss his company. His handwriting was rough and hard to read, just like him. A soft-spoken outlaw—how could that be? He wished she could have joined him. "Adventure. Humph." She thumbed the bills—he left more money than her father made all year. Would he have enough for all the things he needed?

Holding the letter, she sat up and took the lantern by the base. Helping him this last week was enough adventure for this simple girl. It would have never worked; she sighed, taking the staircase slowly. *Such a long trip with someone I barely know, goodness.* After helping a man jump from the grave, she must still be missing the working part of her mind.

Chapter 12

IT TOOK ELIAS a day and a half to walk what should have been a four-hour trek. His hiding spot was good; his home worth all the stops to rest. At one stop it hadn't even been dusk, but he'd curled up and slept all night in the woods. Stiff and sore to rise the next morning, side throbbing, he kept going and made it by noon. Dry tack was sorely lacking appeal when compared to the last week of hot meals served by a curly haired beauty.

His old dugout was probably fifty years old. The woods had grown over it but it provided shelter and storage. He ducked inside and breathed in the musty scent. He sat on his shabby cot and pulled the thick blanket around his shoulders. How long till his strength would return? Carefully lying down, he pulled his legs in, eyes drooping. He didn't want to sleep, dreading the nightmares that were unending and despicable.

Only two thoughts kept his mind alert. Everything Lauren—those round, green eyes, the warmth of her skin on his hand. He let out a shallow breath—and his plan to start a new life. He had carefully moved through Greenlock and been almost invisible. Without his long hair, no one stared and whispered with their soured judgment. It brought a strange swirl in his gut. It had been his identity for so long. Could he really play another role? He had thought that the farther away he got from Lennhurst, the closer would be his deliverance, yet those mocking scenes followed him everywhere he went. Lauren was a lovely distraction. The first angel he'd met since the last time he'd seen his sister, Anna.

Anna was usually so strong, but he'd never seen her crying so hard as that last time. What was he—twelve, thirteen? She had been fine all morning, floating through the wards, greeting and touching all the broken-minded people. Her cheery voice had carried over the constant moaning and crying, and her smile had put the children to task. They would all do anything for her, each one in love with her as much as he was. She had found him loading the coal that day. The way she grabbed his arm and pulled him into a tight hug, he'd known something was wrong. She kept saying she loved him and he needed to stay strong and out of trouble. Something about a letter she'd just read from her family. He had pushed her away, her words and tears had burned into the pain of what was coming.

"Just say it! Get it over with, Anna!" he spat at her.

He'd tried to gage the shock in her pale face.

"That letter from home? You are leaving? Will you be back?" Her vacant eyes and mouth answered his question. She pulled out their birthday trinket, covered in a candy wrapper and held it out.

"I don't want it," he said. His skin squeezed with more pain than all the belts that had met his backside. "If there was any way," she had sobbed. "I could take you . . . but I can't. My family is forcing me to leave, they wanted me here as a child, but now that I'm grown, they want me to marry." She'd barely got the words out that day. He'd never have anyone come for him. He had no real brother or sister or parents. She'd said she'd always be his sister. But now their pretend game was over. Why had he believed they could be family? They were never really blood-related. Only that stupid wrapper was left.

Elias sat up holding his breath to block the pain in his side. Could he stay out of trouble? Dropping his head, he rubbed his hands over a bit of stubble. Did Mr. Campbell realize he had a loving daughter right under his nose?

It was nice to be cared for, but it never lasted. Eventually, Anna would have moved on. She didn't belong there. Shortly after he realized she wasn't coming back, he'd jumped the wall and run away from Lennhurst. In time, anyone he cared about would leave, so it was easier for him to leave first. Lauren had wanted to go west. He'd seen the longing in her eyes.

Somehow, he almost believed he could have a new day with someone to please, someone to do better for. That foolishness was from a lifetime ago. Too many mistakes defined him. His eyes rolled back from the pain in his side. He was smart to go when he did.

By the end of the week, Elias was sure he could make it back to town without stopping and resting. He shaved his face clean and combed his short hair side to side with his fingers. The list in his hand was crinkled from planning and scribbling more items to buy. He placed it and his money in a wallet. After securing today's things, he would come back and spend the last night in his dugout.

He stepped back to the small creek and filled his canteen. Would he miss this quiet, peaceful place? Looking up, he watched as a breeze skimmed over the treetops. Was he ready to follow some sergeant turned wagon master's orders? He'd grown up confined. Prison and the army weren't a whole lot different. At least he would be alone in his wagon and surrounded by wide open space. Following directions was just part of survival. Maybe a kinder group of people would be found than those he usually kept company with.

FATHER MICHAEL HAD stopped by the day before. One of his elderly parishioners had passed and had no close family to prepare her for burial. Lauren fingered the stack of the woman's burial things. She would dress her at the church, and Father would do the ceremony there. A few of her church friends wanted to attend.

Short and simple was about all Lauren could muster. Still ashamed of her actions, she shook her head. She had found every excuse to do something around town this last week. Maybe just maybe, she would catch sight of Elias. Would he dare appear in town, even looking drastically different? With his brown knitted cap concealed in her bag, would she have the nerve to give it to him? What if someone saw her? What if the sheriff saw them talking? Had she become accustomed to being irresponsible? It was better that he was nowhere to be found. He had probably changed his mind about the wagon train. Needing a walk, she blew out a breath. A meandering hour to get to the church might blow the cobwebs away.

Passing by the bakery, she went inside and picked out a yummy pastry for Father Michael. While paying, two ladies came in behind her and looked her up and down. One whispered in the other's ear. Lauren felt the heat rising in her cheeks. The other woman's eyes got wide and pulled her friend back. They gave her a wide berth as she stared at the floor and walked out.

Straightening her shoulders, she walked another

block to get to the back of the church kitchen. It was barren of any cooking and her only friend, Father Michael. She peeked through the double doors into the ornate sanctuary. The large statues of Jesus and Mary greeted her on the left and right. They were impressive art pieces for little Greenlock. Straight down the center aisle, Father Michael was kneeling and praying with someone at the altar. She closed the doors carefully and laid his pastry on the counter. She walked through a side hall to where the dead woman lay in a small room. Setting the stack of clean clothes next to her, she covered her nose. Unfortunately, she'd started to smell. A few wildflowers clutched in her hand might do the trick. She had the time, so she walked to the back lawn of the church. The green grass stretched back to the tree line. Dotted in rows were large thick gravestones and farther back, little wooden crosses. What looked like wildflowers grew here and there beyond that.

She glanced down the last row of wooden crosses, and her steps slowed. *Elias Browne* was burnt into the thin wood. *Why can't I have just have one day without thinking of him?* Even clutching a group of wildflowers reminded her of her escapade to retrieve his box of money. Pulling the group of flowers to her nose, they didn't seem to carry much scent. She tried not to look, but only two people on this planet, except God, knew of those brick bags and jugs of embalming fluid occupying that space in the ground. What had overtaken her that day? She looked up and saw Father Michael coming from the back door.

"I thought I heard something." He smiled.

She caught up with him, and they walked back into the kitchen. "This is for you." She pointed out the bakery bag and set the flowers down.

"Miss Lauren, you are so thoughtful." He opened the small bag. "Mmm, my favorite."

"I didn't see any diggers."

"I know, I didn't have anyone come around today. Not even for my delightful watery porridge." He winked. "I may have to ask a few faithful Catholics to help me after the service."

"I wish I was Catholic." Her brows crossed. "Do your people shun people like me?"

He blinked. "People like you? You mean Protestants?"

"No—I just mean—like me. Someone who works at a mortuary."

"Oh. I suppose all people struggle with judgment, even though we are told not to judge. I would say my friends here deal with the same judgments all people do. I would like to hope they do a better job of getting to know someone and base their findings on a person's merits or godliness." He smiled. "Because I also work with the sick and dying, I never saw anything in you but someone who is caring, kind and respectful to the families."

Lauren raised a slight smile. She didn't mean to fish for a compliment. The people who needed her help were friendly enough. "How do people get to know people? How do people get past what people do and become friends?"

Father Michael wobbled his head and took a bite of his pastry. "Usually some common interest bonds them. The church should be that starting point for people. Mrs. Oden will most likely have only her prayer circle here today."

Lauren nodded, taking up the flowers. "I will get her ready."

Chapter 13

LAUREN GRABBED HER father's stiff clothes off the drying line. In the kitchen, she placed them on the table to fold. In only a few minutes she could easily heat up the iron and give his shirt and pants a press. She tapped her finger on the table, but why? He hadn't been out in public in weeks. Rolling her bottom lip, she put the iron on the stove anyway. She wanted to. She wanted to hand him clean and pressed clothing, hung on a hanger.

He had come to supper yesterday, and they even talked a little about how to make friends. She told him about a few of the friends from primary school, but they had all moved on to marriage and running a home. She didn't tell him about her conversation with Father Michael a few days back. To the poor priest she must have sounded pitiful. Her father asked if the money from the county had come in. Lauren made up some excuse, in all the chaos, she didn't remember turning it in. She said she would look into it.

The next morning, Lauren turned from the dishes to answer a knock at the door. It was the sheriff's deputy who she hadn't seen for weeks.

His thin face was pale and frowning, and her heart dropped to her feet. It was Elias, they had found him, again.

"Ma'am." He tipped his large hat. "I have a body for you. I left the wagon around back." Lauren tried to replay his words. Wouldn't he have said it was Elias?

"It's a sad thing." He pulled his hat forward and held it over his chest. "The priest from Saint Paul's."

Lauren jumped back. "Not Father Michael."

"I think so. Is there more than one priest there?"

"No, only one that I know of." Her head started to spin. "Are you sure?" Maybe someone was visiting him? "I just saw Father Michael a few days ago. He was fine, no signs of illness or anything."

The deputy was already grimacing. "He-he was stabbed. Sometime last night. It looks like someone was after the church money."

"That makes no sense!" Lauren whined, eyes filling with tears. "He gives everything away."

The deputy scratched behind his ear. "I don't know how much they got. It looks like to me like he might have even lived if the doctor had helped him." He grimaced. "Blood trailed from the altar to the back door. He must have crawled all night, but without any help . . . he was gone by this morning when someone found him."

Picturing Father Michael alone on the floor,

crying out for help, Lauren turned from the door and left the deputy standing alone. She went into her numb, automatic place, and slipped down the basement steps, then lit the lantern. Slowly she grabbed the large wooden doors and pulled them apart. The morning sun blinded her, but nothing could hide the hem of his long robe and simple black shoes at the end of the wagon bed. It was Father Michael.

The deputy came around back and found her frozen and staring. He jumped up on the wagon bed and pulled him forward. He was wrapped in a sheet, but now his shoes and black stockings hung off the back of the wagon. The deputy jumped back down and struggled to pick him up. Straining, he lifted him and set him on the ice table. "Do you want me to chip the ice like I did before?" he puffed.

Lauren couldn't feel herself breathe. "No," she whispered.

"The sheriff has already got some ideas. He thinks it's one of those squatters down by the river."

"Father Michael helps those people. Why would," her face burned with grief, "they kill him?"

"Just a robbery gone bad. But Sheriff Dodd has his own way about quick justice. He'll have no mercy for anyone killing a priest. I'm sorry to say, you will have a few more to get buried if he doesn't just send them floating down the river."

Lauren wasn't sure she'd heard anything he said. She finally turned to him. "What?"

"Dodd doesn't like a waste of time and money to feed and wait for a trial. He'll just shoot 'em first. Like those last three we brought ya." He looked back at the wagon. "So just a fair warning. You might have more a commin'."

Lauren felt her neck and head tighten. If he said one more thing, she might just fall into a pile on the dirt floor.

"I've got some church folk waiting for me. I wanted to get him over here before I let them in to help clean up the church."

Lauren didn't move.

"Do you need to get that tablet and write anything down?"

"No," she whispered.

"All right." He walked out and dragged his hand along the wagon bed. "I'll have someone let you know about his service."

The wagon pulled out leaving the silence as demanding as the morning light. Lauren pulled the large doors together. Fighting the shivers and shock, she pushed the lid off the icebox and pulled on the heavy gloves. Grabbing the pick, she tried to raise it in the air but she could not, her arms would lend no strength to the task. Dropping everything, she walked up the base-ment steps. Their front door was still ajar. She closed it softly. Stoic and barren of all feeling, she walked up the steps to her father's room. She knocked softly, "Father, I need you."

He cracked the door, and his breath smelled like rotten eggs. "What Laurie?"

"The priest, Father Michael, from St. Paul's. He's. Been. Killed." Her eyes closed, fighting the pain and loss. "He's in the basement. You will have to tend to him. I can't do it."

"Okay, honey. I'll try." He rubbed his eyes. "You look like you might be getting sick, you're not usually so pale."

Lauren turned around and headed for her bedroom.

He cleared his throat. "Maybe after some lunch, huh? I can try—"

Her door clicked closed.

AFTER HOURS OF laying on her bed staring at the wall, Lauren wondered why she didn't cry. She pinched her arm but didn't feel anything. *Did Father Michael feel pain all night? Did he suffer? Knowing him, he probably forgave the reprobate that took his life. Would the sheriff really just shoot people without giving them a chance to defend themselves?*

What would she do if he brought in the body of one of the diggers Father Michael had tried to help? She had yet to hear her father move about. What if the parishioners came for the body, to hold his service? He deserved the utmost care. Rising with chin in the air, she pulled her apron over her head.

Lighting the other lamps in the basement, she saw her father had not been there. She sighed. Grabbing a bucket, she went back up the stairs and pumped the water to halfway. She went through the steps of laying out the dead as if this was someone else's body. But something happened when she went to wash the blood off his hands. He had beautiful cold hands. Pulling the sponge over and around each finger, tears dripping from her chin started mixing with the water. Gently, she pulled his hand to her lips and kissed it.

"I'm so sorry," she mumbled. "I will miss you," she choked between cries. "You were a dear friend to me and so many others. How will we get along without you?" A wail came up from deep in her being, and she squeezed his hands between hers wishing she could find some warmth, some strength. Why didn't she have any to infuse him with? She pulled the corner of her apron across her dripping face. All those comforting words she'd heard a hundred times, "he's with God now," "from dust we have come to; dust, we do return." "Oh, death where art thy sting?" Did she really think they brought comfort to others? No random sentiment would touch her today. She had gone numb, inside and out. This one person, this only friend, was gone forever.

Chapter 14

LAUREN FOUND THE small mirror from where they had left it the night Elias used it to shave. She had chosen her rust-colored skirt and blue blouse with cream trim for Father Michael's service. Her hair was still damp, and for now, staying in place so she set the mirror down and grabbed her matching bonnet. Today she would walk into the church with her head held high. If she could avoid people looking at her, she would sit in the front row.

"Father, I'm leaving," she called up the staircase, receiving no response. She wanted to feel something, even anger toward her father, but in her heart, she knew it was good that she had been the one to prepare the loving priest. It had helped her to grieve and to give him one last trace of care.

Looking around, she wondered if she should take her bag or a little purse. She'd left her bag with the cap for Elias somewhere under her bed, probably to stay for good. Her small beaded reticule with a clean hankie was appropriate. Grabbing it off the hall tree, she stopped and held her hand on the knob. *Was there ever going to be anything hopeful in this town?* She stepped out and closed the door behind her.

Coming down Main Street was a large, covered wagon with a man and woman of color. She couldn't help but stop and admire. President Lincoln and so many had fought to give the Negros their freedom. They were probably on their way to Independence to start out west. The wagon was larger and higher off the ground than she imagined. As it passed by, the woman on the bench turned and acknowledged her. Lauren nodded back. *How strange. If they only knew.*

She walked on toward the church then looked back. Would that very wagon be meeting up with Elias? It seemed too farfetched. Gripping her little purse, she hesitated again, would she have time to see? She shook her head and set her direction for the church. *"Let the dead bury the dead."* Why did that come to her? One of those things she'd heard at many a funeral. Or not?

She stopped again and watched that wagon. What was pulling her? Glancing back at all the fine people entering the church, she started walking away. It was happening again; someone else was guiding her body. But she had to know, and she just had to see. Was he really doing what he said? Could he really steal her dream like the brash thief he was? Maybe it would help calm down her curiosity. Maybe she hated that he'd left with her curt voice in his head.

She walked faster. Maybe she should run in and grab the cap? His money. It was too extravagant. She flew past her home and saw something in the field past the blacksmith. There was *another* wagon. No not one, there were two. A woman stood near, another packed a box. The large wagon from Main Street pulled into the field, blocking her view. She crossed over and approached the blacksmith's open building. Maybe she could hide a bit and watch. The third wagon pulled around the others and set the break. The two women looked up and went to greet them. Heart racing, Lauren watched their every move. What kind of family or couple was coming from the other wagon? She leaned and strained to see past her hiding spot.

"Lovely Lauren?"

Her hand flew to her heart, and she pushed her bonnet back off her head. Where did he come from?

"Elias." Her mouth hung open.

"You do look lovely . . . really." That gentle voice was accompanied by a slight smile.

His hair was a bit longer and swirled in different directions. She locked her arm to her side and gripped her skirt not wanting to touch that soft, light brown hair.

"What are you doing at the blacksmith?" he asked.

"I-I saw that last wagon come into town. I

guess I was just curious to see it." She stilled as the blacksmith came from the back and handed Elias a metal tool of some kind. "But I am to be at a funeral even now." She nodded, stepping away. "I do have that cap for you." She smiled. "But you don't look too cold, so I just wanted to wish you well, that's all." There she said it. They could part without—

"I'll be by tonight. At dusk."

Lauren swallowed and kept walking backward. Heat flushing her face.

"To get the cap." He looked amused.

"Oh, all right. I will see you then." She turned quickly unaware that she was almost to the middle of the street. "Back alley." She turned, dodging an oncoming man on horseback.

"Back alley," he repeated back as she walked swiftly across the wide street, leaping up on the opposite sidewalk. Had she asked if that other wagon was his? Maybe he was just getting something fixed at the blacksmith? She wanted to turn and look so bad, her heart still pounding from the shock.

For some reason, one look at the only handsome face that had paid her any attention didn't register any anger in her. That felt good. How could she be so selfish to despise someone for changing their life and setting a new course? *Good for him. Wonderful, really,* she mused, trying to find a steady breath.

Down the block, singing so sad and low came through the church doors. She quietly slipped in and sat. Straightening her back, she placed her hands in the middle of her lap. She didn't know the song or what language it was in so she closed her eyes and tried to think reverent thoughts. It was no use; she stared at the church aisle. Her beloved friend, laying there all night, alone. She reached in for her hankie. There is nothing worse than being alone. The pews were dotted with bowed heads, people praying, singing and crying. Why couldn't priests have families? Why had he done this work without anyone by his side? In the thick stillness, she dabbed at her rolling tears. How many were grief for her friend, how many for her own loss, her own disappointments, her own regrets?

ELIAS CRANKED HARD on a steel bolt that kept the water barrel in place on his wagon. There she was. Just out of the blue, peering out to the field while hiding behind the blacksmith's wall. Had she been looking for him?

He licked his lips and shook his head, forcing his rambling thoughts down. It didn't matter, except that he'd just about been able to leave town without seeing her. He knew good and well where she lived, and he'd never stopped in. Why did he say he would tonight? That was one visit he needed to cancel, all around a bad idea.

She looked so pretty today; he remembered that rust colored skirt. Knowing her, she would probably have a piece of pie, maybe some plum cobbler. Just one quick stop. She'd made him a cap. He could abide by that simple kindness.

Elias came around his wagon for the fourth time. The spring days were getting longer and dusk was taking forever. He already checked on his two new horses—they would work well until he got to Independence, then he would buy some oxen. He pulled up and rounded his leg over the tailgate and looked around.

Maybe he should give her something? The money he had promised was from him, but it wasn't very personal. What do ladies like? He flipped open his box of personal things from the dugout. Looking around, he shook his head, a lady wouldn't like anything he possessed. He sat on the bench. Underneath it were all the pots and pans, chains, pulleys, storage for guns and such. Nothing there. He rummaged around feeling his nervousness increase. It was dusk. He wasn't going to step out with her. He was just going to pick up a cap and say his goodbyes. He stepped off the back and pulled a long piece of grass to chew on. This would only take a minute and he would be right back here getting ready to leave at daylight.

Elias maneuvered around the back roads and came upon the familiar back side of the funeral home and residence of Miss Lauren Campbell. A few crates sat by her back door and he looked up as she walked out. She had a heavy coat draped over her arm, a brown checkered case, a full bag hanging from her arm, and the same bonnet back in place. Maybe she was expecting them to go for a stroll.

"Hello," he called. She looked flushed and nervous. "Am I interrupting some cleaning?" He browsed the area.

"No." She let out a shaky breath. "These are my things. Except I need your help with one more large thing."

"Where is this large thing going?" he asked, brows crossing. She looked at the ground, again.

"In your wagon," she said softly, glanced up and then back to her feet.

"My wagon?"

"Do you have one? Are you still joining the wagon train like you said?"

A strange chill ran up his back, a familiar feeling without the ice water. "Are you planning on coming with me?" He went to pull his fingers down his chin coming up short with no beard to pull on.

"Yes, I am. These two crates are the dishes," she nodded at them. "I have all the personal things I can carry. But somehow we need to get the harpsichord."

"Right now? Lauren, I-I thought I was coming

110

to pick up a cap. What about your father? He's permitted you to go?" He rubbed his forehead thinking this has to be a mixed up mistake. She wouldn't be so impulsive. Yet, he stared in disbelief at the young woman who'd helped him jump the grave.

"No, not really. I just made up my mind an hour or so ago. I've written him a letter. I left some money for him to hire someone. Here's the rest." She pulled out the cash from a little beaded purse. "You can have it back. I know it will cost more to include me on your, uh, the trip."

He stepped back. "No, you hold it." He turned and looked both ways down the alley, struggling with his mixed emotions. *Just tell her no.* He bit hard on his lower lip—he had let her believe they could do this weeks ago. Why hadn't he just stayed at the wagon when he'd had the chance? He rubbed his hands back and forth across his short hair. "Are you sure, Lauren? Those dishes will likely be in a hundred pieces by the time we get to Denver City."

"I packed them in extra hay." Those soft, round, green eyes finally met his, sweet as a doe.

"All right." He strained to lift the two crates of dishes. "Get your things, and we'll come back for the harpsichord." He started down the alley.

"Oh Lord, help me." He heard her whisper as she walked behind him.

Chapter 15

JUST PAST THE blacksmith, a small campfire glowed in the dark. Joe Kern and two of the three Utah sisters sat around it. Elias slowed and tried to get a new grip on the heavy crates. If he walked around the other side of the blacksmith building, he could approach his wagon without walking past them. How would he explain Lauren? Going around the building, he sat the dishes down next to his wagon. She looked up and down at the wagon, her arms loaded with her bag, case, coat, and blankets.

"Here." He took the load from her arms and threw them in the back of the wagon. They stood in the dark with obvious, unspoken questions whirling between them.

"So, you still want me to tell everyone you are my wife?" He shuffled his feet.

She leaned away, looking at the folks around the campfire. "I guess."

"The older man with the hat is Joe Kern. He's the wagon master." He pointed. "Those are three sisters trying to join their family in Utah. Joe drives their wagon and then will lead a troop when we get to Independence."

Lauren nodded.

"Let's get this over with." He grabbed her hand and pulled her toward the group.

She stumbled behind him. "Mr. Kern, ladies." He released her hand. "I had mentioned, I was traveling alone—but," he cleared his throat, "my wife has wrapped up some family needs early." They all jumped up. "This is Mrs. . . . ahh . . . Mrs.—"

"Lauren," she said, moving from behind him. "Please call me Lauren." She reached out and shook the hands of the ladies.

"So lovely to have you along. I'm Mabel. My sister, Janet." Janet reached out and shook her hand. "Our other sister, Chrystal, is already sleeping."

"And please call me Joe." He tipped his hat. "The other group is the Littles. I can introduce you in the morning."

"Thank you. So nice to meet you all." Lauren looked to the ground.

"No little ones? Maybe newlyweds?" Janet asked.

Elias opened his mouth, but nothing came out.

"Yes, just married a month." She shot him fearful eyes. "How time flies." Was her lie believable?

"Mmm hum." Mumbling was all that would come out. He pulled his jaw left and right. "Joe,

I have one quick pick up on Main Street in the morning. Then we'll be right along."

"Thanks, Elias, we'll see you here or on the road." Joe grabbed a black kettle and doused the fire. "Everyone sleep well." They all nodded goodnight and turned to their wagons.

Elias stopped by the front wheel of his wagon, pointing to the small footstep. He held his hand out for Lauren to take it and step up. "Are you sure, Lauren?"

She stepped up and held onto the bench as he stepped up behind her. They were so close, he could smell her flowery soap. This whole trip was going to be a whole lot of closeness. Did she know what that was like for a man? He'd told her it would never be about love. Truth be told, even his obligation to help her had faded in the absence. But what a warm, soft-skinned, sweet-smelling woman did to his senses. Did she understand why his heart pounded through his thin shirt?

He pulled the canvas to the side so she could get to the back. She stepped through and began to pick up her belongings.

"That center area where you are standing, I was going to bed down there. But I suppose your harpsichord will go there." He stepped through. "That means that bench is going to be your new bed."

She turned and scratched her nose. The bench

wasn't more than a foot and a half wide. "Lauren, are you sure you want to do this? You could be home and in your own bed tonight."

"Please don't ask me that again." She pulled out her thick wool blanket and laid it over the hard bench. She rolled another blanket out and set a spot for a pillow. "I-I apologize for taking your, ah, area." Her voice wavered as she removed her bonnet.

"Not to worry, I can sleep under the wagon." He could watch her fret and arrange things all night, every move entertaining. If he didn't leave this minute, he'd reach out and grab her in motion, hold her until she relaxed. "If you are good, I'll say goodnight."

"Yes, I am. Goodnight." She sat on her bench bed, back stiff. The moon cast shadows over her fretful face. He grabbed his bedroll and climbed back out the way he came.

"LAUREN." SOMEONE SHOOK her awake. She must have slept on the hard ice table . . . No, she was cold and stiff from sleeping on a hard bench all night. She sat up as Elias pulled his arm back over the back gate.

"I've got the horses ready. Just hang on a bit, we're heading to get your harpsichord." Lauren nodded, trying to loosen her shoulders and neck. She pulled the soft band from her hair and ran her fingers through the curls. Elias sat on the front bench which tilted under his weight. He tapped the reins and led the horses around the field and onto Main Street. She peered through the opening in the back canvas. Barely sunrise, with a few roosters announcing the new morning.

She re-knotted her hair. This was her last chance, was there anything she needed? Her mother's letters, the scarf she had knitted Cammi, everything that was important, she had shoved in her bag. He stopped in front of her house and came around the back of the wagon. He lowered the back gate and reached for her. He easily held her weight as she jumped down.

"Last chance, girl." His grip on her waist was more warning, his calm voice and face questioning.

She nodded timidly. Opening the funeral home front door, he walked past her and picked up the harpsichord, and then barely squeezed himself and it through the door. He set it down on the ground and helped her back up into the wagon. He lifted one end to her and grabbed the other as they slid it into place. Lifting the gate back up, he hooked it closed. With only a few inches for her legs at the end, she watched him take three long strides back to her home and pull the door shut. Staring at the wood chipped brown door, and then up at her bedroom window, something stung in her nostrils. Rubbing it away, she warily looked down the street to see the steeple of the

Catholic Church against the new morning sky. The wagon jerked forward, and she held her hand out to steady the harpsichord.

Blowing out a breath, she said. "Mother, believe it or not, I'm coming."

Chapter 16

LAUREN SAT IN the back of the slow rocking wagon, legs pinched for space by the long harpsichord. She could see the other wagons from last night ahead of them, but she wanted to wait for Greenlock to be well in her past before she came out of hiding.

She hadn't mentioned in her note to her father that she was going to travel by wagon train. Would he assume she took the harpsichord on the train? Would he use Elias's money to hire help or buy more booze? Either way, she didn't see him jumping on a horse to go search for her. He knew she longed to see her mother, and in her heart she knew his timing would never match hers. The dust mesmerized her, swirling up and rolling back behind the wagon. There was something about losing Father Michael . . . she couldn't put her finger on it exactly. Those moments of going numb scared her. To have no hope, no feelings is to be dead. Unfortunately, the dead was something she knew too much about.

Elias took ahold of his new life, and she had helped him do it. Was it selfish to do something so bold for herself? Her eyelids drooped. She had lain awake fretting most of the night; the rocking now smoothed out her frayed edges and made her drowsy.

"Lauren," Elias called over her drowsy state. "You can sit up here." He patted the hard bench seat next to him.

She pulled her skirts over one arm and ambled on her knees along the bench. Elias held the reins in one hand and put his hand out behind his head. Taking his steady grip, she lifted her legs over the back of the seat and sat on the other side next to him. Smoothing her skirt in place, she took in a steady breath. The bright sun hit their legs. The air tasted like dust, and she could see the large prairie bonnets of the sisters in the wagon ahead of them. A quiet nervous emotion squeezed her chest. This was so strange.

"You'll want to walk a portion of every day." He sat taller, nodding ahead of them. "These gals seem nice. Maybe you can walk together sometimes?"

Traveling with these people brought a bit of comfort. "The sisters seem friendly, how strange that they travel separately from their families."

"Their husband had to go ahead with the older children from what I understand. The middle one, Janet I think, was suffering after losing a baby. The sisters stayed behind to help her. Anyway, Joe had said something like that."

Lauren leaned forward to look around,

squinting at the sun. "You said, husband. You mean husbands."

"No, I mean husband. They're Mormon, they all are married to the same man."

Lauren turned and squinted at him. "You're telling the truth?"

"Yes, Mrs. Browne," he smirked. "I only lie when it benefits me."

She closed her eyes and shook her head. "I can see your quick charm has improved with your health."

He flashed her a smile. "Thanks to you."

"Humph," she huffed, but secretly was a little bit pleased at his appreciation.

"Will you befriend them?" he asked, watching the road.

"The other folks, in the first wagon, they are colored people."

"Umm hum," he nodded.

"I think we are all much alike in this group, fleeing from past hindrances. I will look forward to getting to know everyone." She grabbed the seat as they rocked hard to one side. "And you—I wondered if you would change your name? I saw your grave marker. Elias Browne with an e. Your name is standing in the back St. Paul's cemetery."

He rubbed his forehead, pushing his wide-brimmed hat back. "I thought long and hard about it. I don't have much, but I have a name.

I guess I just didn't want to give that up, too."

His stories of a childhood in a mental hospital twisted anew in her heart. He surely had the most deficient past. Why had she decided to trust him with her wellbeing?

"And you, Lovely Lauren. I almost believed you would leave everything for this trip to see your mother. But then I understood why you changed your mind. When you were looking for me yesterday—"

"I wasn't looking for you. I-I was curious about the large wagon."

"Okay." His calm, airy tone was soothing. "Then what happened between curiosity over a wagon and standing at the back door with your bags packed?"

She rubbed her hands together, looking out. The truth of losing Father Michael and her lowly state felt too intimate, too painfully close to her soul. If she was going to have a chance in heaven of keeping her heart intact, she needed to keep her cards close. Lord knows, Elias had become a master of it. The "no love, only loyalty" speech came to mind.

"Too long a story. It would surely bore you."

"I have nothing but time." He flashed a rogue grin.

"Then tell me how the traveling works?" She looked ahead at the other ladies in the wagon. Her biggest fears spun around womanly necessi-

121

ties. These women and hundreds before her had survived this travel. But how?

"We ride six days a week. Up to ten hours if possible. Sabbath is important to Mr. Kern. He said animals, humans, we all need it. If we lose time and have to stop mid-week, then we might have to travel on Sunday. The chores—hunting, and baking—can all be done on Sunday to get us through the week."

"Is Mr. Kern a Mormon?" Lauren interrupted.

"I don't know. You can ask him."

"How does it work? Those ladies can all be married to the same man. Can a woman have many husbands?"

"What are you asking?" He snickered. "All at the same time?" another laugh escaped.

Lauren shook her head. "I just don't know much about the Mormons." His snickers now irritated her. "I didn't mean at the same time like that. Forget it." She hated when she sounded stupid. He looked away but kept laughing.

"It's not *that funny*, Elias. You do like to mock me. I knew it." Her jaw clenched.

"I'm . . . I'm . . ." He couldn't seem to repress more snickers. "Not laughing at *you*." He drew his hand down his face. "In the Bible, like King David, he had many wives. Just never did a woman have many husbands."

"Clearly, God loves women. One man would be *plenty*." She rolled her eyes and watched a group of birds fly from tree to tree. At least those sisters had each other, obviously understanding and caring for one another.

ELIAS CIRCLED THE horses around one more time. He had driven the wagon only a few times before this, and he still was getting used to how wide he needed to maneuver to get the wagon in the right place. He set the brake and rolled his stiff neck from side to side. He jumped off the seat, and when he hit the ground, the jar rattled all through his sore body. *One day down,* he thought, *only a couple hundred to go.* Walking to the back gate, he let it down as Lauren put her knitting back in a canvas bag. She could barely move around the tiny area. The harpsichord seemed such a useless waste of needed space.

He reached his hands out to her, and she freely held his shoulders as he lowered her to the ground. After such a quiet afternoon, he wondered if she was still mad. He liked helping her, talking to her. He risked a quick wink with her so close. She squinted back, fighting a smile.

"Let me show you where things are." He reached behind her to the hard bench bed and flipped up the lid. "Cooking stuff in here, and some food. We'll have to buy what we can until we get out too far from towns."

"Brownes, come on over," Joe called.

Elias came around the wagon with Lauren

123

following. They headed to the common fire in the center as did the other travelers. Elias watched Joe wave everyone closer as Mabel lit a match to some kindling.

"That was a good day today. Thank you all for keeping up. Please be aware of things getting wet tomorrow as we cross the Forks River. The winter runoff doesn't seem too bad, but I won't know till I see it." He helped Mabel put a larger log on the fire. "Mr. and Mrs. Little, have you had a chance to meet Mrs. Browne?"

Lauren caught the eyes of the older woman for the second time. The elderly couple bowed, and she didn't know if she should shake their hands or just what was proper. "Please call me Lauren." She nodded.

"Louie and Ida Bell Little," the older black man said, nodding back.

"I prefer to call him Reverend Little," Joe spoke up. "We go back a bit. This man pulled me down and covered me after a Confederate cannon landed near us. He'll be leading our Sabbath time on Sundays. Oh, and Chrystal, this is Lauren."

Lauren nodded again, her eyes quickly averting from Chrystal's swollen belly to the ground. "Nice to meet you," she murmured. She had learned that pregnancy was visible but unspeakable. It was one society rule her mother had ingrained in Cammi and her early.

Chrystal nodded back, "Wonderful to have both

you, Lauren, and Mrs. Little on this trip. We are just going to Utah. And you?"

"Denver City." "California." Lauren and Elias said simultaneously.

Joe scratched behind his ear squinting at them, while the others looked confused, but no one dared ask about it to Lauren's huge relief.

Chapter 17

"IT'S A SATURDAY eve, leadn' to a Sunday, Sunday." Reverend Little sang as he did a little jig around the small band of friends.

Lauren couldn't help but smile and chuckle. She had found his joyful personality like a balm to a weary body. The firelight danced off each face differently as they sat and visited after the meal. This is what friendship feels like—warm and encompassing; feeling companionship down into her bones. The sisters had taken her under their wing, helping her each night with different chores while the men hunted or cared for the stock. Many times Elias had lowered her from the moving wagon to join the ladies on a walk. Nothing too important, just sharing recipes or stories about their children that were a month ahead on this trail west. The mothers missed them. They had asked her where she'd met Elias. Trying to swallow a giggle, she had said at the hardware store. Who would ever believe their story? She wasn't sure she did.

Lauren covered her yawn and glanced at Elias. He had been helpful, even patient with her when she'd panicked crossing the Forks River. Trying to manage the team and trying to convince her they wouldn't drown was no easy feat. If he only knew what a calming effect he had over her. Whether working together or in the quiet this last week, they seemed to fall into a comfortable pace. Besides a sore backside, it had gone better than she could imagine.

Ida Bell walked by, taking a bucket of water to the back of their wagon. She was the only one who didn't sit much in the evening. Lauren wondered if she could help with her load. The woman walked morning till dusk, and then prepared food and cleaned up. They were all tired, but the load of work kept this poor woman moving until they said their goodnights. Often she could hear voices from their wagon, but not voices or even a wolf howl could keep her awake once her head hit her pillow.

She stood and stretched, then gathered their empty dishes. Lauren leaned over the bucket and washed up. Elias came next to her and rinsed and dried.

"This is a bit reminiscent." He bumped into her side.

She peeked up at him. "Would you like a haircut too?"

He ran a hand through his short hair. "I think I'll grow it back out."

"I assumed your Nazarite vow was long over."

They looked up as the others waved goodnight.

"Sleep well." Elias took the dirty water and tossed it to the side. "We'll leave the coals for a hot breakfast in the morning. Our first Sunday."

"Praise God from whom all blessings flow." Lauren looked to the dots of twinkling white stars filling the night sky. "Minus my blister."

"Is it bad?" They turned to their wagon.

"Nothing a day off won't help." She rubbed her eyes.

Before she could react, Elias put his arm under her legs and lifted her up. She wrapped her arm around his neck. "Oh sir, you are so kind, but my walk is not far. Well—here we are."

Their faces were so close. Her smile dropped, seeing desire flash in his eyes. He stood stoically at the back of their wagon, clutching her, watching her, examining her.

"You are beautiful Lauren, outside and inside," he whispered. "I wish you had a better man to tell you, then you would believe it."

A wave of confusion hit her. "I think . . ." She stopped when he dropped her legs and let her go. "Elias," she grabbed his coat sleeve as he turned to lower the back gate. "Listen to me, I know it's only been a week, but I know I've changed. I've never been part of anything like this before. These people bring out another Lauren that I never knew was in here." She pointed at her heart.

He reached for his bedroll, expressionless.

She pressed her point, "You *are* the better man you've never met. You are strong and patient, lending a hand to these people. Your loyalty to me is dependable."

She tried to hold his eyes, now he was the one to look everywhere but at her. She moved to face him, their coats touching, she boldly planted her hands on the gate, blocking him between her and the wagon.

"You need to move, Lauren."

A quiver ran up her spine. The soft desire in his eyes had gone dark. She stepped back, his lips in a thin line. "Don't ever pin me in again. You'll be sorry."

ELIAS TOSSED HIS bedroll under the wagon and stalked out into the dark away from the camp. He grabbed a rock and threw it hard then another and another. He squeezed his head with his forearms and leaned back then he walked on, blowing out a sharp breath. He had wide-open space now to get his heart to calm down. She wasn't supposed to be on this trip. Messing with his very fragile head would not turn out well. *A torn mind that grew up among the insane and immoral,* the thought rolled in his brain, *I should be ten feet under by now.*

He quickly reminded himself that he'd said he would be loyal and that was it. A friend, and that was more than he could usually keep. Tonight all he'd wanted to do was kiss her. No, that's a lie. He had seriously thought of pulling that stupid instrument off his wagon bed and pulling her in with him. Of course, she would protest, they weren't even married. He didn't care—he could have his way and leave her in Denver City. She thought him some changed man, but if she only knew the darkness that stirred deeper than his outward actions.

"ELIAS . . . *ELIAS* . . ." THEY had the hand-cuffs on him. He jerked up. Something slammed his hand, and he opened his eyes. He came up on his elbow and rubbed the pain pulsing through his hand. He was underneath the wagon, and a shadow was across his face.

"I've learned to stay back." Lauren bent down on a knee holding a cup of hot coffee. "You always jump so hard when you awaken. You slammed your hand on the bottom of the wagon, but you slept in. I saved you some breakfast."

"I just want to sleep." He rolled away from her.

"Are you warm enough? I have an extra blanket." She waited, and he didn't answer. Something was wrong. He was the first one up every morning. He got more done before the coffee was on than Joe Kern. She had done something to upset him. She stood and held the warm mug in her cold hands. Last night, they had been playful one minute—he was the one who picked her up—but when she got too close, he acted like a bear caught in a metal cage.

Mabel waved her over. "We're going to try to heat some water and do a quick scrub in the creek and rinse with the warm bucket water. Gather whatever clothes you want to be washed, and we'll do that after."

Lauren looked down toward the small creek. "Is there enough privacy?"

"We girls take turns holding the sheets around each other. A few frogs might take a peek," she smiled. Chrystal set another kettle of water on the hot grate. Lauren smiled, clutching her coat together. Wagon trail life was about to get even more uncomfortable.

Heading back to their wagon, she noticed Elias was gone, bedroll and all. Only one of his horses was grazing in the field. No one watched her as she searched left and right. She didn't see him anywhere. Did Joe send for him? Wasn't this supposed to be the Sabbath? She stepped up into the wagon and found her towel and soap, wadding up her underclothes to be washed; she stuffed them inside her towel. Stretching around the harpsichord, she had seen Elias drop some of his things in the other bench. Should she offer to wash his things? Would he be mad? Reaching, she lifted the lid and saw his pile. Under his things were three long boxes with locks.

"Lauren."

131

She jumped at Mabel's voice, the lid slamming.

"Coming." Lauren slid to the edge of the wagon and jumped off.

Walking by the campfire, she dropped her things to help Ida Bell as she maneuvered a full pot of water and beans to the fire. Lauren grabbed a rag and moved a kettle to make space for her.

"Thank you, Mizz Browne," she bowed.

"Please call me Lauren. I notice how hard you work around here. If there's anything I can do—my, that's a full pot of beans. Will they last you all week, two weeks? Is there a way to store them?"

"Yes'um. Uh huh, all kinds of ways to keep vittles on the trail."

"Lauren." Chrystal waved to her as they headed to the creek.

"I am thankful to have a reverend's wife on this trip. Maybe say a little prayer for me, I'm certainly not accustomed to bathing outdoors." Lauren smiled, picking up her pile.

"That bath might just get your man from sleepn' 'lone each night," she chuckled.

Lauren's eyes widened. It had never occurred to her that anyone would notice their sleeping arrangements. Of course, people wondered. Did it look bad? Or did she smell that bad?

Chapter 18

MONDAY BROUGHT DARK clouds and a snap of cold wind. Just about the same temperature that Elias had toward her. If it weren't for Reverend Little's riveting Sunday sermon on the ten lepers and how to be the one who is thankful, Lauren would have sunk into a well of complaining.

She had spent most of the day off with the sisters, noting that Elias had returned with some rabbits around suppertime. Handing them off to Mabel, he had walked past her without even a greeting. Hunting was normal, going another day without really speaking to her was not. Sitting on her hard bed, she sniffed under her coat lapel. She thought the fast outdoor bath had been helpful.

The wagon lurched forward as he led the horses out onto the road. For the first time all week, she missed Father Michael, not her own blood father, but Father Michael. It was likely from yesterday's sermon. As reverent and serious as Father Michael talked about God, Reverend Little was loud and bouncy. Elias had stood next to Joe Kern, listening to the message without expression. Reverend Little had held his Bible open yesterday as he moved back and forth. She wondered if he could read, he never really read anything from the Bible, but anyone who communicated about a loving, caring God had always held her attention.

The wind gave the canvas roof a ripple, and she could smell and feel a dampness in the air. She knew she did not have enough knowledge of the Bible but wondered if the God of the Bible could really know her? *I haven't been very thankful about much,* she prayed. *I'm one of those who does more complaining.*

Feeling lonely, while rocking and swaying in the back, she watched how the fabric of Elias's shirt pulled across the thick muscles of his back and along his strong arms. Suddenly, she was thankful for his strength.

Father, I am grateful for Elias, his strength, and his calmness. I realize I constantly complained about my father, never thankful I have a father. She sighed, shaking her head. *I complained about working in a funeral home, yet never thankful for a job. I complained about having no friends, yet now I'm surrounded by women friends—yet so very different from me.* Ida Bell's comment about being smelly flitted through her thoughts and it stung. Surely she was judged a bad wife.

Forgive me, Lord. I am thankful for them and Elias, and for this trip to see my mother and Cammi. A warm sensation comforted her. It was good for the soul to confess her mistakes. The dishes, the harpsichord, to enjoy the family's pretty things once again, God had seen her heart's desire. To be with her own woman folk, to touch them again, hold them, kiss them. Something splatted on the canvas above her. Two more, three more—the rain now drummed against the horses and Elias's legs.

"Can you hand me my coat and that tarp?" He turned, pointing. Lauren crawled to the things, maneuvering around the harpsichord and handed them to him. One of the wheels dipped into a deep rut, and she tumbled into the harpsichord.

"Careful." He turned to her again. "Are you all right?"

Wincing, she straightened herself up, holding onto the back of the seat. "Why wouldn't you speak to me yesterday?"

He jerked his coat on, trading off holding the reins. He threw the tarp over his legs as the rain came down heavier. Lauren watched the wet streams of gray cover the land.

"I was just upset with myself," he said shifting in the seat. "There's a lot you don't know about me."

Lauren opened her mouth to ask.

"And I like it like that way. I want to do right by you and see you to Denver City, that's all that's important."

"Can we be friends?" She needed to know;

it was like food to her. She didn't want to be ignored for months.

"Yes, I'm sorry for yesterday. Being alone was good for me." He turned to her quickly, "Good for what I'm used to."

"Maybe it was good for me, too. The sisters took me in. We baked and washed, and they told me more stories of their children."

"Did you remind them you were already married?" A rogue grin lifted up the corner of his lips.

"They know *that*." She pushed on his shoulder. Teasing her was a good sign. "Ida Bell is another story. Reverend Little laughs and carries on with all of us, but I'm not sure she likes me."

"She likes you well enough. She's had a hard life. Been bounced around from Kentucky to West Virginia. Joe says most of her children were sold off. This trip is all about freedom, but the closer we get to Cincinnati, the harder time they will have."

"What's going to happen in Cincinnati?"

"The good Reverend's a race man. It's a Union State, but it's chock-full of Southern sympathizers. Just don't be surprised if we hear from them."

"I enjoyed the Reverend's sermon yesterday." Lauren leaned back trying to avoid the rain dripping off the front canvas. Dark mud flung off the horse's hooves splashing in the new puddles.

136

"He's a man full of conviction." Elias sighed. "If we don't get separated in Independence, Joe insists we have services with him every Sabbath. Joe says his prayers saved his life."

A gust of cold wind hit her face, and she watched the landscape grow grayer. "How do so many, hurting from the war, from the different sides, travel together?"

He turned quickly. "That's a good question. How do we travel with these folks?" He faced ahead.

Lauren pulled her hair out of the band and quickly fingered it back together. "For one, we don't hate them. None of them killed a brother or son. We don't judge them. I suppose they want to be treated as we do." Leaning back, she tucked in the folds of her skirts. She would miss walking with the sisters today. "I guess everyone wants a chance to heal and forget."

"Humph." He tilted his hat back and then snapped it back in place.

DARK CAME EARLIER than usual. Elias tied the horses near the wet green grass. Watching his wagon mates running back and forth, dodging the dripping sky, he blew out a breath. There would be no cooking fire tonight; each was on their own. Joe pulled a canvas over the front seat of his wagon, forming a tent and a small but dry place to sleep.

A small break appeared in the dense clouds.

Pulling out some dry jerky, Elias chewed a hard piece and looked under their wagon. The ground was saturated. A shiver ran over his cold, damp back as he reached into the wagon seat. He grabbed the tarp and brought it to the back gate. Jerking the metal pins out, he lowered the gate. Lauren fidgeted as he grabbed the end of the harpsichord and began to pull it towards him.

"What are you doing?" She was able to put her feet down stand straight for the first time.

"Get the end."

She grabbed the end and lowered it to him as he pulled it out. He wrapped the tarp around the instrument and tied it to the side of the wagon. Pulling himself up inside, he pinned the back gate and cinched the back canvas closed. He leveled her with his gaze. "I won't be cold and I won't be wet."

She backed up until she bumped into the back of the front seat, which set the lantern rocking on its hook. A stiff alarm shone on her face. "But the harpsichord will ruin if it gets wet."

Could her eyes get any more round and wary? "I've covered it, and I'm sleeping there." He pointed to the large empty space at her feet.

"Can I just point out, that you are already cold? Already wet?"

"Not for long." He sat on the opposite bench

138

and untied his boots. She grimaced at the swirl of mud beneath him, then looked away like she could ignore his intrusion. He pulled off his jacket and lowered his suspenders. He'd never known what propriety really was. But the red in her cheeks was a telltale sign she did. He pulled out some dry pants and quickly unbuttoned the top of his shirt, pulling it over his head.

"You've changed." She mumbled facing away from him.

"How's that?" He found a dry pair of socks.

"You use to talk slow and calm, and you use to move slow and calm."

"I had a hole in my side you could stick one of those knitting needles through."

Her shoulder shuddered. He pulled on an extra sweater. "I'm done. I'll face the back while you get ready." She turned and faced him. "I am ready." As she laid her bedding across the narrow bench, he tossed his bedroll in the middle. She carefully sat. Dress, coat and fancy boots all still in place.

"Lantern out then?" he asked.

She wouldn't look at him but pulled something from her bag. She handed him a brown knit cap.

He took it and pulled it on. Their eyes finally met. "Handmade by you *for me.*"

She gave a quick nod.

"It's really nice." He rubbed his tongue along his bottom lip, a quiet peace warming his body. Reaching up, he rubbed the soft cap, "I love it, Lauren, thank you."

Chapter 19

FALLING ASLEEP KNOWING a harpsi-chord was at your side was far different from knowing a man—not just any man, but this charming yet moody, but confident, yet confusing man—slept below. She had almost landed on him in the basement of the funeral home. It was as dark then as it was now, what if she needed to get up and—

His arm slammed against her bench, and she jerked up heart racing. Was he awake, needing something? She listened, teetering on her thin plank for a bed. His breathing sounded deep. He mumbled something as he sucked in a frantic breath. Was it a bad dream? She remembered the other times when he had been wild with fever. Had he taken a chill?

"Elias," she whispered. "It's me, Lauren. I think you're having a nightmare." Dare she touch his shoulder? "Elias . . ."

"Get off me!" He rolled up.

Lauren pulled away, the wet canvas touching her back. "No one's on you. You're in the wagon."

He grabbed his knees, dropping his head. "I'm sorry. I must have woke you."

It didn't really matter that she had been awake for hours fretting. "You had a bad dream."

Yanking his cap off, he scratched his head. "I'll go sleep outside."

"No." Her voice was soft, calmer. "Just go back to sleep." She tried to see his expression in the dark. "Are you warm enough?"

"Umm hum." He pulled his cap back on and lay on his back.

"Sometimes I have to think of something good but boring before I fall asleep." She lowered back down, facing him from above, waiting, a strange familiarity hung in the air.

"Tell me," he said, sleepily, dropping his arm over his face.

"Mostly sums. I keep all the ledgers for my father's business—what comes in, who he owes. I daydreamed a lot about this trip. But then I'd have a hard time sleeping, the thought of getting to Denver City was too exciting. Oh, to see my mother and my sister. Humm, let's see, rehearsing knitting patterns I wanted to try would always make me sleepy. The one I used for your cap was fairly easy."

She waited, his deep breathing returned. *Thinking of you, looking at you, stretched out below me.* She glanced over the side. His eyes were closed and his arm now lay on his chest. That's of *no help* to fall asleep. Tucking her hands under her chin, she scanned his attractive masculine outline in the dark. Of course, he had a real hat to protect his head. But that simple cap—a strange smile broke out across her face. He said he loved it. She leaned too close to the edge and almost lost her balance. Gasping, she scooted back, squeezing shut inquisitive eyes.

Slipknot, cast on, purl one, knit two . . .

"LAUREN, CAN YOU help me?" She awoke to Elias over her. It felt like she had just closed her eyes and now it was daylight?

"Yes, what?" Sitting up, neck stiff, she pulled her blanket back. He hopped off the open gate of the wagon. "Grab the harpsichord as I lift it in.

Standing on awakening legs, she grabbed the end of the bulky instrument and pulled it back into the center. He waited and reached out for her as she came around the side to him.

"Can you make it quick?" He set her on the ground, his blue eyes meeting her tired ones. "The others are packed up." He turned, hitching the back gate.

She nodded a smile and caught up with Chrystal heading for the bushes, too. "You go ahead," Lauren offered. Chrystal had said she was five or six months along with child. Would she deliver in the back of the wagon after they left Independence?

"Thank you, Lauren." She came out from behind the bushes. "I'll keep watch for you."

• • •

AFTER RIDING A few hours on the seat with Elias, Lauren saw the other ladies slip out of the wagon. The road's steep grade had made the wagons slower. It was a perfect time to walk, relieving the bumps and jolts to her backside. The air was damp and cool, but the rain had held off so far.

"Do you suppose we can cook tonight?" Lauren asked as she walked in step with the sisters.

"I think so," Mabel offered. Janet grabbed Chrystal by the hand and gave her a little pull up the steep road.

"I was just thinking how wonderful it is for you to have each other." Lauren smiled. "Chrystal even guarded the privy for me this morning."

"How long since you've seen your sister?" Janet asked.

"It's been two long years."

"And your new husband is so willing to take you to your family."

"Yes, he is willing." She'd rather talk about them and their children.

"Where are his people from?" Mabel asked.

"Uhh, Pennsylvania, from what I understand."

"What did you think of his family?"

"He has been on his own since he was fourteen. They are deceased."

"That would be hard. In our religion there are so many mothers, aunts, grandmothers . . ."

"Often too many to keep track of." Janet smiled.

"I envy what you have." Lauren didn't mean for that to slip out. "Just how you are all there for each other. I don't know you very well, but I don't sense any jealousy or rivalry."

"We believe strongly that to honor God is to honor our husband and each other." Mabel smiled.

"Mabel is the oldest, the first wife, and she carries a certain place." Janet looked at Mabel. "And we respect that because she's there for us, like staying behind to be with me. My body was feeble with fever after losing the baby. She and Chrystal never left my side. I wouldn't be here without their care."

"Do you and your husband look forward to children?" Chrystal asked.

"I don't know." Lauren shrugged. "I've never asked him."

All three broke out in laughter.

Lauren opened her mouth in confusion. "What's so funny?"

"You are such a dear one, Lauren," Mabel said, smiling.

"You and Mr. Browne are just about the cutest couple ever," Janet chimed in. "You two look like you're still in courtship. The way he watches you, like he's still nervous around you."

Lauren could still hear him demanding a place

to sleep in the wagon; he wasn't taking no from her or anyone. "I think I am more the nervous one. Without my mother's help, nor having my sister with me, I'm not very prepared."

"Ahh, but you have a good man, Lauren. The best way to learn about each other is patience and respect." The wagons came to a stop. Janet took a moment to rub Chrystal's back.

"Mabel." It sounded like Joe Kern calling. "Can you help us?"

Chapter 20

THE OTHER WAGONS had come to a stop, and Elias followed suit. Looking around, he had always had an extra sense of danger, it didn't feel like that, but he grabbed his gun from under his seat and looked back at Lauren. Mabel walked by him quickly, and he motioned to Lauren to step up on the wheel pedal. "Come sit here." He pulled her into his seat. "The brake is on, but just hold the reins firm." He handed them over and jumped out the other side.

He saw Joe and the Reverend looking at something in the woods. Looking past their somber faces, Elias saw a young man bound and gagged, laying on his side. He quickly raised his gun and stalked into the woods. No tracks to be seen, no other bodies. It was strange. He came back to the teen, where Joe had cut his bindings. Reverend Little was rinsing his face with a bit of water. "He has a pulse," he said. Looking up to Elias he asked, "See anything?"

Elias looked around again. "No tracks, no sign of anyone else. Looks like he got dumped here."

"I don't want to lose time," Joe spoke up. "Can

we put him in your wagon, Elias? We'll get him to a doctor in Cincinnati."

"Sure." All three men helped lift him and carry him to the back of their wagon. Lauren sat straight-backed watching their every move. How would she feel about this bruised, nearly dead body on her bed?

"What is *that?*" Joe peered around Elias's back as he jumped inside.

"A harpsichord."

"Good Lord, man," Joe said as Elias took the teen and pulled him in.

"Sell it and get the money. She can buy another one; it will never make it."

"*You* tell her that." Elias tilted his chin to the front of the wagon, "He seems to still be alive."

Lauren's green, dark-lashed glare flashed at him. He cleared his throat. "Just until we get to Cincinnati." Elias carefully climbed over the other side of the harpsichord and over the back of the seat. She handed him the reins and moved over. Joe locked their tailgate in place.

"You *are* good at nursin'." He winked brazenly patting his healing side.

"And keeping criminals alive." He forgot to mention that. Lauren gave him a sidelong look before she crawled along the other side of the harpsichord. The wagon rocked forward, and she tumbled forward again. Hanging on to the giant instrument, she looked the patient over. Maybe sixteen, seventeen years old; a few random whiskers poked out from his chin; his face was black and blue. The cuts looked old, and she didn't see any knots protruding anywhere. She pinched on the skin around his wrist. It raised and then went back, that was a good sign. He seemed cool to the touch, and his hair didn't fall out with a little tug. His eyes twitched, maybe from all her poking and prodding.

"Young man." She shook his arm. "Can you wake up? Hello." His head rolled side to side, swollen cracks for eyes started to open.

"Where am I?" he whispered hoarsely.

"In the back of our wagon about a day or two east of Cincinnati. What's your name?"

"Brody." He pressed his dirty hand into his forehead. "Can you find a real road? One that doesn't separate my bones."

"How are your bones, Brody, besides being bumped by this road? Can you move your legs?"

He touched his knees together.

"Can you move your shoulders?"

"Yes," he growled pulling them up and down. "Do you have anything to eat?"

"Yes. Food next."

Elias had turned, watching them for a moment.

"Tell me why you were beaten up on the side of a deserted, bumpy, as you call it, road?"

"I had some problems with my, uh, stepdad. Do you have any biscuits? Any butter, maybe honey?"

Men and their bellies. Lauren scratched her ear. "You might want to know—I'm Lauren. The man who carried you from where you were dumped is Elias. What kind of problems?"

"Huh?" Brody groaned.

"With your stepdad, surely your mother—"

"She's been gone for years."

Lauren inched back. Her judgment of this wayward teen softening. "I'm sorry to hear that." She kneeled on the end of her old bed and reached down to a basket. "Here's a biscuit from this morning." He practically swallowed it from her hand, butter and honey must have faded from his mind as he shoved it in his mouth.

BEFORE DUSK, ELIAS carefully guided their wagon into the circle in a wide, grassy area and set the brake. Thankfully, Joe knew all the best spots for water and grazing. Usually old wood abounded for the needs of the evening. Lauren watched Brody napping on her bed. After such a demanding day, that warm spot belonged to her. Elias dropped the gate and reached for her. She would never tire of his arms setting her to the ground. They both looked back at Brody.

"Can he get up?"

"I think so, he—"

Before she could finish, Elias grabbed Brody's boot. "Brody, wake up. Get up, and you can eat supper with us."

Brody rolled up on his elbow. "Can you just bring me something in here?"

"Sure." "No." They chimed together.

Lauren dropped her chin. "I don't mind. I can bring him something."

"No," Elias whispered, eyes widened. "Trust me on this; it will show how his recovery is going." Elias pulled on Brody's boot. "Here, I'll help you." Brody rolled up slowly and lumbered to get to the end of the wagon. They both put out their arms to steady him. "We have a wonderful little group." Lauren caught Mabel's eye, and Mabel rolled over a stump for Brody to sit on. "This is Missus—" Lauren fumbled with their matching last names.

"Mrs. Walter Hawkins," Mabel provided.

Lauren spied the other sisters busily preparing their meal from their pull-out kitchen. Do they mind all being Mrs. Walter Hawkins? She decided to let them introduce themselves.

"So what's the story?" Joe Kern approached and pushed his hat back.

"I don't remember much. Got in a fight with my stepbrother and my stepdad took his side," Brody croaked.

"Where's home, son?"

"Ahh, outside of Bloomville."

"That's a ways from this part of the country." They all watched as Ida Bell set a pan upon the fire grate, ignoring them.

"So what brings you out on this road?"

"Yeah, well," Brody dropped his head and rubbed the back of his neck. "I was goin' to Cincinnati to look for work."

Eyebrows raised, Joe cast Elias a glance. Elias shrugged.

"If these fine folks don't mind, you can ask them for a lift that far."

Brody ignored Joe. "What was your name again?" he said to Lauren.

"Lauren."

"You've been all nice." The corner of his slit lip lifted. "So, are you gonna cook me something?"

She nodded as Elias pulled her away by the elbow. "Don't be doing all his bidding," he said softly in her ear. "He's not telling the whole truth. I know his type. He's a taker."

She gave him a bold once over, looking from his grip on her arm to those serious blue eyes. "Really."

Chapter 21

BRODY SLEPT ON and off the next day, seeming to revive every two hours to eat. Lauren handed Elias a slab of dried venison tucked between a thick cut of buttered bread. "Where's yours?" he asked, as she sat on the front seat.

"I'm fine." She watched the road.

"Don't be giving him any extras. He'd eat all our supplies if you let him." He took a large bite. "Here, you can have half of this." He chewed, holding out the smashed sandwich.

Lauren pulled back shaking her head. "I said I was fine."

"I know you know what you're doing." His eyes narrowed, still chewing.

"What do you mean?"

"Like yesterday. You got the information first and then promised him something to eat. Very savvy. My sister Anna was incredible at it."

"Such as?"

"She gave every child a job and then promised a reward. The children who couldn't even speak, she'd have them rub the limbs of the cripples with oil, then she would sneak them a sugar cube, or she would comb their hair."

Lauren glanced sideways at him, "I thought she was there—you know, like you. But she worked there?"

"She *was* there like me. She just had a way with everyone. The staff liked her, and they liked that she could control us. I guess it made their jobs easier." Elias pulled the reins to the right leading the team around a sharp corner. "Can you hand me some water?"

Lauren grabbed the canteen and unscrewed the top. "Your little wrapper in your pocket, was that a gift from her? Did she use it to get you to mind?"

He took a long swig and handed it back. "That little thing was for birthdays. She knew I had no people coming, so she found this gold coin someone had dropped, and she told me how valuable it was. I was a kid, and didn't know any better." He gave a half smile. "She put the wrapper around it and every year would give it to me for my birthday."

"The same little coin in the wrapper?"

He nodded. "Yeah, like I didn't know she would find it, keep it, and then give it back to me each year." He smirked. "It was kinda like a game between us. One year when I was ten, I think, I hid the coin under a loose floorboard. Sure enough, I went to check on it and it was gone, reappearing as her gift for my eleventh birthday."

"She sounds amazing." Lauren sighed, remembering her mother making a layered cake and the family singing. Usually, she had a new dress, or a skein of yarn wrapped in pretty paper. Her chest squeezed. "Are your nightmares from that place?"

"There and a few more." He leaned forward. "We are getting close to Cincinnati. I can see some farms and roads ahead. I think Brody's had enough convalescing; he can hit the road."

"He asked me about going on to Independence." Lauren shot a glance at Elias and then out the other way.

"And you said no, right?" A vein popped in his neck.

"I—um, I didn't say yes or no. This is your wagon Elias, your trip. As long as he sleeps outside, I don't care."

"I care. He's trouble."

"I thought we, of all people, believed in second chances."

Elias scoffed, dropping his chin and shaking his head. "Thank you, Reverend Lauren. If he could show himself useful, I might consider it."

MAIN STREET, CINCINNATI. Heart racing with excitement, Lauren drank in the details. She'd wrestled with telling Elias she wasn't much of an outdoor girl. But since it was her dream to take the covered wagon, she kept her complaints at bay. Even so, she was eager to be in a town again.

A large, bustling mercantile was on the left, and a hotel sat just a few doors down. Children chased each other, playing games in front of a school on the right. Truly, this invigorated her like nothing else. Shopping and a warm bath—she chewed her bottom lip, wondering what a night in the hotel would cost.

Their trio of wagons rolled through as Lauren strained to look past the side of the wagon.

"Can I sit up there?" Brody asked behind them.

Lauren nodded and inched closer to the edge.

"Can you sit in the middle?" he scoffed.

"Oh," Lauren scooted next to Elias, pulling her knees and skirts into a thin line. Brody stepped over and rocked the wagon seat. Lauren stiffened, bumping into Elias. She pulled her hair out of its messy knot, pretending this closeness was normal.

"What's your plan, Brody?" Elias shot her a quick wink.

"I want to go on to Independence. Someone once told me if you don't have a job by the end of the day there, it's 'cause you never looked."

Lauren shrank inside, as they kept going further from all the people and the stores.

"This next leg is nothing but work. Weeks till we even see St. Louis. You'd have to be willing to feed the animals, chop wood, haul water. Nothing's coming to ya for free."

"I understand. As long as Lauren is cookin', I'll do whatever she needs."

Elias looked up and rolled his eyes. "You'd answer to me or Joe Kern, not her."

Lauren squelched a chuckle.

The wagons made a wide turn into a flat area with scrub trees and a small grassy creek. "Joe said we'll take the afternoon to gather supplies and spend one night. Then we are back on the road at dawn." He set the break and wrapped the reins. Jumping off the side, he held his hand out for Lauren as she stepped on the wheel step. "You know how to unhitch a team?" he asked Brody, settling his hand on Lauren's waist even though she was safe to the ground.

"Yes." Brody let himself down gingerly.

Lauren touched Elias's arm, "He might not be up for—"

"Great, you can start now."

WATCHING EVERYONE WORK together to get camp set up, Lauren felt foolish for thinking about a night at the hotel. Elias had left with one of the horses to go hunting, while the sisters talked and prepared the fire for cooking. Joe sat on a rock talking to Reverend Little, writing a list with a stubby pencil.

"Mr. Kern." She scratched her neck. "Would it

157

be possible to join you in town? Elias has agreed to allow Brody to travel to Independence with us. He has nothing. He needs a bedroll and change of clothes." Brody dropped a stack of wood by the fire.

"Can you ride?" Joe looked up from his list.

Lauren looked back at Elias's remaining horse. "Ahh, not really."

"She can ride with me," Brody said. "And both of us can carry whatever we buy."

"All right," Joe nodded. "If you're sure Elias won't mind, we'll leave in ten minutes."

Lauren smiled at Brody, then quickly looked to the ground. Elias was the one who wanted the teen to show his worth to the group. A good bath and some clean clothes would go a long way towards that end. She eyed him again. Should she trust him? *Well, he did say he'd do whatever I said for him to do, and he needs a bath.*

Chapter 22

ELIAS PULLED THE reins back, slowing the horse as he approached camp. His eyes searched for the other horse. Did it get loose? Would Joe have taken it without asking? He slid from the saddle, and smiled as Mabel came out to meet him. Handing her the four dead rabbits, she nodded her appreciation. "Did you see Joe?" he asked. "Did he need my other mare?"

"I saw Lauren and Brody ride off on her. Pretty sure they were going to town."

An unseen force locked his jaw. He struggled to get the words out. "Lauren and Brody?" He bit the inside of his cheek, tasting blood.

"These look like they got a bit of meat," Mabel held up the stringer. "Thanks, Elias. We'll have something ready in about an hour."

Elias stalked back to his grazing horse and grabbed the reins. Looking up, he saw another covered wagon approaching their camp. Mabel looked to the wagon and looked to him. She walked back to him. "Could you see what they need? Joe's still in town."

Elias nodded, trying to hide his rising fury. Why would Lauren go anywhere with Brody, that no good, snotty nosed brat? He should have never agreed to take him on. Where did Lauren keep the money he'd given her? Probably now in the pocket of that lazy squirrel. As he approached the wagon, a middle-aged couple nodded at him. The man jumped down and offered his hand. "I'm Lux Coolidge." Elias liked his strong handshake.

"This is my dear wife, Mrs. Coolidge."

She nodded a greeting, as four heads poked out the front canvas. "We have twins, Martin and Felicia, seventeen. The one with the big bow is Katherine, and the blonde is Eleanor."

Elias smiled and nodded, knowing he was too upset to remember their names.

"We've been told your group is on their way to Independence and we'd like to join up if that's possible?"

Elias was distracted by two very large, white, hairy dogs broke out between the children.

"Oh and two Great Pyrenees, Goliath, and Athena."

They looked like lazy guard dogs to Elias, but his gut was churning too much for him to pay much attention to them. He looked around, "Uh. I can't say. The wagon master is Joe Kern. He should be returning any time."

"Can we make camp for the evening either way?"

They all looked harmless. "I'm sure that would

be fine." Maybe Reverend Little could do some introductions while he rode into town. The kids and dogs all piled out. The wife looked like she'd just come fresh from church.

"Quite the adventure, traveling west." Mr. Coolidge followed Elias. "Where did y'all start from?"

"I—I mean my wife and I started from Green-lock, Ohio."

"You are married, any children?"

"No." Elias huffed, "You'll have to excuse me, I need to get into town before dark."

Janet stood close to her wagon, and Elias got her attention. "Janet, could you or Mabel show these fine people our camp? I need to go." He looked up as Joe rode up to camp with burlap bags hanging off his horse. He jogged over to meet him.

"Thanks, Elias." Joe smiled, as he approached. "I could use some help with these. They're heavy."

Elias grabbed the heavy sack and pulled it free. "Did you see Lauren and Brody?" He sounded winded for no reason.

"No, they had their own list, I'm surprised they're not back by now." Joe swung down. "Looks like we have another wagon trying to join up?"

"Yes, a family with kids, dogs. I don't know much about them, and I told them they had to talk to you."

"What do you think?" Joe lifted the bag over his shoulder.

Elias rubbed the knot in his neck. "It's up to you. You make the call."

They walked toward the wagons. "This happens to me every run I make," Joe drawled.

"What happens?" Elias twitched with wanting to go.

"A natural leader emerges."

Elias shook his head, confused.

"You. You're a natural leader. You're strong, smart and have a good way with people. I'm surprised they only had you setting explosives in the army. If something ever happens to me, you're in charge."

Elias pulled back; this man must be soft in the head. Or, Elias was compelled to be honest, he had only shared what he wanted Joe to know.

"For this trip, *you stay* the general." Elias walked backward. "I've got to go see what's taking Lauren and Brody so long."

"And you don't have a suffocating ego!" Joe called after him.

ONLY TEN MINUTES later, Joe would have a whole different opinion when he saw what Elias was going to do to Brody. The sun cast an orange glow through the trees as he saw them come toward him on the road. He should be happy that Brody was heading back to camp. Lauren obviously riding safely behind him, but nothing would stop the boiling.

He swung off his horse and grabbed Lauren by the arm. Before she knew what was happening, he'd jerked her off the horse and circled his arm around her waist, pinning her backside against him. He didn't notice she was holding anything until the items scattered around them. "That horse goes back exactly where you found it. If you don't want to feel my hands around your throat, you'll do it right now." Elias seethed. Brody was wide-eyed, barely breathing. "Now!" Elias yelled, feeling Lauren struggle against him. Brody quickly kicked the horse forward. Elias's horse wanted to follow, but he reached for the dangling reins, yanking his horse around.

"Elias." Lauren wheezed, pulling on his arm locked around her middle. "You're hurting me." She twisted around pushing against his chest, her toes barely scraping the ground. He let go quickly, realizing how easy it would be to let loose his anger on her. Suddenly freed from his grip, she swayed back, falling in the dirt. He tried to reach for her, but the fear on her face stopped him cold. Shaking all over, she stood up and backed away, rubbing her arm. "Why," her voice breaking, tears forming, "would you do that? I-I—" she sucked in a sob. "Have never seen you so angry."

Elias held the reins up in his fist, opened his

hand releasing them, and stalked away. The shock on her face crushed his throat closed and confirmed what he knew. He was a defective child from an asylum turned man. An old oak tree was in his path, and he slammed his forearms against it and pulled them down until he felt his skin peel loose. The pain quieted him. He could breathe for the first time. Good breaths, full breaths, he turned and fell on the ground his back against the tree. He closed his eyes, with only searing pain and a pounding heart to feel, now he could go somewhere else in his mind.

LAUREN LOOKED DOWN. The cornmeal. It had to be the cornmeal that had broken open all over the road. She bent down and tried to gently scoop it back into the paper bag. Her tears were falling so fast they caused the yellow meal to clump together. Why did she think she could do this? How stupid and desperate could she be?

Hair in her face, wiping her wet cheeks with her sleeve. She sided a glance at Elias. Who is he? Just when she thought she could trust him, believe him safe, he turned colors. A wave of homesickness twisted in her belly, she needed the solitude of her room, her own kitchen, someplace to soothe her shocked and chaotic heart. Any place away from here.

Another wagon appeared to be at camp. There were trustworthy people in that group, even friends, and she felt included for the first time in her life. Could she go on? Could she rely on them? His horse nuzzled her back, a long tongue coming around for a taste of their food. "Get away." She pushed on the horse's nose. Gathering what was left of the torn bag and picking up her other items, she shoved them in the saddlebags. Taking the horse by the reins, she walked to Elias sitting against a tree.

At the sound of her approach, he looked up and quickly rolled his shirt sleeves down. His face was still red, but the fire had left from his eyes. He stood and brushed off his backside.

"Elias." She looked away, not wanting to cry again. Her voice breaking, she said, "I don't understand, why . . . why are you so angry with me?"

"I'm not angry with you." He shuffled his feet, voice composed. "I am sorry for grabbing you off the horse." He looked at the ground. "There is no excuse."

"I wanted to go into town for supplies, and I had a letter to post to my father, but I don't know how to ride a horse."

"I would have taken you." His simmering watery blue eyes captured hers.

"I didn't think Brody taking me would offend you." She sighed, her shoulders dropping. "He's just an innocent boy in a large body."

"Lovely Lauren." His usual tone of endearment,

now condescending. "I admire your pure heart and beauty," his soft words clashing with the forceful slits of his eyes, "and this desire you have to believe the best in everyone, but he could have slit your throat and left you in a ditch." The visual picture hung in the air, causing her knees to shake again. "Can you see me rolling up to your mother's home in Denver City? Here's your harpsichord and dishes, but your dear daughter, Lauren, is dead."

His words stilled her being. He was worried. He didn't know she would be safe. How could his calm tone turn her insides to mush? "So you weren't jealous, just worried?"

Walking toward her, he leveled her with his gaze. She backed up until he reached past her, snatching the horse's reins. "It doesn't really matter, 'cause he's outta here."

Chapter 23

QUIETLY WALKING THE road back to camp, Lauren was glad for the moments to shake loose the baffling emotions still gripping her insides.

"A new family arrived in that extra wagon." Elias glanced at her. "I don't remember all their names. Husband and wife. I think four kids."

"They are looking to join us?"

He nodded. "It's up to Joe."

She followed him to the back area where the animals grazed. It was dusk. The smell of the land intensified by the light dew. The campfire danced with people and food surrounding it, but it held no appeal. She wasn't even hungry. Reaching the back of their wagon, she stopped. "There are a few things in your saddlebags. I don't have much socializing in me. I think I'll just put things away and get to bed."

Elias looked at the group and back at her. His expression conflicted, unsettled. "I wish I knew what to do." His tongue rolled over his bottom lip. "I said I would be good to you."

Lauren couldn't find any words. She reached out and squeezed his arm. He winced and pulled in a quick breath. "What's wrong with your arm?"

"Nothing." He shrugged. "Just a few scrapes."

She turned to pull the pins from the back gate and felt his hands on her waist. He turned her gently and pulled her close, wrapping his arms around her back. Carefully rising on her toes, she stretched her arms around his thick torso and touched his back. His warmth and strength seeped into her very skin. This was the closest she'd ever been to another human. Surely, he could feel her heart pounding. His hands gently pressed her hair back. Regret mixed with his calm breath spoke in her ear. "I am sorry for today, for the way I grabbed you. Please forgive me. If you want to help Brody, I'll settle down. I'll try not to kill him."

She moved back from their embrace, rewarded with his crooked smile, but immediately sorry for the loss of tenderness. Arms dropped, the cold air came in between them like an intruder.

"I forgive you, Elias." She tucked her loose hair behind her ear. "If there was anyone who could help him, understand him, it's you."

He pulled in a deep breath and glanced over at the group around the fire. "You're right."

"Would you give everyone my apologies?" she asked.

"For what?"

She peered up at him and smiled, "You say, my

wife apologizes for not joining in, she was tired and has already retired."

"Oh. Yeah." A slow smile rose. "I can do that."

LAUREN LIT THE lantern and arranged the supplies in the wagon. She noticed Brody's new bedroll was under the wagon next to where Elias slept. After tonight, it would be by the grace of God for them to connect in some civil way. Elias slept hard. Brody would find that out soon enough. She sat stoically on her blankets.

Elias was so complex. His anger had frightened her today. She remembered him dead, well, like dead, yet speaking from the ice table. It had so terrified her, it had knocked her to her backside. As long as he was weak as a kitten, she had some sense of control. Finding peace with his calm side, the other side—completely unpredictable— was a stark opposite and quite unsettling.

Surprisingly, he wasn't mad about the money she'd spent on Brody. He just made her promise to remove the money from her purse and hide it somewhere new. Looking around, she took the remaining cash and stuffed it in her extra wool stockings. Gritting her teeth, she realized her bladder needed the earthen water closet, as the sisters had named it. Necessity made her lift her skirts and climb over the back gate. In the shadows, she made out Ida Bell heading out to the bushes and hurried to meet her.

"Ida Bell, can I guard the path for you and you for me?"

Ida Bell whisked left to right so quickly, Lauren backed up, sorry for startling her.

"Granby?" Little white eyes popped up from the darkness.

Ida Bell jumped to block Lauren's gaze and said to her, "Why you sneakin' up on me? You should be ashamed."

"I didn't mean to. Who is that little one?"

"Granby." Another set of bright eyes and pitch-black skin, came up from the bushes.

"Hush now!" Ida Bell batted her hand behind her, shaking her head. "Lord, come quickly," she mumbled. A small child shot through the brush and wrapped up in the layers of Ida Bell's skirt.

"I didn't know." Lauren tried to sound encouraging. "Are these your grandchildren? They are welcome to come and eat, visit with everyone. I don't think anyone would mind."

"Well, maybeez I mind." She jutted her chin out as a third older child came out.

"Does Mr. Kern know about them? Surely he—"

"Yez, he's knows good and well." She looked past Lauren. "Now you best be on your way and mind your own bidness."

"Yes, ma'am." Lauren scurried around her and smiled at the little trio behind her. "I'm Lauren,

170

so sorry if I frightened you," she whispered.

A few minutes later, heading back to the wagon, she remembered what the sisters had said about Elias. Sure enough, from the campfire, he watched her come from the brush. She nodded to the wagon, and he said something to those talking around the fire and headed her way.

"I didn't mean to . . ." she rambled before he had even stopped.

"What?"

"Ida Bell. She has a bundle of children with her. We've been on the road all these weeks, and I've never seen them?" Elias took her by the arm to the back of the wagon.

"It's a whole family. I think five of them," he said hushed.

"What? There are five extra people in that wagon, and I never knew?"

"There *is* a reason they don't want it to be known."

"But the war is over. The slaves are free. Look at the Littles. They are free to come and go."

"Trust me on this—the Littles have done this route before. They know what they are doing. Not everyone is as free as we think they should be. Just keep it all to yourself. As we add more people and get to St. Louis and then Independence, we need to watch out for each other."

Lauren felt a prick of danger. "Remember when I said we all have our hindrances we want to leave behind? I thought you and I were the imposters."

Elias stroked his chin stubble, nodding back toward the fire. "Mr. Coolidge over there sold war bonds. Supposedly the company went under. Of course, everyone needs money now that the war is over. I think they had to leave town, quick like." They watched as the Coolidges prepared a large canvas tent with cushions and blankets.

"That's a nice tent. I should have gotten one for you and Brody today."

"No, thanks." Elias squinted at her. "Joe told them everything has to be done before sunrise. That's when we pull out. This should be interesting."

Brody came around the corner and stopped short. "Sorry, didn't mean to interrupt."

"You got a bedroll and some new duds I see." Elias spit to the side.

Brody nodded looking at the ground. Lauren could see Elias struggling. "I shouldn't have, um, blown up on you today," he finally said. "Lauren has her own say. She can come and go. I just thought you were gone too long." He swiped the back of his hand across his nose and mouth. "When I don't know where she's at, I think the worst."

Lauren blinked. Was he pretending for show or was he being serious? The way he was tense in body and word, it seemed as if he was telling the

172

truth. The husbandly voice of worry and concern touched her flustered heart.

"It was the bathhouse." Her words broke the tense moment. "Brody hadn't had a real bath. He must have been in there thirty minutes. We didn't even know he had brown hair until it dried." She tried to chuckle, but no one joined in.

"I saw you talking to the Coolidge boy."

"Martin," Brody offered.

"No problem there. Just stay away from the daughter. That family has got nothing in common with you. You eat with us, you work with us, you listen to us, is that understood?"

"Yes," Brody murmured.

Lauren let out a breath she didn't know she was holding and offered Brody a weak smile.

"Joe wants to add a mid-day break this next leg—with children along." He glanced at Lauren. "It will be short, but," he eyed Brody, "we can switch out driving the team. Joe wants me to hunt and scout as often as I can."

Brody nodded his agreement and walked around them.

Lauren rubbed the side of her cheek. "Everything changes out here. Every day a new challenge."

"Tomorrow we leave Ohio, crossing Indiana, and soon enough Illinois." Elias looked down, circling his boot in the dirt. "I know you regret it hasn't been what you thought."

"Oh, no." Remembering where those strange locks had once hung, she lightly touched the bit of hair curling against the soft skin of his neck. He looked up. "It has been more, so much more, than I could have imagined."

Chapter 24

L AUREN ATTUNED A sleepy ear to the sounds of the sisters preparing breakfast before sunrise. She lit her lantern and folded her warm blankets. Pulling her boots and coat on, she flipped open the grub box. Working and cooking in tandem with the Mormon sisters, she knew by a nod from Mabel when her turn to heat the bacon and biscuits would be. Elias lowered the back gate, reaching out for her and helped her out.

"How did you and your bunkmate sleep?" She pulled the wooden bowl forward for making the biscuits.

"He's still alive if that's what you need to know." An insincere grin twisted in the shadows. "And he does smell better." Elias leaned under the heavy wagon. "Get up, Brody, or I'm running this thing right over your body."

"Elias." She stopped whipping the spoon. "You said you would try."

"That was yesterday. This is me trying today." He licked his finger and stuck it in the bit of sugar she'd ground off the block.

"Hey." She raised her elbow trying to block him from her hurried preparations.

"Mmm, so sweet, just like you." He kissed her quickly on her temple and turned. "Brody, the stock eats before you. Let's go!"

Lauren touched her temple. How could that crazy-looking man she'd met at the hardware store have just kissed her? Just a while back she despised his attention. Now it warmed her like the hot coffee Mabel would soon offer.

Just as Joe Kern and the sisters were done eating, the first vibrant crack of sunlight made its way over the low rolling hills. Elias's and Brody's plates of hot biscuits and bacon were waiting as they walked up. The Littles had taken their simple fair back to their wagon. The teams were already hitched, and everyone turned quickly to hear an argument coming from the Coolidge tent. Martin came around from the side of the wagon and made his way to the campfire.

"Go tell your ma this campfire is out in ten minutes. We leave in twenty." Joe swigged the last of his coffee.

"Yes, sir." Martin nodded.

"Brody, go gather their mules and hitch them up. Don't forget to swab their noses."

Brody swayed, his head low. He handed Lauren his empty plate, and tramped off to the pasture.

The group turned as the Coolidge family filed out of the tent.

"Good morning, y'all." Mr. Coolidge waved.

"I will help the missus," Lauren said, nodding to Joe.

Joe nodded back. "As soon as we get moving, Elias, could you take my horse and go ahead and scout a few miles?" The men talked further as Lauren nodded to Mr. Coolidge. "I'm Lauren, how nice to have your family along."

"Yes, Mrs. Browne. It's a delight to meet you. Your husband says you're from Greenlock?"

"Yes, sir." She smiled. The sunrise behind him looked like a painting over the new morning.

"And this is my wife, Mrs. Coolidge, our eldest daughter, Felicia, and next is Katherine and Eleanor."

Lauren nodded, smiling at them, all tidy in their matching woolen skirts and jackets. "Please, call me Lauren."

"They will call you Mrs. Browne." Mrs. Coolidge's deep southern drawl spoke up. "My children are being raised as ladies and gentlemen."

Lauren felt her own back stiffen. Mrs. Browne was the last thing that she wanted to be called, but she understood why this woman didn't want to lower her standards for a wagon train of strangers.

"Can I assist you in any way?" Lauren offered. "We have all eaten. Do you need to use the fire?"

Mr. Coolidge stepped forward, "Yes, we

should." She watched as the Littles pulled their wagon forward. "Ahh . . ."

"Send the children over," Mabel called from the back of their wagon. "We have enough to share." The well-dressed teen and girls followed her offer.

"We've always had domestic help." Mrs. Coolidge huffed. "I thought, possibly, the Negro couple did the cooking." Her cordial southern tone bristled Lauren even further.

"No, we all cook for ourselves. Sometimes we join in a pot of something. Depends on my husband's hunting." She smiled, glancing ahead. "Can we get that tent broken down?"

Mr. Coolidge clapped his hands, looking around. "Yes, thank you so much. The morning just got away from us, I guess."

Lauren walked passed Mrs. Coolidge, as Mabel secured their wagon to leave. "This wagon group is about to get away from you, too."

RIDING MILES OUT from the group, Elias saw two important things ahead. Looming far out to the east, maybe only a few hours away, was a thick layer of gray. Dark gray. Heavy rains could be coming their way. Grabbing the rope off his saddle, he watched something even more important silently nibble the tall spring grass. His heartbeat spiked, just like during his days of running explosives. Now, how to approach the herd of wild horses. He knew he couldn't corral the bunch by himself, but one or two would be a conquest.

Circling carefully, they watched him, jerking side to side. A black mare eyed him like she would take him for a run. A few sorrels had some markings, maybe loose from the army or local tribes. Squeezing his knees to hold Joe's horse in place, he waited, loving the familiar rush that confirmed he was alive. Freedom to be his own man swept up in his nostrils like the serenity of the land. His own mind for his own choices, no lieutenant, and no prison guard dictating the hours of his life. From the moment Lauren helped him off that ice bed, his good and bad flashes of the past seemed in competition.

Reverend Little's voice from the other night, echoed. *Your soul isn't anchored in what you do or have done. Nah, nah, nah, your soul is anchored in whose you are.*

In this moment, he was his own man—no gangs, no running. If he was belonging to anything, God and Lauren were the best he could imagine. Days like this could cause a man to believe.

When the herd had grown used to him, he slipped slowly from the saddle. Pulling a large green shrub from the ground, he never took his eyes off them. Barely moving, he raised the plant, teasing a curious chestnut pony closer and closer until he slipped the rope around her neck.

She had obviously been broken, as he tied her to Joe's horse. One more with saddle markings hung back. Walking the tethered two nearer, it showed some interest.

"Hey friend, you wanna see what I have?" He waited, slowly lifting the shrub. "This smells good. Just like my Lovely Lauren." The horse stepped away, and Elias stilled. *My Lauren.* He grinned. "I'll let you meet her." He took a step forward. "She smells good and feels good." The horse looked up like he was listening. "Real good," he whispered, as the horse dropped its head, Elias slipped the rope around its neck.

"THOSE KNITTING NEEDLES stop clicking every time you look out for him."

Lauren pushed her project into her bag. Brody yawned, probably tired after driving the team all afternoon.

"It does seem like he's been gone a long time." She looked out again from her seat next to Brody. "If you want, I can take the reins while you walk."

"I'm fine." He wiped his nose with his shirt. "You two sure don't like to be apart."

Lauren turned and started to speak. "Well, it's not that." She had made a point to tell the truth to these people except when it might expose their lie. "We are in many ways still getting to know one another." There, that was the truth.

"Betcha didn't know he has a temper. But you probably figured it out after he yanked you off that horse."

She'd never had any qualms with Brody until now. Was he trying to goad her?

"Are you going to lay into him when he gets back?" Brody said, a bit too wide-eyed.

"What? Why?" She straightened her back.

"He's been gone all day. It just seems fair."

Lauren wanted to change the subject. "I assume you've had a difficult childhood. I know what it is to miss your mother."

His eyes bobbed, and he let out a sigh. "She wasn't any great piece of pie."

"And you want to make a new start. All of us on this road want something new and better. What about—"

"There he is, out yonder," he interrupted. "Got two ponies behind him."

Lauren leaned out the front seat and saw Elias in the distance.

Brody huffed. "Probably stole 'em."

Chapter 25

ELIAS JUDGED THE distance between his wagon and the Coolidge wagon and brought the new horses around securing their ropes to the back of his rig. He debated stepping over the tailgate to see Lauren but glanced again at the approaching line of pure gray. Kicking his horse, he rode up to where Joe was driving.

"We got a gully-washer coming towards us." Elias nodded up to the sky.

"I've been watching it," Joe frowned. "Our next crossing is Charity Creek. The only problem is I've seen it swell fast. It could take two to three days before we could cross. That's no charity."

"What are you thinking?" Elias asked.

"If we skip making camp and press through— four, five hours tops—we could get past the creek before that thing comes down on us. Stinkin' muddy roads are one thing, that kind of water in a swift current could take a wagon away. Unfortunately, I've seen it before." Joe let out a held breath. "Ride along and tell everyone. The Littles will be fine, but the Coolidges are a bit green. Have Martin trade out driving for now.

Mr. Coolidge is gonna get a fast lesson when we hit that creek."

Relaying the plan up and down the line, everyone agreed to keep moving. Mrs. Coolidge complained about the new horses kicking up more dust on them. Elias had no words for her, everything riding on a one lane dirt road stirred up dust. He guessed she hadn't figured that out yet.

He walked along behind the sisters' wagon, tying up Joe's horse. They wanted him to tell Lauren they had leftover rice and beans for tonight if they needed them. He smiled his thanks; they had been good friends to her.

Elias drove their team at dusk as Brody slept on Lauren's bed. She had listened intently to his victory over wild beasts. He wasn't sure if she understood how important it was to have another team to switch out when they had a long day like today. He leaned out. "Whoo-wee, that is dark meeting with dark."

"I'm a bit nervous. I didn't like that last river crossing." She pulled her bonnet off and let her hair loose.

"I think we should make it fine. We can ask Reverend Little to pray for a Red Sea crossing." He looked for a smile and found a wrinkled scowl. She quickly pulled her hair back into a bun.

"Take your hair back down. I'll show you

something—help keep ya from fiddling with it."

Frowning at him, she pulled the band out. A cool wind came up, as she smoothed her thick hair behind her ear.

"Come over here, next to me and take the reins." He smiled at her confused green eyes, at least she would look at him now. Scooting over, she took the reins, staring ahead.

"When I was nervous or scared as a kid—" He pulled some of her hair free.

"What are you doing?" She moved from his touch.

"Just hold still." He pulled back on her shoulders and separated a strand of her hair. "This won't hurt. When I was nervous or scared as a kid, some of the other kids would chew their hair or pull it. A lot of hair pullers at the asylum, but I liked hair twisting." He rolled the strand between his fingers. "I know you pull your hair out of place when you are nervous." She smelled like sage and fresh rain, and he liked the strange heat rising over him. "But you have the perfect texture for locks."

"Oh, no, not me." She tipped her head playfully. "That was you."

Holding her hair tight, he pulled her back closer than he should. He'd missed her today. Darkness had fallen around them, and he had a sudden urge to pull her into his lap. His breath was hard to find, as he pulled his fingers through her soft curls.

A rend of white light flashed in the sky, and she jumped. "The reins." She had moved so fast he barely caught them midair. The thunder rolled, consuming the earth.

"Oh, Lord." Lauren rolled her hair back up into the band.

Janet and a lantern appeared in the back of the sisters' wagon, facing theirs. "Joe says we're stepping it up," she called. Chrystal popped out of the back canvas next to her. "And when we get to Utah, could Elias show our husband how to do our hair?" Janet and Chrystal giggled, smiles bouncing off the lantern glow.

"Of course I will," Elias called back.

Lauren dropped her head, embarrassed.

THE WIND WAS first, and by the time the rain started, it was falling sideways. Brody had awoken and traded places with her. She huddled under her blankets. Unfortunately, neither the canvas nor the blankets muffled the sound or feel as the rain came down in buckets.

"The Littles are starting through." She heard Elias yell over the wind and rain. "Steady, stay steady now."

Fearful, yet invigorated, it helped to peek out the front to watch. A large limb flew loose from a tree and bounced off the sisters' canvas. The creek water bubbled wide and swift, "How deep is it?" She strained to see as the sisters' wagon approached the bank.

A crack of thunder popped her quickly back under the canvas. The wagon jerked hard, and she tumbled against the harpsichord. Pain shot through her side as the wagon pitched to the right, dumping her on the other bench. She rolled up to see the team skittering left to right; the horses were trying to bolt ahead as Elias strained to control them.

"Steady now!" he yelled, leaning back to keep them at bay. Even Brody tilted back, legs locked straight, clutching the seat as the horses trotted forward. With noses pressed against the sisters' tailgate, they tried to swing left to get around. "Whoa!" Elias gritted out. They swung back, just as the sisters' wagon started up the bank. Like a shot out of a cannon, they took off up the wide bank, the sisters' wagon only inches from their's as they bounced past.

"Hold on!" Elias's backside was off the seat, legs straining as he muscled the reins back. The horses jerked to the left and were blocked by trees, swinging back to parallel the sisters' wagon. Joe turned his team left, and Lauren dropped her face into her collar and held on. A large slam knocked all of them as the wagons hit then came to a final stop. She opened her eyes to see Joe had blocked their team between the trees and the sister's wagon, safeguarding them in place. Elias set the brake and looked wide-eyed to Brody.

"That was the most fun I've had in a long time." Brody panted smiling ear to ear.

"That was fun." Elias slapped him on the back. "Lauren, are you okay back there? Harpsichord in one piece?"

She opened her mouth to answer when she heard a scream. Elias shoved the reins to Brody and jumped from the side of the wagon. Lauren maneuvered down the back of the wagon and pulled on the cinched canvas as another scream came from the Coolidge wagon. Elias sloshed through the dark, swift water and grabbed the mules' harnesses. The water swirled around his waist as he tried to jerk the team forward.

"Slap 'em hard!" he yelled at Mr. Coolidge. The reins rose up and cracked down upon the mules' backs. Elias pulled hard, and the wind caught his hat and blew it down the creek.

When nothing happened, Martin Coolidge pulled loose of someone holding him, and jumped off the side into the churning water. Hanging on to the wheel as the wind and water tried to beat him, he pulled himself around to the front of the mule team.

"On three!" Elias yelled. "One, two, three!" They both pulled as another crack came down on the mules. The mules jumped forward, and the men pulled, running backward, and dripping with creek water. Elias and Martin dug into the creek bank taking heavy, long strides as they guided the team up the side to where the other wagons waited.

"See that grove of trees ahead?" Joe yelled over the wind as they approached. "There's enough room for us all to tie up." The rain splattered heavily as they nodded in agreement. "We'll let the animals rest and get out at noon tomorrow." He turned to Elias. "Thanks for helping the Coolidges tonight. I used to be that strong when I was your age."

Elias laughed, "I was needin' a bath anyway."

Chapter 26

A FTER BRODY AND Elias led the wagon up a rise, they unhitched and tied the team to a tree. Before Lauren could think of an alternative, Elias had dropped the back gate and pulled on the harpsichord.

"Oh, no," she whined. Three of them inside. She glanced out the front. Maybe the sisters would take her in.

Elias handed the large instrument off to Brody telling him to secure the tarp around it and tie it to the wagon. He jumped up on the back gate and sat on the end. Lauren huddled at the other end as he dumped the water from his boots and threw them in the corner of the wagon.

"Elias," she drew in a breath. "The wet ground will ruin the harpsichord."

He shook out his coat and stepped into the wagon. Everything he had on was soaked by the rising creek. "It will dry out, like everything else." He held his hand out, pulling, as Brody stepped into the back of the wagon. Elias closed the back gate and pulled the canvas together. Lauren swallowed hard, pulling her coat tight as the wagon rocked under their weight. Elias dropped his suspenders and pulled his shirt free. "Sorry, everyone, but I'm a bit wet and need some dry clothes."

Brody lit a match to the lantern, sat on Lauren's thin bunk, and pulled off his boots.

"I think my knitting bag got thrown down here." She turned away from them and the light, pretending to rummage around.

"It's right there under your blankets," Brody said. She turned, trying to ignore the sound of men undressing and dressing only an arm's length away.

"I suppose you two will sleep in the middle. Can I have Lauren's spot?" Brody reached for her stack of blankets.

She snatched her bundle and held it close. "I'd prefer my same spot. Elias has uh—"

"Elias hates to be cold." After pulling a wrinkled shirt over his head, he rubbed his hands together scrutinizing her. "Right now, I'm really cold." He bit back a smile.

Lauren took a deep breath, scowling at him. "You may not have noticed yet, Brody, but Elias has ah, I guess you'd call it, fitful sleep. So . . ."

"Geeze, are you two married or not?"

"Yep," Elias replied, grabbing his bedroll. "You can have her spot."

He knelt, rolling the thick pad down the middle. "Give me the blankets, Lauren." He reached out. Brody stretched out on her pad as a low growl rose from her throat. Elias leaned forward and grabbed her wrist. He pulled, and she resisted at the same time. It'll be fine, he mouthed. He pulled again as she glued her feet to the wagon bottom.

"Can you douse the light before daybreak?" Brody faced the canvas, pulling his own wool blanket around him.

Elias reached back toward the lantern, raised the glass and blew it out. Lauren tossed out a checkered quilt, hitting Elias's legs. Lifting the lid on the other bench, he rummaged through his things and pulled on his brown cap. The rain still beat against the canvas as he came back close to her. Reaching out quickly, he pulled on her blanket and skirt at the same time. Her knees buckled, and she knelt taut before him. He came up on his knees and circled cold hands around her neck, bringing his face to her ear, he said, "I have a plan. I'll lay on my stomach. I can't swing at you that way."

Lauren felt a wave of relief. His voice was calm and honorable, like when she first met him. His fingers wove into the back of her hair kneading her scalp and neck—without permission she noted. Her eyes closed as he massaged her stiffness to a light, heady bliss.

"I can twist these too if you want." He tugged on a strand, and she opened her eyes. Still clutching a lone blanket between them, she shook

191

her head, darkness the only cover to her blushing face and rapid heartbeat.

He turned and laid on his stomach, as promised.

Lauren stared at Brody's back, trying to calm the dizziness. Picking up the checkered quilt, she carefully laid it over Elias, tucking it in around his dry woolen socks. Was this loyalty, she wondered, because her heart was upside down. His touch felt like more, way more. He inched next to the side of her bunk now holding the large teen and patted the space next to him. She wrapped her body in an afghan she had made with all her yarn scraps. Like a baby swaddled tight, she carefully laid on her side, facing away from him.

ELIAS AWOKE ON his side, the fingers of both his hands were tucked under her blanket and tightly tucked under the side of her body. Somewhere in between sleep and sleeplessness, he must have thought that was a safe place to contain his flying hands and arms. Slowly, like leaving an explosive setting, he pulled them out from her. She didn't stir. He waited, listening to Brody snore. The morning had broken, but the gray clouds hid the sunlight. Joe had said for everyone to rest until noon, maybe he could fall back asleep.

Remarkable. He pulled off his cap and scratched his head; he'd had no nightmares.

Actually, quite the opposite. He'd dreamed of a little cabin; it wasn't his dugout, wasn't any place he'd stayed before. It had a large rock fireplace with a blazing fire. Warmth and comfort filled the one small room as he stared at the bed where lovely Lauren slept blissfully on her side. He sat on the corner of the bed as peace seeped into his bones. Freedom pulsed in him to join her, as he pulled the covers back and saw a little pink baby suckling at her breast. His breathing suddenly caught in his throat. It was a dream, but his chest flooded with a certain feeling. *Yes, it was warmth, warmth in wagon loads, but it was so much more.*

Alone. All his life he'd always felt alone. This overwhelming feeling was remarkably different. Like when Anna would hug him as a child. Her arms anchored him to something, like they belonged together. Thinking of his dream, he knew the woman and baby belonged to him. He knew it deep in his being, and he belonged to them. Lauren rolled to her back, eyes closed.

"Ouch." Her nose and forehead wrinkled adorably.

Raising up to one elbow he looked quizzically at her.

She moved her shoulders up and down. "My back," she blinked looking up at him. "I hit my back on the harpsichord when the horses took off."

"I'm sorry." he whispered, "Did I keep you awake last night?

"Horses. I know, I know." Brody sat up in a daze. "Water, feed." Elias opened his mouth but had to dodge Brody's reckless legs pulling his boots on. The teen's eyes were still half closed as he loosened the back canvas and jumped out.

Elias snickered. "I was about to say, 'we're in no hurry. We're not pulling out till noon.'" Lauren pulled her blanket closer and yawned as the cold morning air entered their cocoon. She looked so relaxed, a sight rarely seen. With tousled hair and sleepy, sweet face, he brought his hand under her blanket, caressing up her arm.

"A big breakfast sounds good." She sat upward, his hand falling away. "Yes, I mean no. You never bumped me or kept me awake. I'd ask you if you were warm enough, but I have a feeling . . ." A red flush rose in her cheeks.

"It was my best warm ever." He reached for her again.

"I think I hear the sisters." She pulled her blanket off and sat up on the bench.

Grinning, Elias enjoyed watching her fiddle with her cooking supplies.

"You deserve to be a man of leisure, the way you practically pulled the Coolidge wagon through the water." She glanced back at his relaxed state, then back to gather their breakfast items. He touched the hem of her skirt then

194

gently cupped his hand around her ankle, wishing she would come close again. "I think I have everything." She jumped up fast and stared with wide eyes at his brazen touch. Smiling, he finally rose and helped her with the back gate.

She held her hand out. "It's not raining. Right now, anyway." She jumped out the back and froze. "Is that my harpsichord laying over there in the mud?"

Elias groaned, rolling back down to his bedroll, he covered his face.

Chapter 27

"OH NO, OH NO, oh no."

Elias heard her moan as he slipped his damp boots on and rammed his arms in his half soaked jacket. Jumping off the back of the wagon, he saw it, sure enough. The harpsichord was lying flat in a puddle of water and mud, no tarp to be found. He clamped his teeth together to hold back yelling Brody's name across southern Indiana.

Lauren strained to stand the large instrument upright.

"Here, I'll get it." He moved in and lifted it right side up. Water drained from the top all down the sides and legs.

She whimpered.

"This is my fault. I should have tied it myself."

"Or just never taken it out." She blew out a flustered breath. "It's ruined. I tried to tell you."

He saw the tarp against a tree and picked it up. "This would have helped."

Lauren's chin quivered. "This was my grandmother's, from England. The wood, the finish, the keys," she moaned, "all ruined. Just ruined."

Elias chewed on his bottom lip and watched as

the others prepared breakfast around a large fire. His stomach growled, and he smelled the coffee. "I'll buy you a new one before we get to Denver City." He glanced at Lauren and back at the camp preparations. She didn't move, wasn't she hungry? "Should I grab your things for breakfast?"

She glared out past him, face red, nostrils flaring. Last night a little tug was all it took to get her moving. He reached out, and she jumped like his touch was a bee sting. "Lauren, I said I'm sorry."

"No, you did not!"

Rubbing his chin, he tried to remember. "Okay, well, I am sorry."

"You think you can just buy me a new one? Do you have rocks in your head? This is the only one that matters to my mother."

"I think *you* matter more than that thing." He mumbled.

"No, I don't. This matters a great deal. Her grandmother played it, her aunts, her sisters, it's a family heirloom."

"You know your mother will swoon to see you, more than that thing."

Pulling her hands up like claws, she growled and turned away from him. "You. Don't. Understand." She flipped back around, and he took a small step back. "You've never had a family." Her eyes bored into his. "You've never had a mother." The words slammed into his chest. "How could you ever, ever possibly understand?" The fury behind her words was like venom from a snake bite.

His blood started to run cold, worse than a tub of ice water. *Never love anything. Never love anything. This is what will happen. They will pull your skin inside out and jump on your heart.* It was ridiculous to think they would love each other, want to belong to each other. How insane was he really? Like some goose-eyed lap dog, he'd become tame and soft. He held himself rigid, looked her slowly up and down, breathing in his former resolve of only loyalty, he turned and stalked away.

LAUREN DROPPED ANOTHER slab of bacon in the sizzling grease. Brody had already had three plates full, but Elias was nowhere to be found. Guilt assaulted her. It was Brody's fault yet she hadn't pointed one finger at him.

"Brody, can you tell Elias his breakfast is ready."

"He's out yonder a ways getting those new horses set up with the wagon harnesses."

"Please."

"Hey, Martin," Brody waved him over. "Come along."

Mabel came up to the fire with another pot of water to heat as the teens headed out. "Joe traded with a farmer for some eggs and milk. I was going to boil all these eggs and divvy them up."

Lauren removed the cooked bacon. "That would be wonderful, thank you."

"We almost had our wagons collide last night." Mabel laughed. "Those horses don't like thunder."

"No, that was a rough ride, I'd say."

Mabel carefully placed the eggs into the water. "I couldn't help but hear your harpsichord got left out in the rain." Janet came over to the fire circle and sat down. "I was sad because I thought maybe one night we could ask you to play it for us."

Lauren found a small grin to give the sisters. "I don't really play." She remembered herself fumbling through Amazing Grace at the funeral parlor. "It was more my mother and my sister. I knew how badly they would want it with them. Probably the main reason for this trip." She grew silent.

Brody and Martin jogged back to the ladies. "He says he's not hungry and gave us permission to do some target shooting." Lauren nodded as they ran off, looking to the sisters. "Elias wasn't the one who left it out last night, but I took my frustration out on him."

Mabel and Janet nodded.

"Cause we all know he'd never miss a meal." Lauren tried to lighten the moment.

"There are misunderstandings in every marriage." Mabel poked at the coals.

"I can't imagine you sisters ever having a cross word with your husband."

Janet laughed. "You know there are three of us and one of him."

Lauren smiled, "Yes, but still . . ."

"The thing that has helped me the most is to get rid of the idea we have to agree on everything." Janet nodded at Mabel's advice. "You will always have your strong feelings about something, as they will theirs. We do try to be respectful, but we don't have to agree."

"It helps us as wives, we can all get a different view," Janet said. "So many times, the problem isn't even worth the time to find out who's right and who's wrong."

Lauren felt an abiding comfort at their words as Mrs. Coolidge walked up. "Mr. Coolidge is supervising the young men with the target shooting," she said, her tone terse and lips pursed.

Moving back to allow them near the fire, Lauren smiled at Katherine and Eleanor. "How are you girls doing today? Did that thunder scare you?"

"I didn't like it." Eleanor piped up, big, brown eyes wide.

"We ended up like sardines in a can. I barely got any sleep," Mrs. Coolidge drawled. "But my husband assured me that would be the worst of the trip."

Lauren, Janet, and Mabel took wide-eyed glances at each other. Lauren scanned past their wagon where Elias was working with the new horses. He still had his brown knitted cap on. She should be happy and thankful; she'd slept warm and safe.

Reverend Little joined the fire circle. "Good day, ladies. Gray, but not raining," he chuckled.

"I'll have some of these boiled eggs coming up for you in a few minutes." Mabel took a ladle to the water.

"Why, thank you kindly," the Reverend nodded. Mrs. Coolidge gathered her girls and reminded them they still had lessons to finish this morning. Lauren heard the boys approaching camp. Glancing back, Brody tried to get Felicia's attention—looking cocky with the gun hanging off his finger. Lauren knew Mrs. Coolidge would put a stop to that. The cast iron skillet was awkward and heavy as Lauren poured the grease into a can. She turned to set it back on the grate, but something blew past her, pinging the iron skillet so hard it knocked her and the skillet to her backside.

In a flash of a second, Mabel loomed over her. "Oh dear Lord, Lauren are you hit?" Mabel's face was chalk-white, what had happened?

She waited for something to sting or burn. "I don't . . . think so."

Mabel pulled her up on shaking legs. Looking

over, Martin and Brody had saucers for eyes. Felicia was hunched down, with her arms over her face. Mabel rubbed Lauren's arms, looking her over. "Oh, the grace of God, I think the bullet missed you."

Reverend Little's "Oh nah, nah, nah," broke forth somewhere behind her. Lauren looked up from Mabel's grip; the campfire group was all fine except for their frozen stares. Giving Mabel a forced smile, she took a steady breath and stepped away.

Just as her eyelids rose from the bullet-dented black skillet to the wet landscape, Elias, like a bear loose from a cage, was in full run. Not toward her, but to Brody, the one with the gun hanging from his hand.

Chapter 28

BRODY'S EYES TWITCHED from her to Elias, as Elias sprinted closer. Brody dropped the pistol, and, as it thudded on the ground, he took off running.

"Mr. Kern!" Lauren called. Turning to the people watching, "Where is Joe?" She stepped around the campfire, gripping the Reverend's jacket. "Can you please go after them? Please?" Elias had overtaken Brody, and they rolled in a ball of mud, brush, and rocks. Mrs. Coolidge yanked Felicia up and pushed her inside their wagon with the girls. Martin took off running. "Martin, you get back here this instant! Lux! Get him." She screeched.

"Please, Reverend." Lauren panted. "Elias will kill him." The whole camp could see the arms and knees punching, kicking, twisting bone and body.

Lauren caught sight of Joe in front of the sisters' wagon and ran to him. "Joe, please, please go stop them."

"They're just letting off steam. It's just what men do."

"Please," Lauren whimpered, grasping her

hands under her chin. Joe shook his head. Now Elias was on top of Brody, his fist slamming the teen's face. Lauren gathered her skirts and ran out toward the fight. Halfway there, coming up behind her, Joe grabbed her arm and pulled her back.

"Okay, okay, stay clear now." He raised his gun in the air and pulled the trigger.

Lauren winced, the shot deafening her ears. Joe held her arm steady. Elias jumped up and swiped the mud and blood off his face. Wheezing, he staggered back with a crooked bloody lip smiling his physical release. Martin helped pull Brody to his feet. Lauren came closer, amazed that Brody was bent over but standing.

"Mr. Kern." Lux Coolidge swiftly came up to them. He looked so out of place with a clean white shirt and tweed vest. "I want to believe after all the fighting this country has been through, we could show our young men that there are more civil ways to work out our disagreements."

Joe's hand still rested on his holstered gun handle. He looked confused squinting at Mr. Coolidge.

Elias stared at Lauren, rubbing his jaw. His eyes steel-cold, deeply set with distance. "The next time some stupid kid plays with a gun near your family," he glared at Lux, "and you want to sit down and talk to him about southern hospitality, you go ahead. It's supposed to be a free country." Elias spit blood onto the ground. "Brody, Martin." Elias waited till they looked at him. "You ever play with a loaded gun near camp again, there will be no talking. I will personally string you up by the neck and hang you from the closest tree."

"Say, now." Mr. Coolidge puffed out his chest.

The corners of Elias's eyes crinkled at Lauren, testing something in her. Loyalty. Though Brody was much worse for the wear, she knew better than to help him. His mistake could have killed her today. Truth be told, he looked about the same as when they found him. Elias could have killed him, but he didn't. He'd kept his word. He stalked away. She nodded at the men before trying to catch up with him.

Heavy in step and gait, Elias walked toward the open field. Lauren could not reach him without running. "Elias, wait. Please, slow down." He turned so quickly, she almost bumped into him.

"It's okay Lauren, you can go tend to Brody." He turned and stomped through the wet grass.

"Wait, please." Jogging to grab his arm, he froze, staring out to the cloudy gray field.

"I don't want to tend to Brody," she panted. "I want to say something to you." He touched his tongue to his fat lip, gazing over her head.

"Now you won't look at me," she sighed.

His chest rose and fell, but he dropped his spent eyes to hers.

Throat constricting, she pushed the words out. "I'm sorry for this morning. I-I was harsh. And I blamed you for something that wasn't even your fault." His eyes bounced back to the open field. "Truth is," tears began to pool, and she sucked in a quick breath, "your mother didn't choose to leave you—death wasn't her choice. I've more splinters embedded in my heart and my mother is alive. That harpsichord shouldn't be so important. You were trying to help me understand that."

Glancing at her, his steel blue eyes softened a bit. He opened his mouth and closed it, shuffling his feet. "I didn't see what happened," he said, rasping. "I just heard the shot and saw you fall back." He blew out a short breath, looking everywhere but at her. Clutching his ears then he dropped his hands quickly. He was agitated.

"The bullet hit the cast iron skillet," Lauren now thankful he was talking. "I'm not sure why it knocked me over."

"I saw Mabel help you up." He watched her, reaching out and swiping a slow tear on her cheek, "but I was still going to kill him." His mixture of calm, tender touch and wrath collided inside of her. She lifted her hand to his face, but he stepped back.

"This is why I don't do love, Lauren." He cracked a crooked grin, causing a shiver to run up her spine. "Because it would be like living my life in a cold, hard cell behind thick bars, smelling decay, planning how to kill myself. When I don't care, I can take care of me. Live for me. Think for me. Feel only for me." He chuckled, knocking the mud off his pants. "Of course, when I met you, I wasn't doing that great of a job taking care of me."

They smiled, though nothing was funny. A cold wind brought another round of shivers. An awareness of his vow started to come clear. If he loved her and someone hurt her, he believed he'd have no control. She wasn't blind. She'd seen it, felt it in his hug, his tender smiles, his little touches, that soft kiss to her temple, something was building in him. Turning toward the breeze, she pulled her hair out, raking her fingers through it and shook her head. She wadded her bun back and tied it tight. This was a fine mess; here he stood covered in mud and dirt, fighting for . . . for her life, her protection, loyalty. Did he understand how attractive he was? But was he safe? *He's trying to tell you loud and clear.*

"All right, then." She cleared her throat, remembering her goal was always Denver City. "I just wanted to say sorry for the things I said."

ELIAS SNIFFED HARD, nodding his acceptance. He watched that green skirt as she walked away. Lord Almighty she was everything good and beautiful, and more. That stupid dream. His bed with her in it. A baby, their baby. Why couldn't it just stay a good dream? Why did it have to stir up hope? There's to be no hope, no future. She had risked everything to free him from the grave. He owed her and that's all. He'd promised her safe passage to Denver City. Puffing out a long-held breath, he noticed Reverend Little walking his way.

"Elias, can I have a minute?" The older man looked to the ground, face pinched.

"Yes, sir."

"Your wife is a good woman." He lifted a grin. "She obviously loves and cares for you a great deal."

Elias stilled, befuddled, he had no response.

"She asked me to go and break up you and Brody's fight. I didn't help her, and she may not understand why, so I hoped maybe you would tell her."

Elias tipped his head.

"Yes, the war's over, praise the Lord above." The Reverend chuckled. "But still, where I come from, a black man don't go telling any white men what to do. I don't think I will see that day in my lifetime."

Elias stilled; years of being under another man's rule, he knew the feeling.

"Reverend," Elias lightly touched his worn and patched jacket. "Whether it's when you are pointing that Bible at me or at any other time, you have my permission to set me right. I've learned who to respect not based on past or color. I respect you and what you say. Knowing what you've been through, it gives me hope that maybe God can reach me. I've had to sit through a lot of Bible teaching, but you're the first religious person I can relate to."

"I know you've been through a lot son, I see it in your eyes." The Reverend smiled. "One thing I know when I see it is captives longin' for freedom. To the day I die, I'll tell everyone that will listen, freedom is real, and it's possible."

Chapter 29

THE EVENING BEFORE the group was to enter Indianapolis, Joe spoke to those sitting around the campfire. Everyone was especially quiet. It had been a long week of pressing the wagons and animals. While Lauren enjoyed the time walking with the sisters, sometimes she would daydream about the little farms dotting the spring landscape of Indiana—to just have her own little home, open windows, breeze blowing the curtains in and out. Being gone this long, she could almost erase the dark and damp smells of her home in Greenlock. The idea of her father faring alone still pinched her heart with regret.

Elias stood stoically as he listened to Joe. Hanging back from the inner ring, he looked tired. Like her, did he feel the progression dwindle from their friendship? He had been friendly enough, just nothing personal. Even Brody and he had fallen into a workable routine.

"So then, Brody, you will take the watch till one, then Elias till three. I'll finish up until dawn," Joe said, pushing his hat back. "Indianapolis is a large city. I'd recommend you get your supplies as a group. We'll be circling up by noon. Set up and go from there. Any questions?"

"We might take the family in to stay in a hotel. Will we still leave the same time the next morning?" Lux Coolidge asked. The tired group looked up souring at his question.

"Yep." Joe nodded. "Same time. If you're not packed and ready, we move on without ya. Remember the next leg will be about two weeks out. I can't guarantee there'll be any trading with farmers, or what the hunting might be like, so each wagon is responsible for their own supplies."

Hotel, the thought made Lauren sigh. Hot bath, big bed, a meal with items not infested with bugs. Maybe she could just find a bathhouse in town where she could soak?

"Reverend Little." Like most nights, Joe handed the closing song or prayer to the encouraging man.

"Oh, people now." The Reverend clapped. "How far we have come. Yes, Amen. Our journey, our crossin', our steps are for a better day. Amen?"

Everyone sprinkled amens back at him.

"We walk it out by faith and not by sight, umm hum, that we do." He removed his hat, and the men followed suit. "So Lord, we pray to trust you like never before. Protect us from evil, yes, Lord. Keep the path safe. Amen."

As everyone stood, Lauren offered her arm to help the pregnant Chrystal stand. "Thank you, Lauren, this baby was kicking me the whole evening. Oh." She held her belly, stretching her back. Chrystal grabbed Lauren's hand and placed it on her belly, "Here, right here. It's probably a boy with all this energy."

Lauren waited till a little tap-tap tickled her palm. "I felt something!" Her eyes glowed. "I could feel little kicks." They smiled at each other. She looked up. Elias waited for her.

"Sleep well, Chrystal." Lauren walked toward him. "I felt her baby, just then. It kicked, and I could feel it."

He stared at her in the dim shadows, illuminating the hollowness between them. She sighed, "I suppose that's not something you want to hear about." She sighed again at how many things of late were not sharable between them.

They walked back to their wagon. "With all the hurry and set up tomorrow, I want to take you to town." He lowered the gate for her. "I'll help you get what we need."

She nodded, remembering the mess from the last time she went to town.

EVEN FROM THE outskirts of Indianapolis, the vitality of the city pulsed into their little camp. Mrs. Coolidge sashayed by in a dress suitable for a southern tea party, and Lauren had to fight a pang of jealousy. Drawing her hand down her dusty day skirt, she'd never been to a nice restaurant or museum. Martin and Brody tried to find a way to convince Mr. Coolidge they would be fine on their own. Elias came alongside her with the mare he rode most often.

"Ready?"

Holding his hand out, he helped her into the saddle. He stood up on a log and jumped onto the back of the horse. His arms surrounded her, then he grabbed the reins, his chest bumping her back as the horse trotted. All too aware of their closeness, she tried to focus on the wagons and people soon filling the thick streets.

"Joe said the mercantile is up here, on the left."

"Could we . . ." She couldn't turn enough to see him. ". . . could we look around first?" A large ornate church loomed tall at the end of the main street. "Maybe go see the church?" Her head jerked to the side. "Do you smell that? There must be a bakery near."

"Sure." He kicked the mare forward.

"And over there." She pointed. "Look at the top of that! Is it someone's home?"

Catching onto her wish, he jumped off the horse and lowered her down. "Let's walk, so we can see whatever you want."

Even though she'd walked across the never-ending land, today it felt invigorating to stop and point out all the interesting things they saw. Their conversation flowed with ease, the companionship that had been missing, slowly returned, surrounding them and drawing them closer.

An hour later, she took a bite of a warm, twisted cinnamon bun from the bakery. "This is heaven." Holding it out to him, he took a bite. Snickering, she rubbed some frosting off his cheek. "We could get you a haircut and shave." She pulled on his short whiskers.

He pulled her hand away. "You don't want my strength to return?"

"Humm." She tilted her head to the side. "You seem stronger now than when I met you."

"Oh, if you only knew, lovely Lauren." He took her elbow as they stepped off the walkway and crossed the busy street. "My hair may grow, but I'm weaker in the heart every moment I spend with you." He winked, his smile brash.

For a moment she felt her jaw drop. Either he meant it or was teasing, but her heart fluttered all the same.

Stopping near a fabric and yarn shop, Elias gestured for her to go in. An empty bench in front allowed him to sit back and rest. His eyes closed for a nap.

She checked on him through the glass and then took her time enjoying the different textures. She settled on four yards of a soft gray cotton with a pale blue stripe.

"Lovely choice." The clerk smiled as she measured the fabric. "I noticed your husband," she glanced at Lauren's ringless finger, "or friend, out the window. Is this for him?"

"Yes." Lauren nodded. "And hopefully enough for a little smock for a new baby coming."

"Well, congratulations." The clerk folded the fabric.

"Oh, not for me, just a friend we're traveling with." Something in the clerk's smug smile and eye contact felt like her old life in Greenlock. It had been many a week since she felt unacceptable. She paid, tucking her bundle under her arm, the clerk already walking away. Coming outside, she sat next to Elias. He winked at her. "Good to go?"

Watching the town bustle by in front of her, she tried to swallow the tightness in her throat. Blast it. It had been such a wonderful carefree day.

"Do you remember when you would never look at me?" he said, bumping her shoulder with his.

She loved that calm voice calling her back. "Yes." She took a deep breath and looked at him.

"What's wrong? Did you get what you wanted?" He waited. "Do you need more money?"

She shook her head, staring again out to the street. "I think I need a wedding ring. But then I think, not. It won't fix anything." Pinching her lips together, she almost felt homesick for their traveling companions—the Littles and their hidden family; the sisters and their marriage to one man; the refined Coolidge family, running from poor financial dealings; even Brody—they were all like the scraps of frayed yarn, finding forbearance and tolerance in being tied together.

"Thank you for today, Elias." She stood. "I'm ready to get our supplies and get back."

Chapter 30

WHILE LAUREN GROUND the beans for their coffee, Elias found a simple gold band and purchased it aside from their other items. He slipped it into his pocket next to his childhood wrapped token. He hated that something had upset her, she said the band wouldn't fix it, and he knew she was right. They had lived the pretense in front of the others so well that it was shameful. His life had been a series of disgraceful choices, but she was not used to the depravity. Her soul was pure and honest; the lies must be whittling away at her. A ring would probably make it worse, he thought, as the round token stung his leg through the pocket.

Coming around him, she put the last of the items they needed in a pile, and he added a new hat. Like sensing his unrest, she offered him a sweet smile. "Maybe two giant pickles for the road?" she said, nodding to the glass container filled with the green vegetable.

"Yes." He agreed as the clerk wrapped their purchases, and he plopped the new hat on his head. "We might need to walk back. I didn't think to bring another horse." He threw the large burlap bags over his shoulder. Truthfully, he had thought of it, but he just missed being close to her since the fight with Brody. He could do well for a while, but then like a fox to the garden—he just couldn't avoid being close to her. He loaded the bags on the horse. Today was like a garden party, or what he thought a garden party might be like, all sunshine and sweet smiles.

They moved down the side of Main Street, eating the large pickles until the noise of the city faded, and the shadows of dusk softly appeared.

"I think this was the best day I've ever had." He stepped closer pulling the horse along.

"This one?"

The side of his mouth twisted up. "Yeah."

She glanced at him once, then twice.

"Tell me about being cold. I assume the asylum school didn't have heat?"

"It had heat. I hauled a thousand buckets of coal." He chewed his last bite of pickle. "Picture the letter H. The long hallway in the front was called the front row, a wide hallway went down the middle, and the back building was the other length of the H; we called it the back row. The front rooms and offices were all the paying folk with nice windows and coal stoves. They even had a large garden out front. The back row was for the less, shall we say, less fortunate."

"And they didn't heat the back row?" They

218

stopped and spilled canteen water over their sticky fingers.

"A bit." He flicked the water at her as she spun away. "It was the ice baths that would chill you to the bone. It's how they controlled us." He pulled the horse forward.

She hesitated, the crickets serenading their walk. "They put children in ice baths?"

Elias let out a held breath, this would be the last conversation he wanted to have, yet it would guarantee her a safe distance from who he really was.

"They held us under so they could drown the devil out of us. It's so cold that you feel your heartbeat stop. You know you're going to die, so you quit fighting."

Pressing her fingers over her mouth, she squeezed and then intertwined her fingers. "Being pinned under water, I . . . I can't imagine. Yet," her face lifted, "how did you find the ability to pull the Coolidge wagon through that swollen creek? That had to be cold water, and the wagon wheel could have trapped you."

He scowled. "Nope, nothing is like having someone pin your feet against the outside rim while your hands are bound behind you. I guess as long as I had control over my hands and feet, the cold water didn't bother me."

A shiver raced up and down her spine. "I-can't-even . . . what great courage you have, Elias."

He angled away from her as if he was watching something out in the field. *Why was his throat tightening?* "I've done more cowardly things, than courageous," he murmured. "I've fought and stole from those who did me no wrong. I set explosives that blew arms and legs off decent Yankee men. How many killed, I don't know. I just always assumed I would end up in the same corpse pile as them, just with a gray jacket instead of blue."

A light breeze blew her soft curls around her face. He needed her to stop looking at him. The way her mouth opened in empathy, speechless, her heart feeling some foolish sorrow for him.

"When the war was over, I walked away. I was supposed to go back to prison. But I had survived this long, so I went back to what I knew, just with a new gang. There was more money in stealing explosives and selling them to all the angry men. I had a good horse and a decent wagon. On one run, I had just jumped down to," he finally looked at her, "um, find a tree." She looked away. "A shot rang out. It didn't hit the horse or me, but it hit my wagon and blew everything to rock size pieces. I waited behind a rock until it was safe to come out and see my horse's head missing from its body, cooking and smoldering from the nitro." That did it; her face paled with shock. "I think I was supposed to die that day, too." He shrugged.

They turned at the rumble of a large covered

wagon coming down the road, the Reverend and Ida Bell riding on the front bench. Pulling the loaded mare off the side of the road, they greeted them as the wagon slowed.

"Needin' a ride?" The Reverend called down.

Elias waved them on. "No thanks. We're making it a stroll."

Ida Bell smiled, as the wagon lurched forward.

"You know the day you came up behind me at the blacksmith?"

He nodded.

"I saw this same wagon and the Littles sitting in that same spot. I was on my way to Father Michael's funeral, but it drew me, like a rope around my waist, I had to go. I had to see. And that look that Ida Bell just gave me? It's the same look the first time I saw her. All these weeks traveling together, she's never smiled at me, until now."

"I think she can smile more now. They dropped off a family here in Indianapolis."

"Oh." She stared after the large wagon. "Do they have another family to transport?"

He lifted one shoulder. "Maybe."

The circle of wagons and flickering fire could be seen ahead. Their home away from home. Part of him didn't want to care about these people. They repeatedly appreciated him, leaned on him, and trusted him. Obviously, Lauren did not share his past secrets. Joe and Reverend Little knew all about the carnage of war; those men he felt a comradery with.

"I was just thinking—maybe you're opposite of Samson in the Bible." She smiled, and he looked askance at her. "Once all that hair came off, you changed into the man you were meant to be."

He nodded. "And maybe if it weren't for a funeral that *you* wanted to attend, you never would have seen that wagon and taken the risk with me." He looked at his feet. "I mean to get to Denver City."

A comforting sound wafted near. Singing. Reverend Little's voice, deep and powerful.

Way down yonder in the graveyard walk, I thank God I'm free at last. Me and my Jesus goin' to meet and talk. I thank God I'm free at last. Free at last, free at last. I thank God I'm free at last; Free at last, Free at last, I thank God almighty . . .

Approaching their wagon, they stood back and listened.

On my knees when the light passed by . . . Ida Bell joined the chorus with her rich harmony as she held the Reverend's arm. *I thank God I'm free at last.* An unexplainable presence surrounded them, softening the camp, and the night.

The sisters sat in reverence with their eyes closed, Mabel swiping a loose tear. Elias let go of the reins and slipped his hands around Lauren's waist. Neither moved, so he pulled her

222

back against his chest, locking his fingers around her belly. The gentle rest of her hands over his and the heartfelt spiritual song spread a warmth through his being. Biting his lip, he stared at the flames over Lauren's soft hair. If the Littles' voices could rise with such conviction and proclaim bondage to freedom, if this beautiful young woman would let him hold her, maybe, he swallowed the lump in his throat, just maybe belonging was his truer freedom.

Chapter 31

SOMEONE KICKED HIS boot in the thick of night. Rolling up, Elias forced his eyes open; it was his turn to do watch. Brody handed him the rifle and flopped down under the wagon. Walking toward the small flickering fire, he poured himself a cup of coffee. Swinging the rifle to his back, he took a steaming sip and started to circle the camp.

He had been dreaming of Anna holding him, rocking him, rubbing his skinny boy limbs warm. She was the only one that could comfort the children of the back row. That was one of the new good dreams he'd had of late. He stared out to the blackened landscape. After the Littles said their goodnights, Lauren turned and kissed him on the cheek. He couldn't really see her face, as she squeezed his hands then pulled away from him. Such strange emotions clung to him even now.

Yet he had dreamt of Anna. *Lord, please watch over her, wherever she is. Protect her and love her as she did me.* He smiled at the darkness. Now he's a prayin' man, too? *And a loving man.*

The strange words came from obscurity. He

sucked in a breath. Yes. Yes, he did love Anna. It felt good and honest to say it. Love is of God, maybe that voice was from God. He chuckled. He loved Anna, and he would probably never see her again. He waited, nothing hurt. Something inside felt stronger, like after a hearty, filling meal.

He tapped his fingers against the hot tin cup. *What if I wanted to love Lauren?* That felt false, especially if God knows everything. Deep inside he knew he already did love Lauren. He loved her from the first moment she brought him food and a blanket in that cramped pantry. He'd loved how her face lit up when she talked about her dream to take the wagon train to Denver City. He loved how she didn't want to trust him, but then, in spite of her better judgment, she did. He loved the time and attention she gave to care for others. Her laugh, the way her voice went soft when she wanted something. *Mmm,* her cooking, her soft skin, her lips, her body against his. He yanked off his knit cap and fanned his face; he was wide awake and warm now. Why not be honest with God? *Yes, I love Lauren.* Still no gut punch to the belly. No need to be this honest with her, but it felt good to be true to himself.

The Coolidge family had left their large white dogs tied to their wagon, and Elias let them loose to do their business. They circled back around him and flopped at his feet.

"Ah, left behind, I see." He scratched the bellies of the dogs as their tails thumped hard against the ground. The female's belly seemed larger than the other. Puppies, he guessed. He'd love to have one. "Are you ready to be a daddy?" He roughhoused with Goliath. "Huh?" He remembered the dream with Lauren and the little cabin. He stood as they circled his feet. Would she want to go on with him to California? He had a ring and a Reverend—he shook his head. Her dream was always Denver City.

ELIAS AWOKE UNDER the wagon to find the sun coming up and Joe kneeling down next to him. "We got company coming. I think it's the sheriff or town law."

He glanced over to Brody sleeping and shook him awake. "Did you get into any trouble in town?"

Brody squinted and grunted, "No."

"No bars, brawling, or woman?"

They both rolled out and stood, watching the three men ride closer.

"Nothing that got me in trouble," Brody said, and started toward the fire. The sisters were already up starting breakfast.

"What about Martin?" Elias called after him.

"Him neither," Brody barked back.

The Reverend and Joe were speaking to each other as the men rode into camp. Lauren came around the corner with her breakfast things. Stopping, she froze as the men dismounted.

"Who's in charge here?" the large man with a badge asked. The other two pulled back their jackets to expose their guns and holsters. Elias looked at Lauren, trying to settle her with his eyes. He knew by the pounding of his heartbeat this could be about him.

"I am." Joe approached them. "What can we help you with?" Looking concerned, the sisters stopped cooking.

"First off, I need the names of all those in your party." The sheriff puffed his chest out. Lauren set her things down and came and stood close behind him, slipping her hand inside his.

"In that wagon, we have Reverend and Mrs. Little." The second lawman pulled out a stack of crinkled paper from his satchel, flipping through the papers. Elias felt her other hand on his back. "Don't say anything," he whispered.

"That one there belongs to Mr. and Mrs. Browne."

Elias nodded at the men.

"The Coolidge family spent the night in a hotel, that's their wagon there." Their dogs stood at attention.

"I'm Joe Kern. I'm in charge of that one, leading these three ladies to meet up with their hus—people in Utah."

The larger man came up to the other lawmen

and said something in low tones. "What is your first name Mr. Browne?" He eyed Elias.

"Elias." He couldn't lie, all these folk knew his real name. If one of those papers showed him as wanted or deceased—

"What about him?" The sheriff pointed at Brody, "Who do you belong to?"

"No one." Brody piped up. "Just joined up a month or so back. On my way to Independence to work."

"Huh." The large man looked skeptical. "Craig, Forrest, start in that one." He pointed to the Reverend's wagon. Ida Bell swallowed hard, gripping the Reverend's arm. Elias tried to read Joe's expression. He knew the Littles were friends. Did they have another stowaway family already in there? Lauren pulled on his arm, whispering in his ear. "They have your real name, but you're supposed to be dead." He grabbed her hand from squeezing his arm and held it tight by his side. Then men jumped off the Littles' wagon, and one grabbed an ax sitting by a small pile of wood. He bent low and began to swing up, chopping holes in the bottom of the wagon. The other man jumped into the back of their wagon. Every eye of their tight group stared in shock as the man chopped away. Grabbing an old threadbare quilt, he pulled it down through the broken lumber.

Elias watched Ida Bell's mouth hang open.

228

How did the Littles do this work? Pinching his lips together, he tried to calm himself with all the insane things he'd done in his past. Except now there was Lauren to think about. He heard the lid of the harpsichord slam down. *Please, Lord.* Pulling the front of the canvas back from his wagon, the man leaned out. "What's in those locked metal boxes?"

"Ammunition," Elias said, confidently. The man shook his head, staring Elias down.

"No need to fret, Reverend." Brody piped up. "Whatever they ruin in their sad attempts, we'll help you put back right."

The sheriff's forehead furrowed at him.

"Shut up, Brody." Elias glared at the mouthy teen. The man jumped down from his wagon.

The man chopping at the Littles' wagon came out and wiped his dripping brow. Ida Bell's lips moved in prayer. He dropped the ax and entered the sisters' wagon. Chrystal dropped her head on Mabel's shoulder. If they asked the sisters, would they admit being polygamists? Would the law arrest them? As the fear couldn't get any higher, the Coolidge family walked cautiously up to camp. The other man glared at them and rummaged through their wagon. Even Lux Coolidge knew enough to keep his talkative mouth closed. The little girls looked frightened and clung to their mother's skirts.

"And where are you traveling from, sir?" The sheriff asked Lux.

"Originally, West Virginia."

The sheriff ignored him and took a long stare at the Littles. Joe walked closer to his friends.

"Transportation of *anything* illegal is illegal. No matter what state you're from. Any contraband, breathing or not isn't going through my town. Is that clear."

Elias clenched his jaw. Contraband, transportation, this was all too close for comfort. Even keeping his own name was a mistake. The farther he thought he could get from Ohio, the less his troubles would find him. If they had wind of the Littles' doings, what else could happen?

Chapter 32

THE LAWMEN'S INVASION of camp added a solemn air to the morning. A few simple repairs to what everyone knew was the Littles' secret compartment were done quickly. With heads down and little spoken, they all worked through the breakfast meal and quickly got back on the road. Lauren was thankful the sisters were walking, she was too keyed up to stay on the wagon wondering what Elias was thinking.

"How did your day in town go?" Janet asked, tying her bonnet under her chin.

"Well." Lauren nodded. "It's the biggest city I've ever seen. Quite a few remarkable buildings. I mailed a letter to my father and one to my mother, found a yarn and fabric store to wander in. I could take a day just to touch everything."

"Me, too," Mabel chimed in. "I love to look. Joe had recommended we stay close and rest." Her voice faded.

"Anyone talk to Mrs. Coolidge?" Chrystal asked. They all shook their heads.

"They have that fine tent." Lauren sighed. "Nicer furnishings than I've ever seen. And they all went to pay money to sleep indoors." She huffed, shaking her head. "I'm just jealous."

The sisters laughed. "Did you ask Elias? Tell him with all this dirt and lack of privacy, you needed a second honeymoon?"

"No." Lauren shook her head, looking down. Chrystal patted her back.

Someone squealed, and they all looked to the left. Brody lay on the ground while Felicia strained to pull him up. Martin pretended to drop a large rock on Brody.

"Do you think Brody's all right?" Mabel peered back as they walked past.

"I think he likes to play dead to get her attention." Chrystal rolled her eyes. "And I think the three of them are out of Mrs. Coolidge's supervision. I've noticed they can find certain spots along the road away from her protective eye."

"It will be interesting to see if Brody breaks off at Independence," Chrystal said. "He should be finding his own way."

Lauren knew it didn't sit well with Elias to take Brody in. It still surprised her with everything Elias had been through, that he wouldn't have more acceptance of Brody. Glancing back, he held the reins taunt with his hat low over his head. He looked like he had a thousand things on his mind.

ELIAS HAD CHEWED on it for three days. Talk to Joe or talk to Lauren. Probably both, there had to be a plan if something happened to him. If they had taken him away outside of Indianapolis, he'd be gone a long time. Robbery, desertion, faking his death. His beloved freedom pounded in him like the hooves clomping against the dry road. Nothing had ever felt so good. He'd rather die than suffocate in a cell. And where would Lauren be? Would Brody drive the team to Denver City? That soured in his stomach. He'd caught Brody in more fibs than he could keep track of.

But he himself was also a liar. Should he tell Joe that they weren't really married? If something happened to him, she shouldn't be seen as the grieving widow. She's just a sweet girl that wanted to see her mother and bring the family heirlooms. Would Joe see her there? He pulled off his hat and scratched the hair growing close to his collar. It was a lot to ask. Never on any day of any month should she have climbed on this wagon with him. Before, he had cared so little about anything. Now, his gut twisted, *I care about too much.*

"Lauren." Later in the evening, he took the clean dinner dishes from her hands as she came near the back of the wagon.

"Oh, I'm glad you are here." She smiled. "Could I borrow one of your shirts? Sunday I'd like to lay out the new fabric and make you a shirt."

His mouth swung ajar. *Nope, no sewing for him.* She's making this more difficult.

"Why are you frowning? You said you liked the cap I knit you. You don't want me to make you a shirt?"

A low growl came from the back of his throat. "Make something for yourself, not me." He dropped the dishes back in the kitchen box. "I'm good."

The woman who would never look at him once before now stared him down. "You took the whole day to see Indianapolis with me. You could have been hunting, sleeping, or working with the horses, but you did that for me. Let me do this for you." She huffed, not angry, almost hurt.

Closing his eyes, he quickly bobbed his head back. He'd do anything for her. "Yes." He cracked a grin. "Take a shirt, make a shirt."

She clapped her hands once. "If you don't like it you don't have to wear it. Let me show you—"

"No, wait." He grabbed her arm as she went to reach for her sewing bag. Touching her brought the fierce connection to everything that was good and right. He loved how it fused into his blood. Loosening his grip, he rubbed her arm up and down. "I'd rather be with you than hunting or anything else," he murmured, "but please, listen to me. In a few weeks or even tomorrow, anything could happen. It's dangerous out here— maybe it's still dangerous for us. What you did, what I did back in Greenlock . . ." Moving back from her, he stretched his neck side to side. "I don't know." He let out a long breath. "You still have money?" She nodded slowly. "There are only a few railroads west of the Mississippi, but you would be fine to get to a stage. St. Louis or Independence, then Kansas, Cheyenne, then drop down into Denver City." Her brows creased. "Maybe you should write all this down."

Dropping her chin, she waited. Her round, green eyes piercing him. "Are you leaving?"

"I have no plans to leave. I just want to know what you'd do if something happened to me." How could she understand the surge of protectiveness that riddled him?

"I . . . well," she scowled. "I'd travel on with the group."

The reluctance in her voice matched his next decision. "Then I think we need to tell Joe the truth. Everything, from who I am to us not being married. Everything. I think we can trust him. I'd trust him to see you to Denver City, or at least to the stage."

Stepping out from the back, she looked at the evening campfire. "I don't know." She faced him. "Can I think about it?"

"Your sin shall always find you out," he whispered.

"Reverend Little said your sin, my sin was taken on the cross. We all make mistakes. He

235

says the grace of God will see us home. Does that mean a real home?"

"I think he means heaven. Like those songs they sing. Eternity, forever with God. I'll risk that before I go back to prison." His tone was quiet.

"Do you believe in a God that forgives you and makes you a home in heaven?"

"I do believe in God. I should believe in his mercy 'cause I'm still alive." He smiled in the darkness that replaced the dim evening light. "I even pray once in a while."

"Then pray for us now." She held out her hand. "That we'll know what to do."

Elias rolled his lips, pinching his mouth closed. This new open area of his heart was so personal. Something he'd keep for himself, he thought. He took her hand, challenging himself not to flash to Reverend Little's prayers or the rote words that he'd been required to pray before he could eat at the asylum.

Lord, Lauren and I ask for help. We've made some choices that we thought were good and maybe we should have asked You then instead of now. Anyway, if it's not too late, could you guide us and . . . ah . . . please keep Lauren safe. There it was, all he wanted. God keep her safe. He would never know how Anna's life turned out, but he wanted to see Lauren safe and happy with her mother. That would give him all he needed. *Amen.*

Even through the darkness, her sweet smile met him. "I often picture us making it to Denver City. I daydream about seeing my mother and sister, but can I ask . . . well you can say no," she paused.

"Ask anything."

"Would you come with me to meet them? Stay for supper?" She rushed on. "I know it will be uncomfortable, so, if it's too much to ask . . ." She let her question hang between them.

He thought of the awkward introductions. *This is my wagon guide? This is my friend?* A cool night wind penetrated his being. "I'll think about it."

They both grinned at the repetition of the words.

Chapter 33

JOE KERN HAD said the first twenty-four hours and the last twenty-four hours on the trail were the worst. It had to be true, they were only a day or so from Independence and Lauren thought every bone and muscle must be giving out. The supplies were empty. If it wasn't for some trading with local friendly Indian women, they'd be scavengers off the land.

The sisters had offered bathing and washing with them last Sunday, but sleeping in she'd missed it, and now she was feeling more rancid in body and soul. Tonight she would find water. Even though Independence wasn't the true last destination, they could at least rest and get more supplies. Joe had talked around the evening fires about life on the large wagon road called the Oregon Trail. Lauren watched Ida Bell and pregnant Chrystal listen. If they could find the fortitude for the next leg, certainly she could find it somewhere amongst all her sore muscles and jounced bones.

After supper, Lauren watched Mrs. Coolidge grab a bucket and head down to the stream. The staunch woman hadn't been one to join in much with the ladies, but she supplied Lauren's best chance to wash.

"Mrs. Coolidge?" Lauren grabbed her things and caught up with her. "Would you mind standing guard while I took a very quick rinse?"

"I suppose so, go ahead." She dropped her bucket as Lauren went behind a large bush beside the stream.

"Usually Martin's here to haul the water, but I can't find him. Have you seen Brody around?"

"No. I'm not much at keeping track of him." She sponged her arms and legs, the cold water running down her goose bumped skin. "Are you looking forward to Independence?" she asked.

A long silence held, and Lauren looked around the leaves to see Mrs. Coolidge wiping tears away. Quickly pulling her clean blouse and skirt on, she left her wash by the bank.

"What's wrong? Has something happened?" She wrapped her arm around Mrs. Coolidge's shaking shoulders.

"I-I can't abide this," her cries sputtered, flipping her hand toward camp. "I'm not like you sturdy, ordinary women."

Lauren tried to overlook the possible offense. She'd never seen Mrs. Coolidge break down. "But you've come this far. Your family has done remarkably well."

"Lux wants to go all the way to California. I think I'm going to take the girls," she pulled out her hanky from her bell skirt and dabbed her face, "and go back to my sister's in Kentucky. I would have done that earlier if Lux wasn't in such a hurry to get out of—" she gulped. "It's not my fault he won't ever return." She dropped her head. "Now I've had my fill, and I'll never make it to California." She breathed in a steady breath, and Lauren felt the woman's back straighten.

She slowly removed her comforting arm, searching her eyes. "You would separate your family?"

"They say the train will soon join east to west. When he's settled and has a home, I mean a real home, not a tent or some thatched hut, then we can come out to join him."

Lauren stepped back as Mrs. Coolidge tried to lean gracefully to scoop a bit of water. Being ordinary, sturdy, *and angry,* Lauren grabbed the bucket from her and sloshed into the deeper, running water. She filled it and dropped it back on the bank. "I'm going to tell you something you won't like to hear. I'm a child of separated parents. I don't care how long your excuses are and all the reasons behind them. If you leave, it will ruin everything your family is to be. If Mr. Coolidge hurts you or your children, then yes, leave." She pointed to the road, voice demanding. "But if you care about your children at all, you won't separate them. You are stronger together. All together. You have made it this far Mrs. Coolidge. You can certainly make it to California!" Turning on her wet, dirty heel, she gathered her things and marched back to camp her bucket swinging with every angry step.

ELIAS WAS ABOUT to turn in. The lantern flickered low inside the wagon, but it sounded like Lauren was wrestling a raccoon inside.

"Lauren, are you okay?" He peeked through the back canvas.

"This ridiculous harpsichord is probably ruined anyway." She huffed. "Could you please pull it out for tonight?"

He undid the ties and lowered the gate. Her face reddened, her eyes puffy. "What's wrong?" He jerked it forward as she lifted from her end.

"I stubbed my toe, and I can't stand up. I dropped my sewing, and the thread rolled under the harpsichord." He bore the weight to set it on the ground, while she retrieved her fabric and thread. He stepped up inside and sat on the bench.

"Now at least I can stand up." She huffed, stacking the pieces of fabric. "I don't know why I thought I would have time to sew," she grumped.

He narrowed his eyes on her little feet in dingy white stockings. "Tell me, did I do something?"

Looking down, she shook her head. "No. I had a dreadful talk with Mrs. Coolidge by the stream tonight."

"What?" He touched her hand, pulling her to sit next to him.

"I yelled at her." She dropped her face. "She needed compassion, and I had none to give."

"You?" He chuckled. "Really? Give me your legs and keep talking—I want to see this stubbed toe."

He pulled her calves over his legs and began to rub her feet.

"She wants to take the girls when they get to Independence and-and—oh, my Lord, that feels like heaven. Ah . . . go back to family in Kentucky." Her eyes fluttered closed at his tender caresses.

"That doesn't surprise me." He smiled at her reaction to his fingers kneading her well-traveled feet. "I don't think I've seen her smile or laugh this whole trip. Why would you yell at her?"

"Because she doesn't know how it will affect her children—not to be a family anymore." Her voice faltered.

"Okay, now I think I get it." He worked his fingers around her toes.

HIS SIMPLE MEASURE of understanding melted her, or maybe it was his strong hands working her tired feet into cream. She leaned her cheek onto his shoulder and set her hand on his shirt. "I think you just rubbed off Indiana and

Illinois. Oh my, I didn't know feet could feel bliss."

"Maybe a harsh word will make her think." His calm voice reached back to her early memories of meeting him.

"We've tried to include her. A few times she's joined in." She sighed, as his warm touch seeped up her calves and legs, right into her being. Her eyes drooped heavy, and he placed a soft kiss on her forehead. Maybe he could sleep here again and hold her all night? Awakened by her startling thoughts, she tried to swing her legs free. Jelly-legged, she stumbled forward to the floor of the wagon. He held her firm by the wrist.

"Why do you do this?" She looked down at his familiar grip on her wrist.

"Always, Lovely Lauren, because I want something from you. Isn't that true?"

Nodding slowly, she knew she could free herself from this moment, but weakness in body and soul drew her to those honest blue eyes, the lovely face of a ruffian. Somehow, if she could get close enough, his strength would seep into her being through her skin. While he pulled on her wrist, his eyes glazed with pain or need.

He moved his knees apart, and she surrendered to his wishes, by kneeling close in front of him. Sliding her hands past his knees onto his legs, he cupped her chin with one hand and pulled her hair loose with the other. An incredible craving rushed through her being as he pulled his fingers through her hair. He bent, a slow curving smile coming closer and closer until she moved to meet his lips with hers. She had dreamt of this moment—a man wanting her, kissing her. Pulling on the back of her arms, he held her steady. Finally, backing away from the tender kisses, he reached up and extinguished the light.

ELIAS GENTLY MOVED her back until, thankful for the missing harpsichord, he could kneel before her. He'd never kissed a woman before. With the wanting in Lauren's liquid eyes, it was worth the wait.

This time when he pulled her in, he could hold her close—a warmth beyond understanding. Their lips met again, and a small sound came from the back of her throat as his hands massaged up and down her back. Wanting more, he held her hair back as he kissed and tasted her beautiful neck. She squirmed against him, making him crazy. Likely when she was going to call out for him to stop, he found her open mouth. He kissed her with more incredible indulgence then he knew existed.

He freed his hand and grabbed at her stack of blankets, knocking them onto the wagon floor. His blood surged like nothing he'd ever felt before. Wrapping his arms around her body, he lowered her down to the wagon floor.

Thieves take, a voice from within him said.

Resting on one elbow, wavering inches above her, he stilled, his hand froze from where he'd pulled up on her skirt. *Can I just take what I need? What I want?*

Her lips were still wet with his kisses; their chests rose and fell in unison. Stirring something more than a need for her body—he realized he needed *her*—her heart, her devotion, her love. A battle pounded in his head. He'd lived so long without it, but he had to have it.

For the first time in his life, he believed he deserved to have someone love him in return. Releasing her skirt, he rocked back on his heels and stood, holding his hand out. She took it, and he pulled her to standing. "I guess that was a bit more than what you agreed to." The corner of his mouth tipped up. Still holding her hand, her body shuddered. *Was she about to cry?* Enfolding her again in his arms, he brushed a light kiss across her temple. "Goodnight," he whispered.

Chapter 34

BEWILDERED, LAUREN COULD see the outskirts of Independence. Instead of wide roads and tall buildings, it looked like a vast disarray of chaos. Long poles to the right hung with endless laundry lines. Long johns, jeans, and shirts flapped in the wind. Joe led their small group around the tents and stables of horses, mules, and oxen. Loud piano tunes drifted from another large pine building. Harsh smells contrasted with the Indiana spring wildflowers.

Desiring his security, she broke off from the ladies and walked back to Elias and the wagon. A gust of dirt swirled in front of her, and she turned around to avoid it. He pulled the wagon over and held the horses still as he reached for her arm, pulling her onto their bench. They exchanged the same sheepish grins that spoke of last night. Neither had broken the ice to talk about it. Did he want her, love her? Or was he acknowledging his mistake beyond the bounds of loyalty?

Squinting, his eyes roved over the jumble of their surroundings. "There's a heap of building going on," he observed. "Look there! You can see the Missouri River." He pointed to a spot between buildings where the sun glinted off the water.

"It's so loud and dusty." She slapped the layers of her skirt. "My," she gazed where he pointed, "that's a lot of water." She pulled her hair loose and squeezed the loose ends back in place.

They rode in silence, people waving or nodding as they filed past. Joe led them around to a flat grassy area, not far from the river. The four wagons circled up with their usual space between them—an old fire pit from the previous campers in the center.

Elias tied the reins and jumped down. Reaching out, he lowered her to the ground. "Everything is about to change," she whispered, her excitement now tempered by the reality that their little group would never be the same.

Joe marched toward them with a serious expression. "We need to take shifts going into Independence. I need to check in with the trail office, so I'm going now. Brody can help the sisters and then, as far as I'm concerned, he can head out. Do you need him?" he asked Elias.

"I do not. He's lifted a ride long enough. He's free."

After all the chores and set up, and driving each his own wagon, the men didn't see much more use for Brody. A pang of guilt nipped her. He'd probably been treated this way his whole life.

"I'll check on the departure date but, if it holds

as usual, the Oregon Trail group leaves here on Thursday. Go over the list I gave you, Mrs. Browne." He looked to Lauren, and she realized Elias hadn't spoken to him about their sham marriage. "This is the last place to get supplies for a while. Don't let anyone gouge you with their prices, I've seen it happen."

"Yes, sir." She climbed into the back of the wagon as Elias cared for the horses. Reaching for her bag, she tried to find the list she'd made. Her coin purse was in the bottom, and she snapped it open. It was empty. The last time she had it out was at the fabric store. She had over four dollars left from that day. Dumping the contents of her bag out on her bedding, she sat back. The money was gone. Elias had told her to separate the money he'd asked her to keep. She flipped open the lid to the bench she slept on. An old pair of woolen stockings that were unusable in the warm temperatures were under a stack of her underclothes. Something stiff was still inside, and she released a relieved sigh at finding the remaining money he had given her. She would have to tell him, and of course, he would blame Brody for the theft.

By noon the next day, without even a goodbye, Brody was gone, and Lauren debated when to tell Elias. Their group, including Mr. and Mrs. Coolidge, walked together to the Oregon Trail meeting outside of the wagon train office. Only

Martin remained with a pistol to watch over their things. The group grew larger and larger as an older man with a large cream-colored Stetson hat set a ladder out and climbed up.

"Circle up, circle up." He waved the people closer.

"Think we're all going to get used to that!" someone called out from behind them, and the crowd laughed.

"All right. All right." The older man held his hand up to get everyone quiet. A baby bawled somewhere to the back, and Lauren felt Elias rest his hand on her waist.

"I'm the wagon master for the train leaving Thursday. My name is Edward Kornoski. Calling me Captain K. has seemed to fit for most folk. I'd like my three company leaders to step forward. This one in charge of company A is Mr. Rex Longard." The man nodded, pulling on his long salt and pepper beard. "Company B is run by Mr. Marvin Knox, and Mr. Joe Kern is overseeing Company C."

The three men tipped their hats to the crowd. They all resembled the weathered look of age and experience.

"You'll notice I did not, repeat, did *not* refer to them by their military titles. This is not a Confederate or Union wagon train. You will do well on this trip if you leave your sympathies and opinions here in Independence this Thursday. I will speak for each company. We do not tolerate fractions or debauchery. I understand honor and liberty, but you're not in your state anymore. You may think you've joined the military when you see what we do to any upheaval or variance of the rules. These two men over here are the law. Caleb Kornoski and Bur Goins." The two younger men waved, the first was obviously working with his father.

"For Company A, I need to see the hands of fifteen wagon drivers." He looked to the right of the crowd and counted off fifteen hands in the air. "Please move now to the right and meet with Mr. Longard. Need fifteen hands here in the middle." He counted them off as the crowd moved to follow Mr. Knox.

Thankfully their group was assigned to Joe's company. They moved to follow Joe away from the other trail meetings.

"Welcome, welcome." Joe waved to thirty or forty people facing him. "Can we circle up here? Can everyone hear me?" he bellowed. The group nodded; the fussy baby now asleep on a woman's shoulder. A toddler hung on his father's pant leg. Lauren tried to scan the eager faces of the new group. "Mabel, would you mind noting the names as we do introductions?" Joe handed her a clipboard and pencil.

"As you heard, I'm Joe Kern. You can call me Joe. This is my second trip on the Oregon Trail.

The first question I'll answer is: Yes, we will be traveling as one large group. But one wagon master cannot keep tabs on all the families, so you'll need to come to me with your questions and concerns. I do a count of Company C's wagons each night. Now pay attention." Joe cleared his throat, brow creasing. "Thousands of folk have already made this trip, but you need to know the facts. One in ten of you won't make it. Dysentery, typhoid, and cholera are common. Drowning, wagon accidents, snake bites, violence from Indians, highwaymen, and even inside the wagon train. You're going to see a scattering of graves and even human remains along the road."

Lauren sucked in a breath. Thankfully she'd never heard this talk when she'd left Ohio. Mrs. Coolidge's eyes were wide as saucers. This would certainly push her over the edge.

"The good news is we are a small traveling town. With care and consideration, we can help one another. I'd like you to state your name and any occupation or experience you come from. Let's start with you, sir, and go around."

"We are Leif and Ameal Brooks, we have three children, and while Ameal is a busy homemaker, I am a farmer. We brought our chickens and can sell fresh eggs." Eggs, Lauren squeezed her hands together.

"I'm Corbin Street, and my wife is Sophia. I was a medical assistant in the," he looked to Joe, "war. So I can help a bit with doctoring. My wife brought her guitar; she plays a fare tune." Sophia lowered her head, smiling.

"I'm Reverend Louie Little. So I guess I can marry and bury." He laughed in his deep, joyous way. "This is my lovely wife, Ida Bell. I'm not sure what she can't do." He chuckled again.

"I'm Elias Browne, and my wife is Lauren." She could feel him shifting his feet back and forth. "I can hunt a fair bit and seem to have a knack for horses."

"Elias will also be my second, should I not be available." Joe piped in. "We've traveled together these last six weeks."

Everyone looked to the next family.

"Oh, I almost forgot." Elias raised his hand. "My wife is a trained undertaker. No one's bones will be left uncared for." He grinned.

Two or three snickers were heard from somewhere, and Lauren felt her blood freeze. What did he just say? The sisters looked at her confused. Even Joe glanced back at her as the other folks told their names. The woman to her left frowned at her, visibly appalled.

Lauren's heart thumped out of control, dizziness coming on. She stepped back, words and voices of the others not registering. Backing into a young girl with a wide brim bonnet, she mumbled an apology and turned to leave the crowd.

● ● ●

AN HOUR LATER after Joe's last instructions, the people greeted each other. The crowd began to thin out.

"Janet." Elias lightly touched her elbow. "Have you seen Lauren?"

"No." They looked to Chrystal sitting on a bench. "I saw her slip out during introductions. Were you just teasing her about being an undertaker? I'm not sure she thought it was funny," Chrystal concluded.

Elias rushed to the busy street and looked both ways. Hammers slammed against wood, workman calling out to workman, dogs barking and wagons creaked by. Did she have on her blue skirt or the green one? Cream blouse, he remembered with the puffy sleeves. His eyes widened trying to see through the people. His mouth went dry as he slammed his fist into his hand.

Chapter 35

AFTER THE LAST greasy leathered hand tried to *help* her find her way, she pulled away and knew it was not safe to wander the town. Going back to their camp was like going back to the basement in the funeral home. The scrutiny from the others would kill her. Seeing the river, she checked the road to camp. None of the people looked like her people. With no place to hide, she would have to walk back. Before she had a chance to sneak into her wagon, Elias rode up to her on the brown mare. She ignored him and ran to a grove of small trees close to the water. He jumped off the horse and grabbed her by the arm.

"Lauren, please."

His touch felt like fire and she couldn't look at him. "Get away from me!" She tried to shake him loose. "I don't care if I ever talk to you again." He finally let go, but the only way she could go forward involved deep green water.

"I'm sorry. I didn't think. That part about being an undertaker, it just flew out of my mouth. I never thought to hurt you."

"Well, you did." She spat, glaring at him. "You

really couldn't do anything meaner, really." She tried to stomp to the left, but he blocked her.

"Did I say I was sorry? Now I can't remember. But I am sorry." He weaved every direction she tried to move.

"There aren't enough apologies for this."

"Good Lord, woman," Elias pleaded, "I'll go to each person in the group and say I was just joking and—"

"I despise how lying comes so easy to you, Elias," she growled.

"I'm not lying. You don't work there anymore!" His face turned a deep red.

"It's too late! You didn't see the—" Blast it, *she would not cry.* "The way they looked at me." She sucked in a ragged breath. "It's the way everyone has always looked at me my whole life." Her shoulders slumped, and the tears ran down her cheeks. "Who would befriend the undertaker's daughter? No one! Everyone knows the horrid things that entails. Now they all know, too!" She flung her hand toward camp. "Those people represented the first time in my life I was just Lauren. They treated me like me, plain Lauren. They were my friends." She hung her head, humiliated. "Besides your belief that it was your fine looks and upright standing." Her tone sarcastic. "I believed, like some stupid idiot, that if I could leave Greenlock, get away from it all . . . Oh, who cares?" Her voice faded, the damage was already done. "I'd actually begun to believe it." A sob caught in her throat, "Not anymore." She kneeled down and covered her arms over her head. Her angry cries finally finding the darkness they wanted.

ELIAS STARED OVER the wide green river. He could try to tell her he understood. He'd spent his whole childhood burying his true identity. He looked around for something that he could do to dull the pain enfolding him. Why didn't he say she could knit or sew? Her huddled cries vexed him like nothing else. What a true idiot. Didn't she say he had rocks for brains. Reaching for a rock, he saw Ida Bell standing between camp and their spot by the river. She raised her hand, and her fingers twitched for him to come near.

He nodded at her as he approached.

"Can I talk to your gal?" Her dark face creased with tender caring. "I think the Lord has a word for her."

He hesitated.

"Have you ever had the Holy Ghost breaking up bricks in here?" She tapped on his chest.

Elias wondered what kind of confidential information God gave to people. He nodded slowly.

"The Lord's breaking bricks. It takes some time. You know I'm telling the truth." She raised those don't-question-me eyes on him.

"Yes, ma'am." He stood aside and watched as

she walked to Lauren. Something tormenting him just seconds ago had subsided, like comfort soaking in his being as Ida Bell ambled by. *"I have to trust you, Lord,"* he whispered walking back to the wagon.

"HERE, CHILD." IDA Bell pulled on Lauren's arm, helping her stand. Lauren, red-faced and embarrassed, turned to the face the water.

"Only two people to please in this life," Ida Bell said.

Lauren heard her words but wouldn't look her way. Had Elias asked her to come?

"Just two. The Lord and yous'self. That's it. The Lord lives *in* you and you gotta live *with* you." She chuckled. "I know you don't want ta hear from me cause you thinkin' how can that ole Negro have anything to say."

Lauren faced her, "No, that's—" but Ida Bell held her hand up.

"But can you believe me, child, that I've only known peoples lookin' down their nose at me? That's all I've ever known."

Lauren nodded.

"You's got to believe in the good—the good of God and the good in you. You's got to find the things that no master—no man or woman can take away from you. You are a daughter of the living God. There's more than being a color, or being married to the same man, or running from your past. Those things don't make us peoples. Those things are meant to help us cling to Jesus. So then listen to Him, girl." She shook Lauren's arm. "Listen to him, 'cause He's speaking all the time. You just needs to tell those mean voices to hush," she paused. "Jesus is always speakin', and you'll know it 'cause it's good words, just like Him."

Lauren stared at the ground, releasing a long breath. "Thank you."

RELIEVED NO ONE saw her, Lauren climbed into the back of the wagon and pulled her boots off. She felt like someone had rolled her through a wash wringer. Arranging her bedding, she laid down, pulling the blanket up to her chin, the bothersome harpsichord only inches from her nose. Bringing her hand out, she drew a finger down the warped wood. Fresh tears flooded her eyes, and she pulled her blanket over her head.

"LAUREN." SOMEONE TAPPED her ankle. It was still light, and she wondered how long she had slept.

"I'm going to Independence to trade two horses. I told you about getting oxen for the wagon," Elias said.

Her eyes and body still thick with sleep, she pulled the hair off her face. "Okay."

"Do you want to come, after that we could get some of our supplies, maybe find a bakery?"

"No." Her voice creaked. His attempts at kindness were making her cry again. She pulled the blanket over her head.

After another hour of sleep, waking to relive what had happened, new tears flowed in the darkness. Lauren pulled the blanket down to her chin. The fire crackled and popped in camp, competing with the various conversations. Rolling onto her back, she watched the shadows slowly drop along the canvas, mesmerizing her in her deep well. Her stomach growled, but food and her wagon mates would not win over this lethargy.

She momentarily thought of her father, alone, shuffling through the house in his bathrobe. Her throat constricted as the regret and tears fought for prominence. A runaway daughter, he must be so proud. What would Father Michael say to see her in such a low state? Her dear friend that would listen, most likely. She had cried out to Elias about never having friends, but it wasn't really true. She was just selfish wanting someone her own age. Ida Bell said to please God and please yourself. Lauren rolled her eyes; she'd wanted to give her body, herself to Elias, just to be kissed and held, doing the unthinkable to please him. Curling in a ball to face the canvas, she groaned covering her face with her arms.

"Lauren?" Mabel's sweet voice wafted into the wagon. "Can I come in?"

"There isn't much room," Lauren muttered, hoping she would go away.

"Here, I brought you some supper." Mabel swung her leg over the gate, and the wagon rocked. Lauren didn't move. "I'll just set it here on top of this piano."

Harpsichord. Lauren caught herself from saying it out loud. Maybe Mabel would leave the food and just go.

"Can I sit for a spell?"

She rolled her eyes and pulled the blanket higher. "I'm just not good company, Mabel, I'm sorry."

"You gave us a bit of a scare. We didn't know where you went. I hope no one hurt you in town?"

"No," she sighed.

"I hope you think of me, and Janet, and Chrystal as your friends?"

Lauren let out a slow breath. First Ida Bell, now this?

Mabel chuckled. "I know I've told you a hundred times, it's so strange not to be taking care of children. They really can keep a wife busy, so we've enjoyed getting to know you. We talked about the first time you showed up. Your handsome husband shyly announcing his wife would be joining him. We didn't even know he was

260

married." She smiled. "You've been a breath of fresh air for all of us. When the wagon master was dividing the travelers into three groups today, I felt my heart racing that we wouldn't all be together. The other thing that warms me is what a good friend you've been to us. We know we are different with religious lines most people won't cross. But you're the most giving and generous woman I've met outside our circle."

Lauren's chin was shaking again. She could almost feel Ida Bell gripping her arm. *Listen.*

Slowly rolling up, Lauren clutched her knees under the blanket. "Now it sounds silly, but before I left Greenlock . . ." She wiped her wet cheeks with the blanket. "I worked at my father's funeral home. Except he drank so much that I had to take over the business. I hated it."

"Oh Lauren, that's not silly. That's very difficult for a young woman."

"I expected I'd have to figure out how to travel with Elias," she said, wistfully. "But I've enjoyed being around you ladies, too. You all three have shared sweet things about your families that made five-mile walks feel like five minutes. You are all so dear to my heart that I didn't want you to know about my past."

Mabel stood and leaned over the harpsichord wiggling Lauren's knee. "You've never judged us and yet you thought we would judge you?"

"I know," she sighed. "I think I got intimidated

by the new group. Why did he have to say it in front of *all of them?*" She clutched her hands over her ears and dropped her chin.

"Humph," Mabel said, "men."

Chapter 36

THE NEXT MORNING, the three Coolidge girls held hands and danced in a circle. Their thick skirts belled out until one let go and they all fell giggling in a pile of spring grass. Lauren hovered by the back of the wagon watching them. The two little sisters seemed happy to have Felicia back from the teen boys. Every day that they were still here, she wondered if Mrs. Coolidge had decided to go on. She heard Elias grabbing something from the side of their wagon, and she pressed back into the gate, he came around and stopped short.

"Oh, I didn't see you." He paused. "Is everything okay, you missed breakfast?"

Her emotions rattled back and forth in her chest, part of her wanted to be still angry. She tried not to stare, but he was cleanly shaven with shorter hair. "I think Brody took some of your money." She muttered.

Shifting his feet, he threw a coil of rope over his shoulder and rubbed his barren chin. "How's that?"

"Not all of it. I have the rest hidden like you said. There was some in my coin purse from weeks ago, when we shopped in Indianapolis."

His lips pursed a thin line, and a red hue rose from his neck.

"I mean, I can't prove it was him. Maybe I was careless and it fell out somewhere?"

Elias rubbed his smooth chin gazing at her, then gazing out to the river, then back to her. "As long as you are all right. I'm all right. Are you all right?"

She breathed in a deep breath, shrugging. Many of the words that Ida Bell and Mabel had shared with her had helped to pull her from the low melancholy, but she still didn't feel like herself.

"I know what I did is probably unforgivable to you, but you scared me bad, Lauren. I looked everywhere. I almost passed out when I saw you by the river." He paused, rubbing his hands through his short hair. "And as for the other night—you and me—I'm—ah . . ." His eyes made another sweep of the surroundings. "I'm kinda sorry, but not fully sorry." He bit back a smile. "It was amazing." His face flushed as his hand cupped his mouth and chin then swiped down his mouth as he stared into the distance.

She shook her head and tried to slide left across the wagon gate. He grabbed her wrist and pulled her back. Gently he wrapped his arms around her and touched his lips to her ear. "Lauren, I don't ever want to hurt you."

Her body felt like stiff ice, and when she

expected him to get the hint and let go, he pulled her in closer. "I'm in love with you."

Her chest squeezed so hard that her knees buckled, so she wrapped her arms around his shoulders and buried her weary cries against his shirt. She'd hoped she could make it today without falling apart, and now this.

"Shush, it's gonna be okay." He held her close.

"I feel like a child abandoned in the snow," she cried into his chest, "numb and lost."

He dropped his forehead to hers. "How I know that feeling, but I'm never going to leave you on your own or out in the cold."

BY AFTERNOON THE other wagons in Company C began to join them in the field by the river. Elias had spoken to many of them and dodged the question of where his undertaker wife was. If one more sodbuster said something, they were going to feel his fist. Maybe he should tie a heavy millstone around his neck and go for a swim. Since Lauren had gone back to bed after this morning's declaration, she would probably be the first one to push him into the river.

He'd never imagined what it would be like to tell a woman he loved her, but reducing her to bawling and the day in bed wasn't what he'd expected either. The truth was he needed her. She had taken over all the food rations and organization. He could guess at what they

265

needed, but it wasn't something he wanted to risk. Hearing Reverend Little laugh with some new folks, maybe he could ask Ida Bell.

"Ida Bell!" He jogged to meet her. "Since you have an ability to know and see all things, could you tell me how to get Lauren going? We are leaving at sunrise, and I don't think—"

"I have what? What's you addling 'bout?" She scoffed at him waving her hands like a fan.

"She needs a better word from the Lord, I guess." He shook his head and pulled his hat off. "I tried to talk to her this morning. I told her I loved her."

"Oh, like that'll solve everythin'." She pressed her fists on her wide hips and leaned close to him. "I'll tell you what I can do for you." She nodded for him to follow her beside the Littles' wagon.

"*You* need a word from the Lord, so . . ." She closed her eyes and dropped a heavy hand on his shoulder. "Mighty King Jesus, come now and speak to your son. He's a needin' deevine wisdom. And deliver that poor girl from torment and suffering . . . soon. Amen." She shook his shoulder staring at him. "Well?"

"Well, what?"

"What did Jesus say to do?"

"I-I, uh, I don't know. You think He's just going to drop a letter from the sky."

"Of course not." She waved her hand at him.

266

"Ain't you ever known the Lord speakin'?" She turned to leave.

Strangely, he recalled the words *thieves take* when he was alone in the wagon bed with Lauren. "Maybe," he whispered.

The bustle of Company C was in full swing as he dodged running children and walked backed to his wagon. Before he peeked in, he thought it couldn't do any harm to ask again. *Lord, how do I help her?*

Tell her how you feel, came like a small stirring under his skin. Taking a long breath, he let it out.

"Lauren, can I come in?" He pulled back the canvas, surprisingly she was sitting on her bench, with her legs crossed, gray fabric in her lap.

"Yes." Her eyes were still red and tired.

"I'm not sure if you've eaten all day. Can I get you something?" He pulled the gate down and stepped inside."

"No, I'm not hungry." She pulled the thread through the fabric.

He sat on the corner of her bench, legs crammed against the harpsichord. "Is that for me?"

She tucked her loose hair behind her ear. "Mmm, hum."

How was this going to work? His feelings, right now? She wouldn't even look at him, and his tongue felt permanently lodged in his throat.

"I'm sewing a shirt for you." She paused. Her pauses were multiplying the warmth of the afternoon air. "A shirt that you didn't want." Another pause. "You said you loved me this morning after you clearly said our friendship would not be about love, nope, no love, only loyalty." She spoke so slowly, like a dull saw grinding against his bones. "I think I'm just exhausted from knowing you."

He winced, twisting his legs from the harpsichord entrapment to face the back gate. She was right. Right about everything. Should he just leave? Just like his ammunition, he'd blown up everything he had put in place to stay away from attachments. But they'd been through so much together. He stood, the familiar outside only inches away calling him back to his life—a life where he only had to answer for himself. Biting his lip, he turned and leaned onto the harpsichord, gripping the sides for stability.

"I'm glad you had no friends in Greenlock," he said.

She looked up, stunned.

"If you hadn't worked in your father's funeral home, you'd have been out courting any man you wanted. I would have never seen you in that hardware store. Because you had no friends, you were desperate. Because you had no friends, I'm alive. I should be sorry for you, but I'm not. The reason I can't wait to get up every morning is the thought of seeing you, hearing you talk, seeing your skirts swish around camp. If I could choose anyone in this world for a best friend, I would choose you. You are beautiful and charming. Do you want to know why?"

She stilled, watching him. Her soft lips slightly parted and her eyes, soft and green, gazing at only him.

"Because you don't know you are beautiful and charming." He huffed. "You don't. You don't carry any airs. You don't judge or believe the worst. Your heart is as open and true as the miles of sage and grass on the trail." He raked his hand through his hair. "I thought I could just be loyal."

He let out a curt breath. "But I can't. If I had a silver dollar for every night I sat on watch and convinced myself that love was a waste of time . . ." His forehead banged onto the lid of the harpsichord and jerked it up, "I'd have a bag of silver that would weigh this wagon down to the ground." Rolling his tongue inside his cheek, he shook his head. "I know clearly you are far too good for me." He rubbed his head making the short strands stand at attention. "Then you asked me to stay, to meet your mother and sister. That made no sense unless—" his voice softened. "The other night, you kissed me back Lauren. You could have pushed me out on my backside. But you opened a current of warmth I've never known. How could I not dream that maybe you wanted me, too?" He stood, his wide shoulders making the tight space even smaller. "I know what I said in the beginning, but I didn't know . . ." He groaned in his throat. "I didn't think I would ever be this powerless against my feelings. I do love you, and I don't blame you if you don't feel that way about me."

She gripped her quivering chin and then sighed. Her eyes flickered with tears.

"When I tell you how I feel, you cry." He shook his head, looking up for help from somewhere above the thick canvas. "And I hate it when I make you cry."

"My problem," she swiped her eyes. "Is that I think I do love you, too." Their gazes locked. "But I'm scared, Elias. I've only dreamt of seeing my mother and sister. I'm frightened by your temper, your past, the things that haunt you— they scare me." She sighed. "Maybe I'm just not strong enough."

A gunshot rang out, and they jumped. "Circle up in five," someone yelled outside.

"Joe wants another meeting before tomorrow's departure. While I do that, can you get the last of our supplies?" He pulled cash from his pocket.

"Yes." She set her sewing back in the bag. Walking on her knees to the gate, she sat and pulled her boots on. He jumped out and lowered her to the ground. His hands didn't want to move from her waist; she still looked so sad. "See if one of the sisters will go with you," he said.

She nodded, and he had to let go.

Chapter 37

ELIAS STRUGGLED MOST of the night to sleep and awoke before the sunrise gunshot. Like a child let loose in a candy shop, he jumped out from his bedroll. The challenge, the hardship, the crisp air, the smells of the stock and wagon train pulsed inside of him. The harder the road looked, the more he wanted to conquer it.

Last night, though Lauren had worked on their supplies, she still did not join in with the group. Her melancholy was the only thing that brought his enthusiasm into check. They both wanted freedom. They both longed for a fresh start—she even had the promise of family to cling to. As he swabbed the noses of the oxen, he looked back and saw her talking to Mabel as they worked on breakfast. People and children began to appear from the wagons, scurrying to meet Joe's strict departure at seven.

Looking down, she handed him a hot mug of coffee. He nodded his thanks as he sank his teeth into bacon wrapped in dried bread. "How do you feel today?" he said, swallowing a thick bite.

"My stomach hurts." She gripped her waist. "I think it's just nerves. If I die, I've written a letter to my father and one to my mother. They are in my sewing bag. Would you—"

"Lauren, you're not going to die. Just remember you've made it over half way from Ohio to Missouri. Those that go on to Oregon, yes, they have a long way. The sisters are only going to Utah." He chugged down his last bite with coffee. "Do you want to ride with me or walk?"

"I hear you're barely able to breathe, the dust is so bad."

"Good then ride with me." He smiled and gave her a quick side hug before he turned.

"Wagon ho!" someone yelled. Elias clapped his hands. "Let's go, Lauren." He smiled back at her then swung forward slapping the reins. "Your future is that a way."

BEFORE THE NOON meal stop, Lauren had jumped down to join the sisters walking. The early summer sun beat down on her wide bonnet as they walked in quiet peace, each of them amazed by the length of the line of wagons. Some men even pushed their own small carts. Janet had said many of the Mormons were poor but dedicated to finding their way to Utah, pushing and pulling if they had to. Even Mrs. Coolidge walked with her girls, the big white dogs pulling the smaller girls by leashes. Mrs. Coolidge donned a lighter cotton day dress, and all of them in the wide brim bonnets like the rustics wore.

The new day and excitement seemed to lift Lauren's spirits. A few of the other women from Company C introduced themselves, not one mentioning her former occupation. Though he seemed truly remorseful, she doubted Elias had asked them not to bring it up. Glancing to the sisters walking in time with her, she longed to ask them about courtship and love. But since they thought she was already married, there didn't seem any way to bring it up. Should she wait to talk to her mother about it? Her mother who didn't want to keep her own marriage vows. Truthfully, her feelings were as wide and changing as the green prairie grass that framed the long line of emigrants. Attraction was an interesting thing.

Even at home, daydreaming about being on the wagon train, she pictured meeting people her age, especially young men. Now that seemed the last of her desires. Elias's kisses, his touches, even his protectiveness had marked her in a strange way. But what if a woman kissed the wrong man? Surely it had happened to someone. A few of the girls in school spread rumors of kissing before they were spoken for. Her heart jumped, she'd never see herself in anyone's arms but Elias's. Was it because of his declaration? It's a mighty commanding thing for someone to love and want you. Was that causing the beads of sweat on her brow just now?

"Hard to believe we've already walked from

Ohio to Indiana and then Illinois." Chrystal sighed.

"And next Kansas," Mabel said.

"Just like the terrain, week after week it changes." Lauren dabbed her brow. Almost as unpredictable as the heart.

IT WAS UNDERSTANDABLE that on this first night it took some jockeying to get the wagons circled for the evening. For the most part, Company C was in place like Joe asked. Elias liked how the oxen pulled. Of course, there was no speed, but his arms didn't ache as much from holding the horses at bay. He led the oxen to the grass to graze. The last two horses were next. He looked back over his shoulder, seeing Lauren approach.

"Did you have a good day?" He grinned.

"I did." She looked down. "The fresh air did me good. Supper will be ready soon."

He didn't want to move because he wanted to touch her. She pushed her bonnet back, and his hand started out to caress her cheek but landed on her arm. "I didn't sleep much last night. When I'm done here could I take a nap on your bunk? Just like twenty minutes." He let go. "You can wake me when the food is ready."

She scrunched the corner of her mouth up. "I don't know, that bench is my private bedroom, parlor and sitting room."

He loved that her teasing tone had returned. "Then don't leave me unattended in your chamber, you could skip dinner and take a nap with me."

She squeaked, as her stomach flipped. "No, no. Food—is-is—important."

He smiled at her over his shoulder as he jerked the horses forward.

SITTING UP, ELIAS listened. It wasn't dark, so he couldn't have slept long. Was it a child crying or playing? All the new sounds of the traveling town were hard to sleep through. It wasn't a child, maybe an accident? He opened the canvas wider and jumped out. Hearing it again, he headed to the backside of the Coolidge wagon. He blinked hard. Why was Brody here, pulling Felicia by the arm? Her panicked eyes found Elias and locked on him.

"Brody, what are you doing here?" He questioned, walking closer to the dust-covered teen. Had he jumped in unseen with one of the other companies?"

"Get back, Elias!" He jerked her back with him. "She said, she would come with me to Independence. We made plans," Brody panted. "I got off work and rode hard to tell her. I already got a job at the mill. Thankfully, the Confederates ruined most the buildings, so I'll have plenty of work," he huffed, with eyes darting back and forth.

Mrs. Coolidge came around the corner and gasped.

"Don't come any closer!" Brody barked as Martin and Lux heading toward him.

"Let her go, now!" Martin demanded, glaring at Brody.

"No, she wants to come with me. You were there Martin—we talked about it." Brody swiped the sweat off his forehead.

Shockingly, Martin turned and walked away. Lauren and the sisters approached carefully from the left.

"Can we make sure this is what she wants, Brody?" Mabel asked gently.

"Over my dead body!" Mr. Coolidge bellowed as he stomped toward the two from around the other side of the wagon. "Felicia Renee Coolidge, get over here at once!" He pointed to his side. Felicia had tears streaking down her white cheeks as Brody jerked her further back, grabbing for his horse.

"Brody, please," Lauren eyed a terrified Felicia. "Just sit down with the Coolidges and talk."

"Oh, like that would do any good. They think they can control Martin and Felicia. But Felicia already said—"

"Martin!" Mrs. Coolidge cried out as Martin came around their wagon pointing a pistol at Brody.

"Brody, I said, let her go." Martin seethed.

"Brody, just let her go," Elias urged, taking a step forward. "If Martin's hand gets to shakin' any harder, you're going to get a bullet in the leg."

Brody unsheathed his knife from his belt. "Get back, Elias, I mean it." His nostrils flared, but his hand was steady as a rock as he brandished the knife.

Elias held his hands up and backed up. "Felicia, do you want to go with him?"

She whimpered, head tremoring, "No."

Brody slid the knife up under her chin. "You're lying," he snarled. "You should have come with me when no one was looking. Now, look what you've done." He wrapped his arm around her waist, trying to get her to the horse. "Put your foot in the stirrup. Now!"

Martin shook so hard the gun wobbled in his hand.

Brody turned away one second to push her up. Galvanized, Elias took three long strides and tried to grab the gun. A loud pop and caustic smoke assaulted his nostrils. His eyes flashed to see blood spattered all over Felicia.

"Oh God, no," he growled. Brody jerked twice and fell in a heap at her feet. Screams from the left and right competed with the ringing in his ear. Elias jerked the gun free from Martin and pulled on the back of his neck. "No matter what happens boy, I pulled the trigger." He pulled the pale, sweaty teen nose to nose. "Do you hear me? I shot Brody."

The words were barely out when Lux jerked his son away. "Oh, dear God," he panted looking at Martin and then running to Felicia. Mrs. Coolidge had Felicia enveloped, rocking her back and forth.

Joe ran around the wagon and skidded to a stop. "What happened?"

"I shot Brody," Elias spoke up, letting the gun swing down on his finger.

Chapter 38

LAUREN FELT HER body sway back and forth as Mabel rolled Brody over from the blood-soaked ground. Taking a moment to get a pulse, she pursed her lips and shook her head to everyone staring in shock. The Coolidge parents gripped Martin and Felicia, huddling on the ground.

The gunshot brought more onlookers and the older lawman, Bur, jumped off his horse.

"What happened?" He grimaced at Brody crumpled on the ground.

"That one shot him in the back." A man Lauren didn't recognize pointed to Elias.

"Joe, did you see what went down?" Bur reached for the gun swinging from Elias's finger.

"I shot him," Elias said.

Lauren's mouth flew open. It happened so fast, but the shot came from Martin, she could swear. The disgust on the lawman's face as he roped Elias's hands behind his back assaulted her with a wave of nausea. *Why aren't the Coolidges rising up and telling the correct story?*

"No, I heard the shot, but didn't see what happened." Joe frowned.

Mabel stood, blood on her hands, and Lauren tried to open her mouth. No air could be found, and her feet would not move. *Someone speak up, Brody had a knife to Felicia's throat! Why?* Her eyelids slowly blinked at Elias then back to Brody. So much blood, so much cleaning to do. The clothes, the body, the smell—darkness overtook her.

"LAUREN, DEAR, CAN you open your eyes?" Janet rubbed her face with a cool cloth. The evening had replaced the dusk. She struggled against the fog in her mind. Wasn't she helping with a body on the ice table, just a moment ago?

"Oh, my. Did I faint?" Lauren tried to sit up, drawing her fingers through her hair. "I haven't eaten much the last couple of days." She searched the area. "Ouch." She pulled her wrist in close. "Where's Elias?"

"They took him, the lawmen." Janet gently touched her wrist. "I think you landed on it when you fainted." She let out a held breath. "Joe went to speak for him. Mabel told Joe what happened. Of course, none of us wanted to see Brody die, but we were all worried he'd hurt Felicia, or what if Martin misfired and killed his sister? The Coolidges have all been in their tent. I suspect as soon as the lawman talks to them, they'll let Elias free." She helped steady Lauren as she stood. "Let's get something for that swelling."

• • •

THE WAGON WHEEL supported his back as his wrists were chained to the spokes. He had enough movement to scratch his nose, but that was it. Discouragement darkened his insides or the fact that his stomach hurt from missing supper. Watching Lauren faint in a pile and not being able to get to her, could be the worst. Just the sight of the chains tried to pull him more into the past pit of desolation. He dropped his head to his knees.

"My son!" A familiar voice called. "Lift up your head. Your redemption draws near!" Reverend Little's chuckle made him smile. The Reverend held onto the lawmen's wagon, struggling to sit on the ground.

"Oof." He plopped down next to Elias. "How are you farin' here in the wagon train pokey?" He slapped Elias's leg. "I told 'em I was doing a clergy visit."

"I'm hungry."

"Well, I didn't think to bring anything. It was a bit of a walk from Company C. I'll go back."

"No, forget it. Did you see Lauren? I think she fainted, but they took me away before I—"

"Yeah, yeah. I saw them sisters heppin' her. The first wagon train commotion and I missed it. They were already diggin' a hole for Brody. We said he didn't have any people. Did you know of any of his people?"

"No. I hope they ask you to say some nice words." He blew out a long sigh. "Martin had the gun shakin' so bad I thought he might shoot his sister, so I grabbed the gun and shot Brody. It was my fault. I know it's a sin to kill a man." He shook his head, the painful sound of other travelers singing and laughing around their campfire, was depressing. "He wasn't my first. You know I was in the war; you probably didn't know I set explosives." The metal chains rattled as he rubbed his forehead.

"Mmm, mmm." Reverend Little moaned. "Is it a sin to protect another from harm? Isn't that what we all fought a war for? Thought we were doin' some protectin'?" Reverend Little blew out a low whistle, touching Elias's shackled wrist. "Seein' me a few years back wearing these. Makes for a long night, if your back's been . . ." He cleared his throat unable to speak the words.

Elias's inside darkness suddenly cleared, this was a good man to come to visit. They had a lot in common. All his years in the asylum or prison, no one had ever come to see him before. Smiling at the dear, crinkled face, he appreciated the reminder that his redemption was from God. He had to keep hope in something besides himself. If this man could do it, he could do it. And for the first time since Anna, he trusted that people cared for him. But a blanket would be nice for sleeping out on the ground tonight. "Reverend Little." His own eyes found the watery deep brown eyes. "You are a man I am honored to call a friend."

SOMEONE KICKED HIS heel, and his whole body jerked up before his eyes cracked open. Every fiber in his being felt frozen and stiff, he hoped the yellow sliver to the east meant it was morning.

"Joe has spoken for you. The witnesses say the young man might have kidnapped the girl if you didn't step in."

Elias squinted, waiting.

"But we have a strict code of conduct here. Word's already traveled through the Companies that you shot a man in the back and killed him." Bur scratched his chin. "So we're releasing you to Joe's supervision. You can drive your wagon, but you can't leave his sight unless he goes with you." He pulled out the key and undid the cuffs. "You'll have to stand before the Captain at Fort Kearney."

Elias rose, now alert, rubbing his wrists. "Can I go?"

Bur nodded. "We didn't want anyone seeing us let you go. If it weren't for Joe, we'd have to keep you. So I recommend you stay low and don't be seen with a gun."

"Understood." Elias wanted to shake his hand but turned and headed back to his group. The morning gunshot went off calling the beginning of the new day.

As the sun shed a fresh glow, the sisters and Ida Bell moved around the campfire. He looked for Lauren. Was she all right? Maybe she was at the privy, he circled behind their wagon and jumped up on the back gate. The wagon rocked, and she screamed, grabbing her skirt off the floor.

"Shush. It's me." He swung a leg over.

"I'm dressing!" She clutched the skirt under her chin, exposing just enough white leg to remind him how lucky he was to be free.

"They let me go." He smiled, heart thumping to see her. "I wanted to see if you were okay? Why are your hand and wrist wrapped?"

"That was so awful." She groaned, pulling her arms into the thick folds of her skirt. "I've seen a lot of death, but never alive one minute and then . . . like that. I don't think you had any choice." Her eyes narrowed. "But the Coolidges never came out to defend you. I don't understand how they could be so callous. You saved Felicia and likely Martin from killing Brody."

"Felicia may have led Brody on. Her parents are probably hiding the fact that something went wrong. They seem a bit strict. What's with this?" He gently touched her wrist.

"I think I must have fallen on it wrong. Nothing broken, it just may slow down my knitting and sewing." She smirked. "I was frightened I'd have to drive the wagon with one hand. Probably taking the oxen to the right all day." She smiled, gesturing what a one-handed driver would do.

"I'm here." He cracked a smile. "And you know how much I like your wrists." He ran his hand down his face. "I'm sorry you had to see that last night. I'm just released under Joe's supervision. I'll have to stand before the Captain at Fort Kearney."

"Oh, no! Your name, your past." She sighed. "What if someone finds out?"

"I know I'm going to sound like Reverend Little, but I have this strange faith that God's not through with me yet."

She searched his face, slowly nodding.

"Lauren?" Mabel peeked in. "Elias! So glad to have you back." She passed a pan of warm biscuits and ham up to them. "Thought you could give that cooking arm a rest this morning."

"Wagon, ho!" Joe's voice called outside, and Mabel bid a quick goodbye.

"I missed you something terrible last night. I'd never had that for anyone." He touched her cheek then brushed his fingers through her hair. "The only real suffering was the thought I might be kept away from you."

Her eyes pooled, feeling his touch. This week had been rough. The stupid harpsichord blocked him from grabbing her close. He leaned over it, hoping his eyes were communicating his desire.

She blinked and leaned forward, touching her lips to his—the salt in her tears mixed with their soft, breathless kisses. Good Lord, thinking of this moment, he'd need no blanket tonight.

Chapter 39

THAT AFTERNOON, LAUREN walked along the tall grass watching the horse Brody had ridden in on. It was a nice tan gelding, content to follow behind Joe and the sisters' wagon. Did he steal it? Did he use Elias's money that he'd stolen from her? How could he be so desperate as to force Felicia to go against her will?

The sisters walked and tried to lend their compassionate reasoning to the whole ordeal, yet they were all shocked and confused. The first murder on the wagon train would probably be more likely to exclude them, in case Lauren was still worried that her reputation as an undertaker would separate her from the new people. More likely it would be that her husband had shot a man in the back.

She didn't have a minute to press the issue with Elias, but the sisters agreed with her, Martin had pulled the trigger before Elias's hand wrapped around the gun. But what if Elias's hand trying to remove it spurred the shot? What if Brody had succeeded in taking Felicia?

The silence from the Coolidge family boiled inside of Lauren. One small hint of gratitude to

Elias, one short discussion with Joe, was all that needed to happen. How dare they coil in with their fine things, while her husband took the brunt of the whole episode?

"Husband." She chuckled. Her protectiveness seemed to stretch the bounds a bit. Even if they had to break away from the group at Fort Kearney, she would do anything to see justice through to the end. Knowing Mrs. Coolidge's fragile state, she could only pray they all didn't disappear from Company C.

After a long week or more of traveling the upper land of Kansas, the large group circled in a place they called Alcove Springs. The tragedy of many days past seemed to fade as the excitement of the beautiful water and springs awaited. Their Ohio group gathered after chores to take a walk to see the Big Blue River and famous waterfall. Adults and children jabbered and weaved around them as they came around the walking trail to see a large ledge of flat rock with a long stream of water tumbling over. Children splashed in the pool below while other brave souls stood under the cascade of water. Lauren scanned the surroundings. "Where's the Big Blue River?"

"That's it." Joe pointed to the stream flowing from the pool of water. "It gets bigger."

"Oh." Lauren hid her disappointment.

"If you look closer at the rocks and trees you'll see signs of many trains gone before us;

the people marked their names. And it's a clean water source compared to the muddy waters of the Platte River."

A mother pulling two wet children behind her climbed up the hill towards them. She stopped and stared at their group and jerked her children sharply to the left almost bumping pregnant Chrystal.

"Joe, I'm taking Lauren just down there." Elias must have read her expression. "Maybe she'll put her feet in the water."

Joe nodded as their group walked closer to the falls.

"Elias, did you see that woman glare at us?"

"Probably mad her kids went swimming." He held her hand, taking her down the bank to the little stream. They sat on a flat rock. "Your wrist is better?" he asked.

Rotating it in a circle, "Hardly hurts unless I knit too much," she said, watching the people enjoy the waterfall.

"I like it when we sit on our wagon tongue at night." He picked up some rocks, leaned forward, making a little dam in the water. "I suppose you'd rather join in with the music and dancing."

"No, I don't want to join in. Funny, I thought I would."

"The circumstances." He nodded.

"No," she smiled, "contentment." She pulled off her boots and stockings resting her feet in the cool water. "I like the few minutes with you after walking all day. I enjoy the time with everyone from Ohio." She caught her tongue from saying, *Except the now unfriendly Coolidges.* "I've got Chrystal's baby blanket done. It's too warm for summer, but she's assured me it will be lovely for the long winters in Utah. I'll give it to her tonight and then finish up your shirt for next week."

"I'll wear it proudly when we get to Fort Kearney."

"Please, please don't talk about it. It makes me fearful."

"You been dozing through Reverend Little's sermon on Sunday?" He splashed a fingertip of water on her.

"No." She flicked some back on him.

"He's been preaching on faith, expectancy, and hope. Remember, there's always a *solution.*" He held up his finger and sang out in a preachy voice enjoying her smile. "Thankfulness changes our outlook from doubt to faith." He bumped her shoulder lightly, and she linked her arm around his, resting her head on his wide shoulder.

A black and orange butterfly danced off the stream in front of them. "Did I ever tell you about the girl at the asylum who thought she was a butterfly. No wait, she thought she was a fairy. Story told, she had jumped out of a top window of her fancy house. Thought she could fly."

"Oh, my." Her head rubbed against his shoulder. "Did Anna help her too?"

"Yes, some, but she was front row—had a nice room and a doctor who looked after her. I used to talk with her when I delivered coal. She seemed normal enough."

Lauren wistfully observed the families frolic and enjoy the water. The more she got to know people, normal seemed such an outlandish word to describe them.

THAT EVENING A dozen or so campfires glowed along the wagon circles. Elias had been in deep conversation with Joe around their fire. Music from the others drifted over her. Chrystal had loved the finished blanket, and Lauren debated between a loose weave shawl for Cammi or Mabel. Time allowing, she could probably get one done for Mabel and Janet before Colorado. She wondered if Cammi would recognize her own sister with her tanned face and hands, chapped lips and windblown skin. Thankfully there were no mirrors on the wagon train.

Martin stepped out from the front flap of their tent. He called the two large white dogs out to the field. She stood and watched him, maybe this would be a good time to talk to him. Walking further out, he threw a stick, and the dogs ran to compete for the flying prize. With only shadowy moonlight, she could barely make the white dogs out, but she heard a loud yelp. One of the dogs spun in a circle and tried to find its way back to Martin. Elias strode briskly by her when she stopped in surprise. Had the dog been injured? It was too dark to see much but the outline of rocks and tall grass. Lux Coolidge came out of the tent looking for Martin.

"Martin, freeze, listen," Elias called. They all froze, even Lux stopped to listen. Ever so faint a rattle could be heard. "It might've bit the dog. Call him to you."

Martin patted his leg and called. Only the second dog tried to respond but then circled back and laid his chin on the dog laying on the ground. Elias slowly approached the downed dog and grabbed it by the furry skin of its neck, and dragged it to Martin and Lux. It was the pregnant female. "There on the leg, see the blood, those are the puncture wounds." Elias backed up, shaking his head.

Lux sucked in a breath. "What can be done?"

"I don't know," Elias said.

Martin knelt to comfort the agitated dog then pleaded with his eyes, "There must be something. These dogs were part of our future income."

"I just can't say."

"Or you won't say." Martin snapped. "You're so helpful with firing guns. But can't help with a snake bite?"

"If it's a rattler—"

"Are you going to help clear his name, Martin?" Lauren cut in. "Huh? You've ignored all of us, while we all saw what happened. How dare—"

Elias grabbed her arm and pulled her back with him. "Stop, Lauren." He leaned to her ear. "Their dog is dying, give them some peace."

"Why do they get peace?" she snarled while Elias tugged her back. "He was probably supposed to fight in the war!" She called back at them. "Did your parents keep you home for that too?"

"Lauren," Elias said forcefully, shaking her arm. "Stop it."

Joe walked to meet them. Elias still gripped her arm as she glared at the Coolidges. "The female dog, Athena. Snakebite. A rattler," he said to Joe. "Do you want me to find it?"

"No, better not. That involves a gun in your hand." Joe shook his head.

"All right." Elias slapped Joe's back. "Lauren's a bit overtired. She needs to get to bed."

"I'm *overtired?*" She grunted as he pulled her to their wagon.

"Or something." He finally let go. "You can't go callin' a young man a coward."

"But he is one. Why isn't he telling the truth?"

"I told him not to." His mouth set in a hard line. "So let it go."

"Why? Why would you protect him? He defended his sister."

293

"I didn't want it scaring him the rest of his life. It was hard enough for the boys who survived the war to let go of those ghosts. Martin's different. Brody and him were friends."

Rubbing her forehead, she let out a sigh. "I guess I don't understand."

"If you had a mad bull in a pen, who would fare better a kitten or a fox?"

"A fox, of course."

"My days have been full of mad bulls. I'm a fox; I'm used to getting myself out of things. You of all people should know that." He drew his finger across her cheek and under her chin. "Martin's a kitten; life could just eat him up. Murdering your friend could just eat you up unless you are a fox. I haven't thought twice about what happened to Brody."

She looked so perplexed at his words. Too late, he realized, those words just cost him a good-night kiss.

Chapter 40

GUILT, LIKE THE crisp sunrise, assaulted her the next morning. The Coolidges' fine white dog was buried close to their wagon. The young girls' cries couldn't be muffled as the family stood around the new grave. Their remaining dog, Goliath, looked around attentively, waiting for his partner to suddenly appear. She nodded to Janet as she approached the early morning campfire.

"Have they had breakfast?" Lauren asked.

"I don't think so. Lux dug while Martin pulled the tent down. The Missus looks about ready to drop."

"If Reverend Little preaches on love your neighbor this Sunday, I'll bury myself in a hole. I've been so unkind."

"Here, I've got time, take this pan of Johnny cakes and bacon over, and I'll start a new batch." Janet held out the platter.

"You are wonderful." Lauren squeezed her arm taking the platter. "I'll pay you back." Turning, she cautiously approached their area. Mrs. Coolidge made eye contact and looked away. Felicia forced a smile and stepped forward.

"Some breakfast for your family." Lauren

handed the platter over. "And I'm so sorry about your dog."

Felicia looked back to her family loading their wagon. "Thank you for this and thank you for your help that day. I've never been more frightened in my life. I know you tried to help Brody, but he wasn't who he seemed to be." She hushed as her mother walked up behind her. Lauren couldn't help but feel sorry for the young woman behind those innocent, round, wounded eyes. Just a few months ago she was this same young woman, confused and wary of right and wrong. Look at the things she had done for Elias.

"Wagons, ho!" Joe yelled.

"I'm just glad you're safe," Lauren said, stepping back, "And again, I'm so sorry about everything."

"GOOD NEWS AND bad news." Joe rode his horse up alongside Elias as they headed into the Nebraska territory. Elias huffed, tipping his hat back. They'd already been slowed down by Company B and someone's brake block cracking in half.

"Like?"

"The scouts ahead found some elk and sent two hunters out."

Elias felt a pang of frustration. He'd love to get in a saddle and be hunting right now.

"The bad news is the western trail is gone.

Probably gone in a flash flood. Good news there's plenty of water. Bad news it formed a cliff no wagon can maneuver without flipping. We got a couple more scouts goin' north to find a way around it. Going south around it leads us right into Pawnee territory, and *that* we don't want to do. Besides a bit of trading, we've kept our nose out of unwelcomed visits." Joe pulled his horse back to pace with the wagon.

"And what do you think of those clouds to the east?" Elias nodded up.

"Yeah, if those come on us, we got more water and more problems."

"If the scouts can't find a crossing, let me know. I might have an idea."

"Well that should be interesting. I will." Joe tipped his hat before he rode on.

The next afternoon the air cooled with the encroaching thick gray clouds. The rain was starting to pelt the powdery dust as Lauren ran to the wagon. Elias reached over to pull her in on the bench seat with him. Grabbing the tarp from under the seat, she pulled it over their legs. "The rain's good for some things, I guess. My gracious it smells good and such a relief from the dust." She inhaled the sweet scent of fresh rain on parched ground.

"I think it's going to slow us down. Joe says the trail is washed out ahead."

"I've been thinking we are in no hurry to get

to Fort Kearney," she said, with a weak smile.

"This train can't stop." He stretched his back. "If these people don't get to Independence Rock by July fourth they won't make it over the Rockies or the Sierras. Did you ever read about the Donner Party?"

She barely nodded. "I did. I just was wondering . . ." She grabbed the side rail as the wagon hit a rut. "What if we left the group and skipped Fort Kearney?"

"No, Lauren." His eyes narrowed. "I'd rather face the soldiers at the fort than be out on these flatlands alone." He pulled his hat forward, and his jaw worked for a moment. "I'm not running, no sir. I've come too far." He dipped his chin and watched her. "I know you're worried about getting to Denver City, so I can still talk to Joe about how to help you."

"I'm not worried about Denver City. I'm worried they will arrest you." Her eyes widened, "What's a wife to do then?"

A slow smile creased his face and his eyes crinkled with joy. With everything in him, he didn't want to live a minute without her. Hesitantly he asked, "Would you want to marry me, Lauren?" He swallowed the constriction in his throat. Life was short and unpredictable, why not risk the hardest question he's ever asked.

"Elias Browne, with an E. I would very much like that. But I'm so afraid for you."

Joe rode up, rain dripping off his wide brim. "So we have a problem. The scouts report the north route would take us an extra week. Watching the clouds move, I think this thing will only be a day or two. The likelihood of wagons stuck in the mud could double the time. But leaving the trail could lead us off a cliff. So I'm listening, Elias. What are you thinking that no one has considered?"

Elias wiped the puddle of water off his tarp and looked to Lauren, and then back at Joe. "Let's blow the cliff up."

"Blow it up, you say?"

Elias didn't need to look at Lauren. Her eyes were surely as wide as Joe's.

"I have dynamite, but that won't work with the rain. So I could set an explosive and try to set it off with a gunshot."

Joe looked out to the line of moving wagons and back to him. "You have everything to do that?"

"I do."

"And you won't blow any wagons up in the process?" Joe chuckled.

"No, sir." Elias could feel Lauren's eyes burning into him.

"How far out does the train need to be?"

"A hundred yards or so. Might be some dirt rain, but nothing else."

"So how do you set this thing off a hundred yards back?"

"I don't. I have to be at twenty, thirty yards to hit it square on."

"I know you told me you were in munitions in the war. So I'm assuming you've done this before?"

Elias nodded.

"Let me go talk to the company commanders." Joe rocked in his saddle, giving his horse a nudge. "I had a feeling I was going to be surprised by you." He turned and smiled back at them. "And I am."

Elias waited then finally risked a glance toward Lauren's way. She stared straight ahead, lips in a straight taunt line. If he couldn't see her chest rising and falling so quickly, he'd wonder if she was breathing. She turned her head quickly, opening her mouth and shutting it, looking back to the gray landscape. She broke the long cold silence, "Where, can I ask, are these things, these explosives you are talking about?"

"In the wagon."

"Our wagon?" Her voice quivered.

"Well . . . it was my wagon before I went to your home to pick up a cap and you invited yourself along."

"What!" Her eyes popped. "The wagon train was always my idea. *You* were going to help *me!*"

"But then *you* chose to stay home. I never thought I would see you again. Then you came spying on me." He raised one eyebrow and smirked.

Her mouth hung open searching for a response. Obviously not catching his tone of humor, she flung the tarp off her lap and grabbed her skirts. Trying to steady herself against the swaying wagon she climbed through the canvas opening. A huge thud and a sad moan of flat harpsichord keys, made him cover his mouth to smother a snicker.

Chapter 41

ELIAS AND JOE'S boots squished in the wet prairie grass the next morning. The rain had let up most of the night but had now started up again.

"So you're goin' to make us a landslide?" Captain K. walked toward them.

"Yes, sir." Elias felt the flash of being back in the army.

"We got the wagons all back far enough?"

"They're good, maybe just a few guards to make sure no children run out past the perimeter. The wagons make a natural break."

"Sounds good." Captain K. squeezed his shoulder. "Joe says you got a pretty young wife. You got a plan not to leave her a widow?" The captain stepped back, eyeing him.

Elias missed the warm grip on his shoulder. Never having any father figures before, he'd seen a lifetime of them these last months. Somehow it felt good. "I can't guarantee how much is sand and how much is rock. But I'll have the Reverend Little say a prayer for me."

The captain smiled. "All right then, you have the hour. We'll keep everyone inside the circle.

Joe, I need you alive, so let this young buck do the work."

Joe chuckled and turned with Elias toward Company C.

"Joe, if something did happen to me, Lauren has some money. Would you help her hire someone honest to get her to Denver City?"

"Like she was my own daughter."

Elias let out a long breath and checked the surroundings. Not one large rock or tree big enough to hide behind littered the distance he needed. He just might need more than one Reverend Little prayer.

LOOKING UP EVERY five minutes, Lauren almost burnt her hand on a hot water pot over the campfire. The water was warm enough for the morning dishes, so she grabbed a wad of apron and poured the hot water into a bucket for washing. In a glance, she saw Elias and Joe walking back to their area. *Please God, have another idea.* But from the way Elias stared out to the prairie, he looked like he would be setting off this explosive. As he walked closer, she kept her head down. Showing her anger never stopped him from doing as he pleased. Some little girls screamed a few wagons over as they played chase. Everything seemed to be fraying her to shreds as she scrubbed the tin plates with more vigor than needed. Peeking up, the sisters seemed to all be conveniently missing.

"Lauren." Elias stood next to her.

Huffing, she dipped the dishes in the clean water.

"I've spoken to Joe. If anything happens to me, the rest of the money is in the other bench. There's a panel underneath the tin boxes."

"The tin boxes that have explosives in them? Humph." Plunging the rag into the basin too hard, water splashed out on her skirt and feet.

Elias caught the rag and pulled it from her hand. Taking her hand, he pulled her away from the fire circle and toward their wagon.

She jerked free and pounded her last steps to the wagon. "I can't abide by this." As she turned to face him, her eyes swelled with tears. "You take too many risks, Elias. You have no regard for your life. And what about mine? I've been traveling over rutted roads in a wagon full of explosives? I can't live with so much disregard." She regretted the harsh words as soon as they spewed out. "I have no-no-no *security*. I need love *and* security."

"I know . . . you're right." He shuffled his feet. "It's just hard to give away something you've never had." He reached into his pants pocket and took a deep breath. "I want you to hold the only two things I love." He held out the little trinket wrapped in an old dingy wrapper. She remembered it from the first day she met him.

"Keep this and keep this." He held out a simple gold band. "One is my past, and this one I can only dream will be my future. If something happens to me, promise me you won't bury them with me." He leaned close to her sinking expression. "After you make sure I'm really dead." He winked. "Just knowing that you'll keep them, I feel better."

Tears spilled down her cheeks, her jaw twitching. She held up her left hand. "Put it on my finger." She locked her eyes on his.

He bit down on his smile and slid it on her fourth finger.

LIKE A TOWN of people who were hungry for a horse and pony show, the folks lined around the outer wagons watching Elias's every move. He'd spent more than thirty minutes setting the explosives in place then another twenty finding the right angle for the shot to make contact.

Ida Bell had sidled close and linked an arm through Lauren's. "The Lord knows how to part the Red Sea. I'm sure He'll help Elias make a path through rock and dirt."

Lauren tried to find a smile, but her face fell into a worried frown. "The sisters are making some bean soup. I might as well go help. I can't stand to watch this."

Unfortunately, though far away, he was in full view of Company C. Even the Coolidges hung on to their stock to keep them from being spooked by the explosion. Lauren shook her head, watching the fire, the black cast iron skillet bumped her toe. Jerking the weight of the heavy pan up, she held it in front of her. *That bullet had just bounced off the thing. What if . . .*

She met Mabel's curious expression then took off like a deer with wings over the mud and wading through the tall, wet grass toward Elias, the heavy pan gripped in both hands.

She opened her mouth to call out to him. He laid on his stomach and held three fingers in the air. As his name escaped her panted breath, the crowd yelled "three, two . . ."

"Elias!" She tried to scream as the crowd yelled one. He placed his cheek against the rifle and pulled the trigger.

Like falling down a dark well, her head and body slammed into rock and dirt walls. Darker and darker it became until she could no longer find the sides. Her body fell back thumping her head and shoulders then her face against the solid darkness. *Oh death, where is your sting?*

From ashes to ashes. The old harpsichord music faintly played somewhere. *To be departed from this earth is to be with the Lord.* Grit and gravel. How could death be so painful? Muffled voices from the darkness. Was it Mabel? Ida Bell? Someone calling for the medic? Had she gone to war? Did a cannon shoot her?

Many hands lifted her out of the dark pit. She tried to open her eyes, but gray shadows danced around her thick lids.

"Lauren, honey, can you hear me?"

She raised her hand toward the sound and was met with a warm grip. Why couldn't she get the dancing gray light to focus? "I'm here," she whispered.

"Oh, thank God," Mabel said. "Just keep ahold of my hand. The medic is rinsing your eyes and cleaning up the last of your cuts. Have you ever had stitches before?"

The whirling in her brain caused things to go spotty gray, white, and then black.

A GROUP OF men pulled Elias out of the hole he had dug for protection. After the rumble of the earth, he was thankful his head was still attached. He looked past the revelry to see that the cliff which had separated them from the trail was now laid flat. Sodbusters he'd never met were patting him on the back and dusting the dirt and rock off his clothes. Their accolades were enjoyable, but only one smile mattered to him. One rock, like a bullet, could have made him a dead man, his sweet unofficial wife a widow. He tried to step around the crowd to see her.

Something was happening with the Ohio friends. Was that Lauren's green skirt on the ground? Did she faint? Out in the field? He broke into a fast sprint.

"Get the medic!" Chrystal commanded him before he reached them.

Chapter 42

RUNNING BACK WITH the medic, Elias could see someone had already pulled the harpsichord out of the wagon and left it on the wet grass. Still confused, he wondered why the Coolidges and Littles were hovering outside their wagon.

"What happened?" he asked the Reverend. "Did she faint?"

Janet reached out for the medic to enter the wagon. "Here, sir." Elias tried to follow him in. "Give them a minute; she looks pretty bad." Reverend Little tugged on his arm.

"What happened?" Elias felt his blood pounding in his ears. Ida Bell placed a hand on his back. "She was upset and said she was goin' to help with soup. The next minute, I look up, and she's runnin' out to you with an iron skillet in her arms. Not sure if she was goin' to clock you over the head," Ida Bell chuckled, "or thinkin' it would shield you."

"Just some poor timing," the Reverend added. "You were already on the ground doing the countdown. She called out your name, but the crowd was louder."

"I-I never saw her or heard her." Elias raked his hand through his hair still full of dirt.

"I closed my eyes during the blast. But it must have knocked her clear off her feet." Ida Bell sighed. "She was out cold when we got to her."

Elias spun on his heel, gripping his head and spun back. "Has she come to?"

"I can't rightly say. Haven't heard." Ida Bell looked to the ground.

The urge to punch something overwhelmed him. He stalked out from the wagon and saw a large rock.

"Elias!" Joe called, veering around the Coolidges. "You did it!"

Elias couldn't think. What had he done to Lauren? Even Martin and Lux looked contrite. It must be bad.

Joe slapped him on the back. "Looks like no one here's happy for you." He smiled, gripping Elias's neck.

"Lauren got hit. I haven't heard if she's okay."

"Oh, dear Lord." Joe stepped toward their wagon. "How did—" he cleared his throat. "Are the sisters with her?"

Elias raked his hand down his face and nodded. "And the medic. She was running to me with the iron skillet."

Joe jerked back, wide-eyed, "Wha—"

"Remember the gunshot that got near her in camp?"

Joe nodded, frowning.

"I think she was running that skillet out to me to shield me from the fragments."

"Clever woman, I would have never thought of that."

"I never saw her. I thought everyone was clear." Elias's fingers gripped what little hair on the back of his head they could, his face white with shock and worry.

"Reverend," Joe turned to the group around the wagon. "Lead us in a prayer for Lauren."

WATER TRICKLED INTO her mouth, but her lips felt swollen and tight.

"Lauren," Mabel said gently, "can you take another sip?"

"Did I fall into a bee's nest?" Her voice was hoarse. She heard the familiar chuckles of Mabel and Janet. Were her eyes swollen shut? She tried to crack them open only to find more floating bubbles of gray and black.

"No, silly goose, but you got blasted by flying rock and dirt. Do you remember running out to Elias?"

"Oh, that," she croaked. "Probably wasn't the best idea. Is he okay?"

"Yes, he's fine. That skillet might have saved your life. I've seen blows to the chest that stopped the heart."

"Who's in here?" Lauren squinted, trying to get her eyes to clear.

"I'm Corbin, ma'am. Worked in the field hospitals back in West Virginia. I didn't see any broken bones. We've rinsed your face and eyes. I'm afraid you didn't have a chance to turn from the blast. Besides the holes in your face, does anything else hurt?"

"I have holes in my face?" she wailed raising her hand to check.

Mabel intercepted her hand. "Nothing that won't heal," she squeezed it. "Do you want to try to sit up?"

Lauren pulled against Mabel's strong grip and rose to sit. "My eyes feel like ice and fire, off and on. I can't seem to see anything but shadows." Someone gently rubbed her back.

"We can't be sure if your eyes were closed against the blast."

There was a strange silence that hung in the air. She broke it, "Will my vision return?" She turned to where she had heard his voice come from. A scraping noise with a change of distance from her told her he stood up.

"It's hard to tell for a few days. You'll need to rest and not force anything."

"How could I force my vision back? Either it works, or it doesn't. Right now all I can see are rolling shadows of gray and black."

"I mean just be patient with yourself. It seems

you have wonderful friends to tend to you." The wagon rocked as he jumped out the back. "I'll check back tomorrow." The sisters chimed in their thanks.

"Lauren, can I come in?"

Her heart flipped a beat. She'd know that calm voice anywhere. There wasn't any use hiding her appearance from him. The sisters bade goodbye as he entered. She could smell the gun powder and earth on him as he sat on the wagon floor. Lightly and carefully his hands took her neck and pulled her until she felt his lips brush her ear.

"I'm so sorry. I didn't hear you or see you."

Something caught in his throat making it difficult to find his breath. Was he crying? Did she look that bad?

"I—" she sniffed. "I faulted you for being reckless and disregarding of your life," she whispered. Feeling his face rest lightly on her shoulder, and his hand kneading her back. "And yet, I did the same thing."

"You are so beautiful, so giving and merciful," he said, voice cracking. "I never want you to be in danger again."

She reached over and fingered his hair. The shoulder of her blouse felt damp where he rested his face. Truly, his remorse was sobering. He lifted his head and held her hand. Finding her gold band, he twisted it around her finger and brought it up to his lips. Sucking in a ragged breath, he kissed each finger. "I love you so much it hurts."

"I love you, too." She whispered. "Did they tell you I—" She swallowed hard, took a deep breath and then said, "I can't see anything but shadows?"

"Yes."

Chapter 43

SITTING ON THE bouncing wagon bench, Lauren fingered her yarn. "Elias, is this the green?"

"Yes," he answered. "Another woman is walking toward us from Company A, I'd guess."

"What is she carrying?"

"I'm thinking a pie. No, it smells more like a chicken pot pie of some sort."

Lauren tried to prepare a smile. The word had traveled fast around the wagon train. The man who had set the blast and enabled the group to go forward had also injured his wife, causing an unfortunate blindness. *Temporary blindness,* Lauren corrected herself. She turned toward the sound of the kind woman's voice and smiled. "So very thoughtful of you. We are so thankful for these blessings." Lauren struggled with where to face as the wagon trudged forward. Was the woman still walking alongside them?

"Yes, thank you." The bench creaked as Elias reached over and received the food.

"It smells wonderful," Lauren boomed.

"She's already moved on," Elias said.

"Oh." Lauren fingered her knitting needles

fighting embarrassment. "If you see the sisters, I enjoyed walking with them yesterday." They had linked arms with her and even sang a favorite hymn with their rich harmonies. It was the most carefree she had felt since the accident. Without being able to read Elias's expression, she never knew if he was tired of being her constant caregiver. His care and concern had been reassuring, making every concession for her needs. How could he know that seeing his simple smile had the power to melt all her fears?

"We'll be at Fort Kearney tomorrow." He cleared his throat. "I still have to answer for killing Brody."

She dug her fingers into the soft yarn and squeezed, just like her heart was painfully squeezing in her chest. His hand trailed down her arm and rested on her leg. "Captain K. mentioned they might have an army doctor on hand. We can have him take a look at you."

"It's been a week, and nothing has changed." On such a warm day, a strange chill ran up her spine.

"That's why we need to see a real doctor."

"How will *we* do that, if they arrest you?" Hopelessness wrapped around her like a dismal fog she couldn't seem to escape.

"Lauren, I wish with everything in me, I could give you answers. I know you hate the insecurities. Insecurities that *I* cause."

"Elias." She went to grab his hand, but it was gone.

"For a while there," he said, "it seemed this weird pattern of I prayed and then God would find a way for me. I have been praying every day, every hour. I even borrowed the Reverend's Bible. Did you know there's a story of a blind man that Jesus healed? I guess I thought if I could find some formula, I could get God to answer. I confessed every sin I could think of." He chuckled. "That took a while. Then I thought of your sin."

"Mine?"

"Well, we have been lying to everyone on this wagon train."

Lauren slouched back against the bench. The truth was as hard as the wood bench. They'd traveled five states and every minute was a lie to these sweet people, to friends they had made. Was God teaching her a lesson? "I should never have left Greenlock," she mumbled.

"The Reverend says, 'God's grace doesn't work on our past, cause it's over and done. And there's no grace for the future.' I guess no grace for Fort Kearney or how your sight will return. All we have is grace for today."

Lauren delicately found each itchy scab healing on her face. "Grace for today. Just this day? Humph. Yesterday, the sisters sang, *'Just as I am without one plea.'* Have you heard it?"

317

He nodded, "They would sing it on Sundays at the asylum. *Just as I am, poor, wretched, blind; Sight, riches, healing of the mind, Yea, all I need in Thee to find, O Lamb of God, I come, I come.* Huh, maybe I should have paid attention."

THE NEXT AFTERNOON Lauren heard a man calling out "Pony Express" up and down the wagon line. "What is it?" She turned from the sun's painful brightness.

"He'll take the mail. Do you have any letters for your mother or father?"

"No." She dropped her chin. "Not with everything that has happened."

"I can see the fort." Elias stood on the wagon bench. "Do you remember your thoughts on the size of the Blue River?"

"Yes," she sighed.

"I see maybe five or so unpainted houses and a couple of rows of sod buildings. It looks like they surround an open square in the middle. There's a large corral to the left. I can see the Platte River. The only brush or trees for miles lining its banks. It looks like they have some blockhouse guns. Not bad artillery defenses. The nice two-story building in the back is likely the officer's quarters."

Lauren sat silent.

"Try to keep your chin up, Lauren. We get to rest here for two days. We have to keep the faith.

It's been a long road, but the next leg is going to see you to your mother and sister."

"I long to *see* them, Elias. Really see them. I haven't seen them in two years." Her chin started to quiver, tears only blurring the gray and black shadows more. Standing, she reached back trying to find the opening to the wagon.

"Wait till we stop, just a few more minutes, then I can help you." His arm steadied her attempt to climb through the canvas.

"I can do it." She jerked away from his hold. Clinging to the canvas, she swung her legs over and landed in the wagon's open area. *Thank goodness I didn't crack my toes against the harpsichord.* Then she remembered earlier, Elias told her the Littles had had room for the harpsichord so she could rest as they traveled. Sitting crossed-legged on her thick blankets, she pulled her pillow to her chest, dropping her face into the soft comfort. The wagon lurched to the left, and her arm slammed against the long bench. Elias mumbled an apology, saying they were circling up Company C.

THE NEXT MORNING, Lauren awoke, missing the familiar shot into the air. Fort Kearney, she reminded herself, the wagon train wasn't moving today. Blinking against the familiar gray and black spots, she debated on staying abed all day. Voices spoke low and careful outside the wagon, and she rose up and straightened her rumpled clothes. Sitting on the bench, she pulled on her boots and heard Mabel and Janet outside. She hadn't helped them with any cooking or chores all week, but all the extra food they had received was shared among the Ohio friends.

"Lauren."

Of course, he could look in and see her, oh how she longed to see him.

"Yes."

"Bur is here. He's taking me into the fort."

Stunned, her back jerked straight. "So early?" Lauren stammered. "I want to go with you." Emotions betrayed her as her eyes swelled with tears. "I haven't finished the buttons on your shirt." She stood and dragged her hands along the canvas to the end, where he grabbed them both.

"I'm wearing the gray shirt." His familiar calm, soft voice was close.

"But I can get Mabel to help me. It will only," a sob escaped, "take a few minutes."

"Lovely Lauren." He lifted her from the back and set her on the ground wrapping a warm arm around her shoulders. "What you can't see is all our friends are standing here with us."

"We're right here darlin'." Ida Bell patted her hair. The Reverend's "umm hum," sounded right behind Ida Bell. Mabel, Janet, and Chrystal all chimed in squeezing her arm and hand. "We're all going with you. Every step of the way."

"We've come this far together," Joe said to her right.

"And I, Mrs. Browne, have our entire family ready. We can only hope that we will have a chance to speak up for your husband. I believe he's why we have our Felicia safe and sound."

Lauren was astounded at the sound of Mrs. Coolidge's voice. These people, these were true friends. The generous warmth and strength from those who circled them seeped into her empty soul. She buried her face in Elias's shirt and sobbed.

Chapter 44

THE SOUNDS AND smells of the fort were overpowering her senses. One minute someone shouted orders, the next a group of men laughed. A dog barked over the sound of a baby crying. The charred smells of iron works assaulted her nose. Her group spoke in low tones, Mabel and Janet leading her steps by linking their arms through hers. She tried to block the sound of the metal chains that Elias wore, Bur leading him somewhere out front. The ladies slowed to a stop as Lauren sensed a group walking in front of them. Low whistles and a comment about needing a pretty lady to dance with tonight, made her look to the ground.

"For heaven's sake," Chrystal clipped. "I'm obviously spoken for." The men had passed, and the sisters giggled at her curt response.

Lauren heard a squeaky door open and close.

"He went in with Bur and Joe. I saw a few other people standing in there." Mabel released Lauren's arm and led her to a bench. "We might as well take a seat and get you out of the sun."

"I know I look like something that got dragged behind the wagon, but I want to go in and speak of what I saw. Are the Coolidges still close?"

"Yes, we are all here."

With each hour, the door squeaked open and closed. Military and civilian came and went. Mabel tried to see inside, reassuring Lauren that Joe and Elias were still inside. The Littles went back to eat lunch, and soon the Coolidges left also saying they'd be back later. The heat and dust were overbearing, and Lauren knew the sisters were as uncomfortable as she was. The next time the door opened, Mabel jumped up and walked inside.

"Joe said the testimony time is over," she said, returning to where they sat. "They won't be calling for any of us."

"Because we are Mormons," Janet added. "Or women?"

"And a wife would be too partial, Joe said."

Lauren felt Mabel pull up on her arm. "Let's go back to camp and get some water and food."

"I don't want to leave. I have to know something," Lauren sighed.

"Joe said to go on, and Chrystal's back is killing her. Come on, let's get you out of this heat."

MABEL HELPED HER into the back of the wagon and brought her some chicken pot pie from the other day. The heat was stifling, so after her lunch she pulled her heavy skirt off and laid down. She hated being dependent on the others but was so completely in awe at each one who surrounded them today.

Dripping with sweat, she awoke without any idea how long she had slept. She billowed her blouse and wiped her tender brow off with her sleeve. Surely Elias would have woken her if he were free. This could mean only one thing—they were keeping him. No wonder Joe had told Mabel to take her back to camp. He knew it was bad news with nothing their Ohio friends could do. She pulled her skirt and boots back on and felt her way to the end of the wagon. Unclasping the back gate, she heard it flop forward then jumped out. Without orientation of the camp, she was at the mercy of the others' help. She felt for the first iron wrapped wagon wheel and felt her way further until her boot hit a barrel of some kind. She felt around the rim and moved, hanging on to the second wheel. Had anyone seen her?

She listened, no talking, just the sound of a low moan. Someone was in pain. Was someone tending to that pitiful sound? "Hello. Is anyone around camp?" More silence. Then another heart-wrenching pitiful moan.

"Mabel? Janet? Anyone?" She felt her way past the bench out to the tongue of the wagon. "Hello, Chrystal?" She tried louder. Another animalistic growl came from the area to her right. Was she still dreaming? Oh, how she wanted to squeeze her face to make her eyes work. What was going on in her camp? Who would be torturing another person? Her body began to tremble in the low afternoon heat, and she felt her way back from where she came. "Please Lord, what is happening? Please!" She found the back gate and clutched it, out of breath. Would they come after her next? A loud scream pierced the air and Lauren bent low and hovered under the wagon gate.

"One more Chrystal!"

Was that Mabel's strained voice from across the camp? Another low guttural cry came from the same area. And then silence. Heart thumping in her chest, she listened like never before. A tiny squeal, like a little bird, came from the same direction. Lauren fell back on the ground. Another little muffled cry sounded across the camp. She hugged her knees, smiling and catching her breath. A baby, Chrystal had had her baby.

The new baby boy was a delightful distraction from such a long day. Chrystal had done wonderfully in delivery and slept peacefully while Mabel showed off the little bundle to those in the camp. Lauren forged a smile as the oohs and aahs ebbed and flowed. The sound of music drifted in with the cooler breeze as the sun began to set.

"No word yet?" Mabel handed off the baby to Janet.

Lauren shook her head, fighting her plummeting hope.

"Here, take my arm." Mabel pulled her up. "Let's walk to the fort. Someone must know something."

Lauren stumbled along hooked to her arm. "If he's in the stocks, will you tell me?" The music grew louder, and the movement of people all around her was disorientating.

"Yes." Mabel held her close as someone approached.

"Hey missy, pretty gal in spite of that run in with buckshot. Wanna dance?"

Lauren could smell fermented cider on his breath.

"No, she doesn't. She's looking for her husband." Mabel pulled her away. "I don't know, Lauren. Every soldier looks at you like a hungry wolf. Maybe this wasn't such a good idea. Hang on to my skirt as I try the door." There was the rattling of a wooden door. "Fiddlesticks, it's locked," Mabel said, exhaling a long breath.

"It's okay, Mabel. You've had a long day. You need to get back to the baby."

"It's getting dark, too." They both jumped as someone shot a gun in the air. "Come on." Mabel pulled her further from the sound of music and merriment.

They stopped, and Lauren took a full breath of the evening smells of prairie grass and camp smoke. "Thank you for trying." The lack of sunlight eased the tension in her forehead.

"Wait here and don't move." Mabel's firm grip was missing before Lauren could protest. Each second seemed like an hour, how could this caring friend who'd taken her to the earthen privy, helped her bathe, met every need with true diligence just leave her standing alone? "Mabel?" She whispered despairingly. "Please." Close to tears and collapse, she felt thick hands wrap around her waist pulling her back. Someone dared to . . .

"Don't scream. It's me."

Lauren spun bumping into the large hard body. Her hands pressed against his chest, then squeezing his arms. Could it be?

"I shouldn't have taken advantage of you not seeing me approach, but I waved Mabel on."

"Elias! Oh, dear Lord." Her hands gripped his neck, fingers finding his hair. She embraced him like he was back from the dead. "What happened?"

He wrapped her in his arms and lifted her off the ground. "Dance with me?" He spun her around. Her hair flew off her neck, and her skirts swirled.

She clung to him, the smells of smoking tallow and cold ashes on his shirt.

"Wait." Her feet finally felt the ground. "Are you free?"

"Oh, yes. I am free indeed. Like the Reverend says. 'Lift up your head, God's not through with you yet.'" His hands gently pressed around her face. "I have to kiss you. I missed you so bad today." His lips were hungry, yet tender, each kiss leaving her more breathless.

"I—Elias!" Her heartbeat rattled in her chest. "I suppose no one is around." The sounds of the music and revelry faded each time they kissed.

"I don't care." He whispered against her cheek, taking her lips captive again. He pulled back, foreheads touching. "Let's find the Reverend and get married right now."

Chapter 45

SOMETHING KNOTTED IN Lauren's gut. She tried for just one blessed moment to be a woman in love with a strong, desirable man. He wasn't going to jail, wasn't going to leave her high and dry. Why couldn't she just lose herself in the warmth of his body against hers, the arms that enfolded her? She knew that tonight he wanted to be alone with her, doing the things only married lovers do. She didn't need to see the desire in his eyes, she could feel it. Her gut knotted again. Her arms slackened, a warm ache rose in her belly.

"I'm not ready for what you want."

"What do I want?" His breath tickled her ear.

This was too hard, she pushed back against his chest, only gripping his hand for connection. "You want a wife who can see you. See the frowns and the smiles. You have an endearing smile, Elias, it melts me. It assures me everything's going to be all right. Your eyes, the blue is bluer than the prairie skies, the curves of your dark lashes—" A gunshot rang out, and she jumped.

His arm came protectively around her. "Just some folks carrying on."

"I," she whispered, "can't remember what I was saying."

"Something about my eyes and smile. I kinda liked it." He tucked a loose strand of hair behind her ear.

"I—" She exhaled and closed her eyes, her knuckles rubbing her temple. "I have to see you to marry you."

His arm slid off her shoulders.

"I'm sorry." Her voice dipped.

"That hurts, Lauren. I want to take care of you. Sight or no sight." He shuffled his feet. "I'd already made up my mind. I will take you to every doctor you want, but it doesn't matter to me. You'll have your memories of my eyes and smiles, and we'll just have to adjust to everything else."

"Adjust?" Her jaw went slack. "I held Chrystal's baby today. Mabel put him in my arms. What if I was to have a baby? I couldn't take care of it." She bit her bottom lip. "One day the baby would crawl and walk. How would I know where? What if she got outside? What if he got near a red-hot stove?"

A loud group of young people laughed coming near them. Elias grabbed her elbow and led her toward Company C.

"I can't cook. I can't find the privy by myself." She stumbled when her boot caught some brush. "I can't walk without help." Tears began to sting her eyes, disgusted she jerked to a stop pulling her elbow free. "My mother and Cammi will help me."

Elias growled and pressed his temples. "*I* want to help you. Look what you've done for me, Lauren. Think about it, please." He shook his head and gripped her shoulders. "I shouldn't be my own man. I shouldn't get to love a beautiful, amazing woman. I shouldn't have gone free today. I shouldn't be loved by a perfect God. But you rescued me from darkness. Please let me rescue you. Please. I'm not saying it will be easy. We might need help." He blew out a breath. "I don't have any expectations. I didn't grow up in a family. But whatever it is, it will be ours. We stay together, and we figure it out together."

A strange flash of his words echoed from so many months ago. *I will be good to those who are good to me.* It seemed to ring true. Fatigue dizzied her head, and she leaned against his chest. In an easy motion, he picked her up and carried her to their wagon. Setting her down, he opened the back gate. "Also, I was gone so long today because the Corporal heard about the blast and the ammunition I have. It's gone. I sold it all. You and the harpsichord will be safe." He tried to read her face in the dark, helping her up. "Okay?"

"Thank you," she whispered. "I feel better."

• • •

THE NEXT MORNING after breakfast they waited outside of the fort's doctor's office. Just like sitting for hours listening to all the law-breakers and disputes, Elias was reminded how large the traveling town really was. Lauren would be appalled if she knew the other despairing sickness and injuries that had happened since leaving Independence. He couldn't help frown at the mothers holding their sick children. Some so pale and thin, it would be a miracle if the doctor could remedy them. If Lauren could see all the woeful looks on these faces, she would give them all her spot in line.

He remembered the conversations with the other folk who wanted to head to Colorado as a way to distract himself from the long wait. "There's a group already forming," he said, "for Colorado. We need numbers and protection for our welfare when we separate from the larger group."

"When would we break away?" she asked.

"Ten days, maybe twelve—depends on the trail. Then another two weeks. You're close now, Lauren." He rubbed her shoulder. "What do you think your mother will say when you come walking in the door?"

"Next," a soldier with a white apron called out. The line shuffled forward.

"I try not to think about it. It makes my stomach hurt."

He let out a weak laugh. "Why?"

"You know when you said you have no expectations?"

He nodded but remembered to speak. "Yes."

"I guess I've had too many. I was such a silly ninny about the great wagon trail." She pulled her hair out and knotted her bun. "All I could think of was getting away from the mortuary. You even tried to tell me, remember? Dirt, blisters and some other things?"

"I did." He drew his finger lightly over her healing face. "But I knew you had it in you. Any woman who would help a man out of a coffin and replace it with bricks and jugs is a force to be reckoned with. I wondered if you'd be stronger than me."

"Stronger?"

"I knew I could do the physical work. But I'm not that good with people. Brody is a painful example." He sighed. "But people accepted us because of you. You are not just likable, you're also a bit loveable." He bent and kissed her cheek. "Did I tell you that Lux and Martin spoke up at the hearing yesterday?"

"No, I thought they had left."

"Evidently, they came back."

"Next," the man called out again.

They shuffled forward as a baby fussed behind them.

"Anyway, I think I need to go to Denver City

with no expectations." A small grin appeared on her face. "I can almost feel it." She chuckled tugging on his shirt. "You were about to say the Reverend would tell us to 'keep our hope in the Lord.'"

"Amen, sister."

Thirty minutes later, Lauren sat on a high cot in the fort hospital. It smelled like lye and a bit like the old embalming solutions she remembered. Her hands started to itch.

"So you report that they cleaned your eyes out immediately with water?"

"Yes, sir. I was knocked out for a few minutes, so that's what I was told."

"Private, please pull the curtains," the doctor asked. "Now can you see the change in the room?"

"Yes, sir."

"Good, good. Now I'm going to pass something by your face, and I want you to try to follow it with your eyes."

Lauren could feel the warmth and blurry glow of a candle as it passed.

"Good, good. Please hold still as I look closer."

She took little shallow breaths as his presence was inches from her face. He pulled on her eyelids.

"Look down, look up, to the right and now to the left. Good, good. One more time." He finally moved back. "Please open the curtains, Private."

Lauren straightened her back to prepare for whatever he was to say. He opened a drawer and came back to her.

"I want you to try these." He placed the thin wires around her ears. The weight of the glasses pressing against the bridge of her nose. "Close your eyes for a few seconds then open them again."

A small sprig of hope dared to rise in her. She opened her eyes and saw images and color. It was Elias who stood to the right. She could make out his height and sandy colored hair. She pulled the glasses closer to her eyes. "I can see better. Not clear, but I can see the three of you. Your private has on a white apron; he's standing right there," she pointed. "You, sir, have gray hair, I believe. And I think you are nodding at me?"

"Yes, I am. I think what you have is temporary. There are some fine eye doctors I would send you to if you wanted to travel back east. But if the glasses help, they are yours." He placed a small box in her hand. "Because you can't see details yet, it's very important to keep them in a box. Visually impaired folks are the first to lose their glasses." He patted her on the back.

"Thank you, doctor." She closed her eyes and opened them again. The colors and men were still blurry but distinguishable.

Elias stepped forward. "Thank you." She could

335

see his arm and hand reach out and shake the doctor's. She faced him as he helped her stand. Blinking, she wasn't sure if he was smiling, but she knew she was.

Chapter 46

THE NEXT WEEK the entire wagon train slowed in the hot mid-afternoon. "Now what?" Elias shook his head. Looking around, he saw Lauren walking with Mabel and Janet. He pulled the oxen to a complete stop and swung around to the side of the wagon. He pulled the lid off the water barrel then strained to reach the water with the cup. Tempted to pour it over his head, he knew the best use was to drink it.

"Third wagon wheel this week." Joe pulled his horse steady next to their wagon.

Elias handed him a cup of water. "With the others, we just kept moving."

"Take a look to the south." Joe gestured leaning over his horse.

Elias hung off the sideboards, one hand blocking the sun. "How long have they been following us?" He turned to Joe.

"Just today, that's why the captain doesn't want us moving on with anyone lagging behind. Word from the scouts is, there are about a thousand buffalo over that low ridge. And unless they are sharing, we aren't invited." Joe tipped his hat and rode on.

Elias jumped down from the wagon's side-boards. He saw Chrystal look out from the back of their wagon. "I think your driver has got the break on," he said, walking to the back of their wagon. "You want to get out?"

"Thank you, Elias. We could use some air."

Before he could unlatch the back, she handed him a little bundle. Taking the baby from her, he brought it quickly to his chest. He'd never held a baby before, it was light, and felt like something from a china cabinet. He wanted to extend his hand to help her but wasn't sure how to keep from dropping the little sleeping thing. She swung her leg and skirts over and jumped down.

"Do you mind if I take a quick run to the water closet?" She smiled and moved away before he could say anything. Stepping into the shade of their wagon, he looked at the tiny, squishy face. "So what do you think of being out?" His question sounded ridiculous, and the baby's chin quivered. "Your mama is coming right back, so don't worry." He tried to do a little jiggle like he'd seen the women do. The strangest wave of helplessness swept through him. "Mamas are good people," he whispered, lightly touching the five wisps of hair on the baby's head.

He never contemplated the loss of his mother much. Most of the children at the asylum had no parents that cared for them. He'd like to think that his first three years his mama had held him and loved him. It certainly was a powerful thing holding a little life in the palm of your hand. Looking around to make sure no one was watching, he placed a gentle kiss on the baby's head. "Grow strong in the Lord and the power of His might," he whispered.

The sisters and Lauren came up between the wagons. "Is that Elias with the baby?" Lauren pushed her thick round glasses up on her nose.

"I didn't drop him or suffocate him or anything." Elias carefully passed the bundle back as the sisters laughed. "Does he have a name yet?" He could feel his body relax with his hands free.

"Not yet." Chrystal shrugged. "I thought I might wait till my husband meets him." Elias had heard of two other infants born and buried already on this trip. He wondered if it was easier to wait. Maybe Lauren was right about waiting till they were settled. He wanted his babies to have a good home. He smiled at Lauren as she cooed over the little bundle in Chrystal's arms, glad she couldn't read his thoughts.

THE WAGON TRAIN circled up later than usual, and the men in each company were told to keep armed at all times. About an hour after dinner, a group of Indians rode into camp. Stopping, they looked over Company C with stoic expressions. Joe, Elias, and two other men approached them.

Elias glanced back to make sure the women and children had stayed inside the wagons. When he turned around, a buck from the back dismounted and jerked a horse forward. It was heavily laden with a dead buffalo. The leader with a fine feather headdress signaled for them to accept it. Joe pursed his lips then blew out a short breath. Carefully, he pulled it onto the ground nodding his thanks to the group. Elias could smell the odor of unwashed bodies and raw meat. "They want to trade," Joe said.

"Maybe blankets?" one of the sodbusters said.

"Not in the summer, Leif."

Joe backed up and invited the chief to sit at Company C's empty campfire. The older Indian with black and gray hair that dangled down the center of his bare back swung off his horse. The Company C men moved back as he walked by feeling the honor and rank he carried. Elias watched as a younger muscular buck searched the camp area. His gut twisted, wishing he knew what he was looking for. Carefully Captain K. and his son Caleb swung from their horses and approached their circle. Caleb had a bottle of whiskey in his hand and gave it to the chief sitting by the fire.

The chief nodded his thanks and seemed to be waiting for more. "Lakota Sioux." Captain K. said, standing next to Elias. "Rumor has it you sold all your ammunition?"

"Yes, sir." Elias never took his eyes off the group still on horseback.

"I would have liked to put a little show on for them." Captain K. chewed on the corner of his thick mustache. "Got anything else you can spare?"

"I've got an extra chain in my jockey box I don't use."

"Perfect, get it." The captain's brow crinkled. The fire popped as Elias moved toward his wagon, his nerves tensing.

"The missus got an extra bolt of fabric," the Reverend said from the shadows of his wagon.

"Yep, bring that, too."

"I got a pouch of tobacco, Cap," another man said.

"Yep, bring that." The captain moved slowly gathering the extra items and taking them to the chief.

The chief stood and looked over the items. He turned and stared at Reverend Little standing near Elias. Elias inconspicuously shifted his feet. Did the chief expect something more from him or was he just curious? Signaling to the group, one of his bucks jumped off the horse and helped carry the items back to the others.

After some discussion among the Indians, the chief mounted his horse. A greased Indian with thick beads around his neck yelled something shaking the bottle of whiskey. Elias watched

Captain K. shake his head no and he raised empty hands. The Indian yelled something back, spitting on the ground. Just when Elias felt the tingle of his finger on the trigger of his rifle, the group yanked on their reins and swung the horses in the direction they had come. Watching them leave, the silence of the camp was filled with relief. Everyone felt the reprieve.

"Let's pull some more buffalo chips together," Joe said to the tense wagon folk. "The faster we can get this meat cooked up, the faster we can turn in."

Lauren huddled on her bench, leaning her shoulder into the returned harpsichord. Gripping her box that held her glasses, she knew she would be no help with only firelight and shadows. She spent the last hour repeating every request to God she could think of. It was going to be a long night for all of them, why not pray for another hour?

Chapter 47

THE MORNING GUNSHOT rang out making Lauren jumped from a nightmare of the wagon train being attacked. She found her box and slipped on her glasses. The clearing of the blur did little to bring reassurance. Last night was close. They all should be thanking God the Indians only wanted to trade. Grabbing her apron, she threw it over her head as Elias lowered the back gate.

"Good morning." His voice was quieter than usual.

"Good morning." Gripping her waist, he lowered her to the ground.

"The coffee beans and the grinder are right here." He placed her hand on the items.

"I know where they are. I put them there each night." She sounded snippy. "I'm sorry. I didn't sleep well."

"I know." He pulled her into his arms. "None of us did. After my watch, I couldn't sleep so I stayed up and talked to the Reverend through his watch."

"Oh Elias, you must be exhausted." She rubbed her hands over his back.

"He's going to talk to Ida Bell. They've been doing underground work for so long, his dream is to have a settled place, maybe a church. We talked about Denver City, not that I know much about it, but they might go with us to check it out."

"Really?" She pulled back. "That would be wonderful. My mother's past letters say everything's growing. Even after the miners all left, they had a terrible flood and fire, but the town's folk are trying their best. I can't really say, but I hope they would be welcome." Her voice trailed off.

That evening around the campfire, a lot of talk and opinions about Denver City flowed. Even Lux and Martin were asking questions. Lauren had been so preoccupied with all the needs of late, she had almost forgotten in two days' time they would be breaking off from the large group.

Chrystal stood up behind her sister-wives swaying the little baby back and forth. Mabel talked with Joe, and Janet did French braids for the little Coolidge girls. Lauren's heart sank lower, watching the blurry images of these dear ones. She had relied on them for her every move, even before the accident. Resting her elbow on her knees, she dropped her chin and looked out over the prairie. A long line of yellow light grew thinner and thinner. These sweet people were her friends. After bathing, washing, meals and the earthen privy, you can't get much closer to folk than what she felt for these dear ladies. Her eyes fluttered closed, and someone pulled on her wrist.

"May I walk you home, Miss?" Elias stood next to her. "Unless you want to sleep here in the dirt?"

Smiling, she rose and bid everyone goodnight. "You're pulling my wrist again."

His hand slid down and intertwined with her fingers. "May I always count on you to remind me?" He pulled their hands up and kissed the back of her hand. They stopped at the back of the wagon, and Lauren sighed.

"I keep forgetting to give this back to you." She let go of his hand and pulled his little trinket from her skirt pocket. Pulling on the pocket of his canvas pants, she let it drop in.

"This feels a bit familiar. Having you reach in my pockets brought me back from the dead."

"I didn't reach in."

"Not this time. But trust me I'll never forget the first time."

"Elias." She shook her head and stepped back.

Grabbing her waist, he pulled her against him. "What is it? Just tell me. You said you wouldn't marry me if you couldn't see." He carefully set her glasses further up her nose. "Did you mean see perfectly?"

"I know you were excited and carefree that night—"

"You don't think I was sincere?"

"No, I mean yes. I think you are truly sincere."

"But you're still not ready?"

"I don't know what to think." She dropped her head against his chest. "Is there a difference between now and a few weeks?" She leaned back to face him. "I just have this rock in my stomach when I picture myself introducing you to my mother. I've never said one thing about you in any letters. How do I explain our meeting, our courtship, our travel together? Have we had a courtship?" Her brows creased.

"You've always cared what everyone thinks." He dropped his hands from her waist. "Humm." Stepping back, he took a deep breath and blew it out.

"Of course I do, she *is* my mother, not just some acquaintance. What if she thinks the worst of me?"

"The more I hear about Denver City, you might be the one who thinks the worst of her."

Lauren flinched. "What are you implying? That is terribly rude to—"

"Good night," he said, already walking away.

THE NEXT TWO nights the group breaking off for Denver City met and talked about the lack of provisions and travel schedule. Lauren's excitement plummeted. Even the sisters got quieter. They knew the time together was ending.

The morning of their departure, Elias still barely spoke to her. Joe approached and dropped a thick hand on his neck rocking his big frame back and forth. He let go of Elias and reached out for Lauren as she set the clean dishes down. "Going to miss you, dear one." He hugged her like a father, making the tears rise. "Take good care of your man."

She hugged him back. "Thank you for everything." A terrible ache squeezed within her chest. Elias looked to the ground—the sisters all stood behind Joe, tears running down all their cheeks.

"I just didn't think this would be so hard." Mabel cried holding her tightly, finally releasing her to Janet's waiting arms.

"We tried to fight off the sadness knowing you will be reunited with family," Janet said, kissing her wet cheek. "We love you like you were one of us, except you have your own husband." They all looked at Janet and laughed through their tears.

"Chrystal and sweet baby." Lauren reached out, noticing he was wrapped in her knitted blanket. "I will miss all of you."

"Utah and Colorado are not that far. We will write and keep in touch." Chrystal sniffed. "I just know God has great things for you and Elias."

Lauren stood back wiping her nose and face in her apron. Each of the sisters hugged Elias like he was a brother, then on to the Littles. The Coolidges huddled together watching the tears and goodbyes. Lauren stepped toward them, feeling the wave of love and tenderness for the six of them.

"No need for such a display." Mrs. Coolidge raised her hand freezing Lauren in stride.

Lux raised a smile. "We've decided to go on to Denver City with you all." He nodded to Elias as he came near. "We had no people waiting in California. You all have given more forbearance and acceptance than any friends we've ever had. If you don't mind, we think we'd like to give Denver City a try."

"We'd love to have you along." Elias reached out and shook his hand. Watching Felicia blink back tears, Lauren wrapped her arms around all four females. "This is wonderful," she whispered.

Chapter 48

THE NEXT WEEK Martin had filled Elias's spot driving their wagon. Without the companionship of the sisters and the little time she had with Elias, the days seem to drag on forever. Little Katherine Coolidge ran next to their wagon and reached out as Martin pulled her up.

"Hello there," Katherine's sweet voice straightened Lauren up. "I'm glad Mr. Browne and Mr. Colder are out protecting us. Indians scare me."

"Me, too." Lauren patted her back as she sat. "Elias likes to be out from the dusty road, I think."

"What's that pattern you're working on?"

Lauren breathed in, trying to appreciate her distractions. "Probably a bunch of knots." She forged a smile, touching the yarn.

"No, it looks like something. Can you teach me?"

Pushing her glasses up on her nose, she set aside her melancholy and tried to remember how her mother taught her to knit.

THE EVENING ENCAMPMENT sounds diminished. Camp sounds that used to be loud and raucous like a large band coming down Main

Street now waned to a single instrument. Without the bustle of the large wagon train, the Colorado landscape seemed larger. Elias had gotten into the habit of catching some sleep right after dinner and waking for the first watch. The Coolidges had their fine tent, and when the Littles rose to retire, Lauren bid everyone goodnight, too. Ida Bell graciously took her arm and helped her to the wagon.

"Ida Bell? Do you think it does any good to worry about what other people think?"

"That's too big a question. What do you really want to know?" She unlatched the wagon gate.

Lauren sucked in a long breath. "I'm fretful over seeing my mother." She blew it out. "I've never written her anything about Elias."

"You don't think she'll approve of him? As long as he's good to you, I can't see the bother."

"Elias thinks I care too much what everyone thinks of me. I know he's right. I've always been like that."

"I think I was about your age, been kicked around enough to lose hope in people. Must have been Jesus," she chuckled, "cause I started to believe in myself over what them were sayin'. You might be about ready, too. Maybe you could believe and trust yourself 'cause the Lord he done lives inside you. What else you waiting for?"

Lauren felt the question from her head to her toes.

"Besides all that judgment and guilt you rehearsin', that's just the devil trying to get you to chase your tail. *What if* they thinkin' this, or *what ifs* they thinkin' that. This er that. Harumph." She rambled, holding Lauren's elbow as she climbed in. "I'm old and got to get to bed. Our Jesus done shows us what He thinks of us each morning. We's got breath and light from the sun risin', giftin' us with a new day, I fall asleep each night with that comfort."

"Thank you, Ida Bell. I look forward to introducing you to my mother."

"Humph." Ida Bell squeaked. "Won't that be somethin'?"

THE LAST LEG into Denver City and the sun beat down like a torch. Far away a range of huge snow-covered mountains loomed. Lauren wished she could see clearer, were there any little farms or ranches to be seen? How she missed the sisters and their walks, so many sights seen through their eyes.

Her backside ached, and their water was so low, she wondered if Elias could find some soon. Pulling her bonnet off, she moaned, trying to fan her face. Without the sisters' help to bathe and wash, she could hardly stand her own odor. "The first day out and the last day in are the worst," she remembered Joe saying. The man knew what he was talking about.

Elias rode up next to Martin. "I've asked every-one, since supplies are so low, they all want to push straight through supper and get into Denver City. Can you do that?"

Martin agreed, and Lauren couldn't tell if he looked her way. Missing their closeness, tears started to form. She stood to climb back to her bench, maybe she could find some dried bread.

"Lauren." His voice now on her side of the wagon bench, startled her. "Do you want to ride with me?"

"All right." She wiped her sleeve across her face.

"Martin keep your eyes on the road now. There might be some sweet woman's leg that you are too young to see."

Martin snickered. "Yes, sir."

"Hike your skirt up and give me your arm, Lauren."

Lauren was about to change her mind when he grabbed her arm and pulled her onto the back of the horse.

She grabbed his waist and caught her glasses from sliding down her nose. The horse was as hot and sweaty as she was.

"You okay?" He led the horse between the wagons and out from the road. Closing her eyes, she felt a small breeze. "Better, thank you."

"We should be in Denver City by dark. Do you have an address? I'm sure we can find it."

"I don't know." She tried to loosen her grip on him. His shirt was wet from the heat.

"You don't know the address, or you don't know if you want to do this. Thinking you might want to turn around and go back to Greenlock?"

"Oh, heaven's no." She wasn't in the spirit for his jokes, but at least they were talking. "I have the address. My mother had an uncle who never married or had children. It's really his home. He passed away about a year after she moved."

"Think about it, Lauren, you could be asleep in a real bed tonight."

"And what about you?" Did she mean to say that out loud?

"I will be with my wagon people or soaking in a cold creek somewhere."

"But you don't like cold water."

"Maybe you could leave me an extra blanket, one that smells like you. As long as that harpsichord is gone."

"Elias, please." She dropped her forehead on his back. "I can't do this. Can we just stay at camp tonight? Maybe I won't be able to get any sleep, but I need a bath and clean clothes."

"It's up to you. I think you look beautiful. Those little round glasses make you more adorable. But, I understand, gettin' the trail off ya."

"Then you will go with me to meet everyone? In the morning?"

"How will you . . ." he turned in the creaking saddle, looking at her, ". . . introduce me?"

"Do you still want to marry me?" she whispered, looking down at her leg next to his.

His jaw twitched. "With everything in me."

That calm voice. Suddenly she was sitting on a box in her pantry in Greenlock. Their first conversations marking her forever. "Then we are engaged or betrothed. Is that okay for me to say?"

"As long as it's the truth. The time is up on living the lie."

Chapter 49

LAUREN REDID HER bun for the fifth time waiting outside their wagon the next morning. Elias approached, clean and neat, wearing the shirt that Mabel had helped her finish.

"Ready?"

She gave him a weary smile, trying to remember something Ida Bell had said about believing and trusting herself. "The Lord lives in me," she whispered, fanning her face against the rising summer heat. "The house is on B Street. I couldn't make out streets in the dark last night."

"I'm guessing it's not far from A Street. Do you want to walk or ride?"

"Let's walk." She gripped his elbow. "Do I look okay?" He led her across a field toward the small town.

"You look beautiful."

"I know that's not true. These boots, this skirt's almost threadbare."

"Those boots have walked across about six or seven states. She'll understand." He patted her hand as a large wagon full of goods drove by them. "There looks to be a lot of building and hardworking folks here. Maybe they have a bakery like Indianapolis. We could walk to the end and—"

"No, I couldn't eat anything," she snapped. "I'm sorry. Maybe later?"

"Sure, I see a sign for A street, let's cross here."

Lauren was thankful for the glasses from the fort doctor. They truly had been helping her see, but to really see her mother's face and Cammi . . . she felt her throat tighten. Walking by a row of homes, the noise of Denver City faded a bit.

"B Street, Lovely Lauren, we are close now."

"Wait." She pulled her arm free, trying to breathe in deeps breath. "Will you hold something for me?"

"Of course." He rubbed the tension in her neck.

She slipped the gold band off her finger and handed it to him. "Just for a short while?"

"I'll take it only if you kiss me."

The corners of her smile rose as he placed a soft kiss on her lips. Her hands rose up his thick solid arms, body and soul missing these sweet moments. Tingling, he pulled her closer, deepening the kiss and embrace until embarrassed, she pulled away. "You know I can't see if there are people watching."

"I just don't want you to forget how much I love you."

"I could never forget what we have. I promise."

• • •

"THIS IS IT." Elias instinctively went to pull his hat off and realized he wasn't wearing it. "Now, you've got me nervous."

Lauren went to knock on the door, but stopped and waved her fingers in the air.

"There's a sign in the window; it says this is a boarding house," he said.

Lauren finally knocked, shook her head and puffed out a breath. "Does my hair look okay?"

"Did you hear what I—" The door swung open and a middle-aged woman with a pale blue flowered dress looked at them.

"May I help you?"

Lauren pushed up her glasses and squinted, awkward silence hung in the air.

"Are you Mrs. Campbell?" Elias asked.

"Yes, are you looking for a room?"

Elias glanced at Lauren, her mouth hung open, but no sound came out.

"No, ma'am. I'm Elias Browne, and this is Lauren Campbell, your daughter?" The woman grimaced and jerked her head quickly to the side.

"My Lauren?"

With a shaking hand, Lauren removed her glasses and folded the wire ear holders down. "Yes, have I changed that much?"

"Yes. No—I-I got your letter so long ago. I think I am in shock." She finally stepped from the threshold and wrapped her arms around Lauren.

"Yes, yes, of course, it's you. You're so thin and tan, you poor thing. Please, please come in." She stepped back as they entered a foyer with dark rugs and brown settee. A long table with tall chairs was to the right.

Mrs. Campbell looked Lauren up and down. "Something's wrong dear, you look about to cry."

"I—can't really see you without my glasses. I'm not sure. They are not really mine." She opened them and slid them on. "I got them at Fort Kearney, probably off some poor soldier who died."

Elias wondered if she could see her mother's eyes widen, it was probably a bit too much information. "And so you can see better now," he tried to help with explanations.

"Yes, yes." Lauren stumbled. "You look well, Mother, is Cammi home?"

"Please, please have a seat." Her mother pointed to the settee. "I'll get us some tea." Her skirts swished down the center hall.

Elias grabbed her arm to sit. "It's a nice home. Stairs here in front of us and nice wood." He looked out the front window. "Nice street, flowers and—" he turned and Lauren stood as someone bounded down the stairs.

"Hello." The young woman nodded and turned the corner. Hopefully, that was not Cammi, Lauren didn't fare well not to be remembered.

"Mrs. Campbell, I'm off to work," she called

and lifted her bonnet from the hall tree. Elias nodded and wondered if he should open the door. She smiled at him as she left, and he turned to see Mrs. Campbell balancing a tray as she came toward him.

"Here, let me take that for you."

"Thank you. You can set it on the serving tray here."

They all stood still looking back and forth at each other.

"Please," she gestured for them to sit, "forgive me." Mrs. Campbell went to pour the tea. "What was your name again?"

Elias frowned, taking the little flowery cup and saucer from her. Like holding a tiny baby, his rough hands looked completely out of place. "Elias Browne, ma'am. Lauren and I know each other from Greenlock."

"Oh, I see." She handed Lauren a matching cup and saucer, and Lauren sat.

"We left Greenlock over three months ago." He tried a faint grin, hoping Lauren couldn't see her mother's true facial expression. Hearing the stiffness in her voice, was enough.

"Umm hum and a few weeks." Lauren blew out a long breath. "I had my heart set on bringing you a few family things. I've brought your dishes and grandmother's harpsichord."

"No. All the way from Ohio?"

"Many people bid Lauren to give it up. But she

never did." Elias took a sip of the watery tea.

"It, unfortunately, has a bit of water damage from a heavy rainstorm. Maybe there's someone here in Denver City who could fix it." Lauren swallowed.

"That old thing wasn't worth much anyway. I thought your father could use it for the funerals." Her mother's voice was curt.

Elias watched Lauren crumple, gripping the teacup in her lap. All the effort and discomfort to bring it this far, a familiar desperation hung from her face. Her shoulders shuddered and she straighten her back. "You never said if Cammi was here."

"Cammi is married and gone."

"What?" Lauren squeaked. "You never said anything in your letters."

"Probably because I hoped she would change her mind, she only knew him a few months." Mrs. Campbell shook her head. "I'm sure she wrote to you, but it sounds like you've been gone so long, it never got to you."

Lauren gazed out the front window, and Elias set the little cup and saucer on the tray. Unfortunately, he sensed her earlier fears were coming to pass. "Maybe I should go get the things you brought, do you have room for Lauren here?" Lauren stilled, eyeing him like he had just traded her to the Indians.

"Of course. I run a boarding home for respectable young women. Miss Call, who just left, she has an extra bed in her room."

"I don't want to be any bother, Mother." Lauren rose and set her cup down.

"Nonsense, I haven't seen you in over two years. A warm bath and proper clothing, you'll feel and look like a new Lauren."

Elias felt the room go stuffy along with an overwhelming desire to be outside again. Now he saw why Lauren cared about what people thought. Did all mothers do this to their children? Or maybe Mrs. Campbell had had to be tough to survive. He hoped Lauren wouldn't bring up their plans to marry. Not today anyway. He watched her closely until he saw her give him a small shake of her head. "Good. I'll go then," he took a step towards her to touch her but stopped and turned back to the door, "and see how everyone is doing."

"The boarders eat around five, come back for supper at six."

"Yes, ma'am." Blast it, he reached for his hat again and scratched his head instead.

Chapter 50

LIKE A WET-EARED pup, Elias nervously pushed his unkempt hair down. Standing in front of Lauren's mother's door at six sharp, he willed himself not to sweat. At least with the Indian visit, he had a gun in his hand. Before he could knock, Lauren opened the door and held it close behind her. She'd donned a pretty pink dress with a soft bun higher on her head. Little whispy curls laid even on both sides on her ears.

"I know, I know, my mother insisted. She believes my glasses had three months of dirt on them. I wanted to tell her I haven't had them that long." She popped up on her toes and kissed him quickly. "She wants the things on the back porch, can you bring the team down the back alley?"

"Yes, but I'm hungry." *Or another sweet kiss from this pretty gal would suffice.*

"Good, I'll meet you by the back door."

Grumbling at the heat of the early evening, he wiped the unwanted sweat from his brow. At last these things had returned home. Standing back, he shook his head at the small porch holding the crate of dishes and warped harpsichord. A miracle they had made it. In the back window of the house, three young women watched him, whispering and smiling to each other. Had they never seen a harpsichord before?

Lauren opened the door and walked him back into the formal room with the table and tall chairs. Her mother nodded to him, and he noticed she had a different dress on. He did take another soak in the river, was he supposed to change his clothes, too?

They all sat in unison, and a young woman from the window came in and placed a bowl of soup in front of each of them. She had such a sweet smile for him he almost dared to ask if this was it for the meal. Giving Lauren a frown, he wondered, out of all these chairs if she could sit beside him.

"Do you pray, Mr. Browne?"

"Yes, ma'am," he said, confidently, bowing his head. "Lord, we thank you for bringing us here safe and sound. We pray for our friends that you would watch over all their travels. Bless this meal and all . . . the . . . peop . . . ladies who live here." Sure enough, he lifted one eye, the same three faces hung off the kitchen door frame watching them. "Ah, Amen."

"I was able to tell my mother about the wonderful people we traveled with."

"And I shared some of the stories from when Cammi and I took trains and stages to get here," Mrs. Campbell said.

"Are you originally from Greenlock, Mr. Browne? I might know some of your people." She held her spoon in midair.

"No, ma'am." His sip of soup was like swallowing air, and his stomach growled.

"Where do your people hail from?"

Glancing up, Lauren rubbed her brows.

"Pennsylvania."

"What did your father do there?"

"I never met my father and my mother passed when I was about three." He looked toward the kitchen door; it sounded like plates rattling. Unbuttoning the top button on the shirt Lauren had made him, the room without a window had become stifling.

"Oh, how very sad. Who took you in?"

Thankfully a plate of peppered chicken pieces came in with mashed potatoes and fresh green beans. The aroma caused his mouth to water. *What had she asked?* Picking up a fork and knife he smiled, trying to lighten Lauren's stoic expression.

"I grew up in a, ah, home for children." Taking a bite off his fork, his eyes almost rolled in the back of his head. The potatoes were worth a hundred dollars, he hadn't had fresh butter in so long.

"And how did you end up in Greenlock?"

Did this woman realize this was the best meal he'd had in months? Conversation had no place in this moment of bliss. "Ah, business. I met Lauren in the hardware store."

"He teased me about something." Lauren looked down. "I didn't know what to think."

"She didn't want anything to do with me." He swallowed another savory bite. "My hair—"

Lauren choked and grabbed her glass of water.

"Anyway, we both were interested in catching the wagon train. My sights were on California, Lauren only had sights for here."

"So then you are here to drop her off and head on to California?"

"No, ma'am." He tried the chicken. It melted in his mouth. "I'm staying here." He stared at Lauren. This was her mother. His timing to talk about their plans might be off.

Lauren speared a green bean. "These are wonderful; vegetables were hard to come by on the—"

"How do you feel about my daughter, Mr. Browne?"

Elias bristled. Her tone was like talking to the staunch Mrs. Coolidge. "What do you mean?"

"I know my daughter skirted around the issue all day, so I might as well ask you."

"Mother, I didn't skirt." Lauren dropped her napkin next to her plate. "I just haven't seen you in so long. I wanted to hear about you, and Uncle Ross's passing, and how you started this business, and how Cammi liked it here. I'm not even mad about you leaving father. I admire your ability to set a new course. That's what I have done."

"With a handsome, strong beau to travel with?" Mrs. Campbell dropped her chin.

"You're making it sound as if Lauren has done something wrong." Elias reeled in his strained tone. "She has done nothing but withstand hardship, and change, and tragedy. She cares and loves others, she works hard, and smiles, and sees the best in people. I'm the one who couldn't make it without her."

"So you sound like you admire her." Mrs. Campbell pursed her lips.

"I admire her, and I love her."

The loud clank of a metal pan hitting the floor came from the kitchen.

"Maybe I should see if they need any help." Elias rose.

"No," Lauren and her mother said simultaneously.

Lauren took a deep breath. "We were acquaintances in Greenlock. We traveled with the group I told you about. And through the weeks together we fell in love." She touched her napkin carefully to the sides of her mouth. It was like looking at the same Lauren, but the room and clothes tried to confuse him. His first purpose was to see her to this place. Was it right for him to come in and change everything for them? Lauren looked ready to cry.

"As you can imagine, living estranged in my marriage is something no woman wants to do. I have a protective stance when it comes to my daughter's choices. I wish someone would have pulled me aside. I am not a mother that hurries her daughters to the altar."

"You need to remember, I have been a young woman without a mother," Lauren said delicately, her eyes pooling.

"Exactly, for what you've said about your father, I feel you have been remiss without any guidance. Allowing you to run the funeral home, dressing the dead is—well, it is just appalling. I'm furious when I think about how obscene—"

"Please, Mother." Lauren stood. "The work, like what I told you about Father Michael, was my gift to them." She bowed her head gripping the back of her chair with white knuckles. "My torment was living in a town worrying day and night about what people thought of me—and to find out that those lies even went with me on the wagon train." She breathed out a smile at Elias, a warm understanding in her eyes only he could read.

Mrs. Campbell rose. Lauren tilted her head at Elias. He rose quickly and tried to help her with her chair.

"No, no. I'm already up. But may I have a private word with you?"

"Yes," he said, glancing at Lauren's crumbling expression. He followed Mrs. Campbell back through the kitchen, suffered the other ladies' stares, and out the back door. He suddenly grew uncomfortable, like the many times he'd been taken somewhere against his will.

"I want to thank you for the safe delivery of my daughter and these things."

Elias nodded, finally breathing in the cooler dusk air.

"But if you love her as you say, you'll need to show me." Her cool tone made his back straighten.

"You have had her to yourself these last months. I want two months with her to myself. I don't want you to contact her or sway her in any way. In fact, I'd like you to take the wagon away from town. If you want to live here, you will find a job and a home for my daughter. I can tell by our conversation tonight, that she won't agree to this. So I'm going to ask you to leave now."

Chapter 51

L AUREN WRUNG HER hands and watched out the front parlor window. Her mother and she were separated for the first time in a month. Taking a pie to a sick neighbor, her mother had gone out without her. She stood and went out the front door watching her deep blue dress round the corner.

Taking her to the only doctor in town that treated people with eye problems, her protective mother may not have thought that through. Her first week with her new glasses had brought another level of clarity to her vision. Never before would she have gone out on her own, now she debated on which way to walk and how much time she would have. At the end of her street, a familiar couple came toward her. Could it be? Was it Martin and Felicia? Were her new glasses playing a trick? She stepped toward them until with true clarity she ran into their arms. "Oh, my goodness, how I have missed all of you." They hugged.

"You have been greatly missed also." They smiled and patted her back. "I love your dress and your new glasses." Felicia squeezed her arm. "You look so different."

"Oh please, it's the same me." Lauren couldn't stop smiling; it was like finding long lost family.

"I've got an errand to run," Martin said. "Would it be all right, Mrs. Browne, I mean, Miss Campbell, to leave Felicia with you for a while?"

"There's nothing I would love more. That is my home with the white trim." She pointed. "We'll be there." She linked arms with Felicia. "How is your family doing?" *Did Martin just call me Miss Campbell?* They walked to her home. Felicia smelled a bit like campfire. Were they all still together?

"First thing, I promised like fifty times," Felicia giggled, "to tell you. Elias is here. He has not gone anywhere. There, sometimes it's funny to see such a big handsome fellow fret so."

"I thank you. I've probably thought of him fifty times an hour. He probably told you what my mother asked. I understand her reasoning, she wants time with me, but I think I would rather walk the wagon trail again than be without him." Lauren opened the front door, and they took a seat in the parlor. "Can I get you some tea or lemonade?"

"Ooh, lemonade would be wonderful. Your home is beautiful."

Lauren rushed to the kitchen, her heart pounding to hear the news of late. Handing Felicia the glass, she wondered what to ask first. "Did Martin call me Miss Campbell?"

Felicia smiled enjoying her drink. "Yes, Mr. Browne told all of us that you were not really married."

Lauren sat, slumping back against her chair. "He did?" She wasn't sure how she felt about that. Her new corset constricted her breathing. What would they all think of her? She caught hold of her sinking thoughts.

"Everyone understands. We always wondered why he slept under your wagon."

"Humm." Lauren squeaked. "We didn't know any of you. The more we grew together, the more it felt wrong to keep such a falsehood."

"I know, believe me, my parents didn't tell ya'll everything either." Felicia drank her lemonade.

Lauren had missed her sweet southern accent. Rising, she looked out the window for her mother. "And the Littles? How are they faring?"

"Well. I think Denver City agrees with them. Elias found a rundown building with a shanty attached. He bought it and is helping them fix it up. They want to have the first mixed colored church here. Mrs. Little says she just wants a real bed and a real stove and she'll feel like she's gone to heaven. Everything in town has to be built with brick. Everyone from Ohio agree that that old muddy Platte River's finally good for something."

Lauren remembered trying to separate the water from the silt. This month with her mother felt like she'd been dropped into a different life.

"And your parents? How's your mother doing?"

"Good. Martin got a job at the newspaper the first week. We found a little house to rent. There's a school over on Elm that my sisters will go to. We've been busy setting up house. I saw my mother smile, so I think she's doing well. I'm not sure we will ever try to raise dogs again. Elias is helping my father with a store or business on Main Street. I'm not sure what kind but things are looking up here. And the mountains are beautiful. I'm happy to be gone from the south."

Lauren smiled and looked down at her mother's fine carpet. It sounded like Elias was busy helping everyone. Stability was something he'd never known. Maybe he didn't know how to provide it for himself or their future? Had anyone told him how cold it gets here?

Martin returned before her mother and, though difficult to say goodbye, she felt relieved not to have to explain what felt like another lifetime. Felicia agreed to come back with her mother as soon as possible. Waving goodbye, she stood, watching them walk away and sighed.

All she had previously wanted was to see her mother and Cammi, but how fickle she was. Now all she wanted was to go back in time. Many nights she dreamed of the Mormon sisters reuniting with their children—how overjoyed they all must be to be together again. They often talked fondly of their husband. Did he understand what strong wonderful wives he had? She wondered if Chrystal's baby had a name yet or whether Mabel's oldest daughter had married. Picturing the Ohio friends sitting around the campfire, she sighed. The journey was the hardest thing she had ever done, and yet their time together brought so much life, filling the corners of her soul. But Elias, stirred her heart like nothing else.

She smiled at the envelope from Felicia in her hand. Elias had written it and it tried to melt in her hand. Quickly, she hiked her dress and jogged up the stairs. Only a private moment with no interruptions would work. Four weeks without word had tried to play tricks with her confidence. Without her mother's constant care and frivolities, the isolation wanted to claim her just like her days in Greenlock. She held the letter to her heart and prayed a simple prayer.

Before she opened the paper, she flashed to him lying on the ice bed in the funeral home basement. He frightened and compelled her at the same time. Drawn to his calm voice wrapped in a barbarian body, he was like that silly coin wrapped in an old wrapper. Funny the things that hold value to the right person. If her mother only knew his past, the shock would send her reeling. She unfolded the paper and squeezed her eyes shut. Maybe love makes us all reckless—reckless enough to believe the best, see the best and hope for the best. She was not the same uncertain Lauren who had run away from home. She held her arm outstretched to the bright sunlight able to read the uneven script of her betrothed.

Dearest, Lovely Lauren,
I've asked Feleesha to read you this.

She smiled and thought how he must have labored to write this note and she was thankful to have this moment to herself. She touched each dear, little, misspelled word.

Thow dificult on my heart, body and intnsions. I will abide by your mother's wishes not to come to you. I can obey hoping someday she will acept me as family.

Family. The word sank into her comfort, like she sank into the real mattress she slept on.

I have been busy helping the Littles get setled. Their new church shoud be ready when we are reunited. Would you like to be married there?

"Yes," she whispered, a lone tear falling on the paper she'd brought to her lap.

Your mother's demand has ended up being a good thing for me. With Martin's job at the paper, and wanting to keep busy, I've found some investmnts to make. Who knew I would be good at buying and selling? And none of these things xplode, you will be releeved to know. Lux will oversee them. I pplied for an abandoned land grant and got it. One hunderd and sixty acres.

I've timed it from the front acre to town, it's only twenty-five mintes by horse.

His crooked handwriting made her love him more.

The Rocky Mountains at the flank will take your brath away. It has an old soddy on it, but I already have a plan for the home I will build. I'd like to rase horses and, if it's okay with you, someday bring the Littles to live there when they need the help.

Four or five more tears dropped onto her lap.

These are just the things I've been doing this month without you. I hope your mother will aprove, but more than anything I care about what you think. My heart belongs to you. My plans are nuthing without you. I would like to say more, but Felicia may not want to hear my words of indearment, so I will save them for when I see you.

I love you more than warm blankets,
Elias

Lauren fell back onto her bed, clutching his thoughts to her heart; misspelled words making her croon. Four more weeks, with all that he was doing for them, what could she do for him?

Chapter 52

LAUREN, PLEASE." HER mother leaned into the parlor. "You've been up since dawn. I didn't give him a time, but I would hope he would not come until supper. Looking out the window every five minutes is going to make a long day." The other three boarders came downstairs where Mrs. Campbell had laid out pancakes and coffee. Lauren pulled away to join them.

"I don't know how you did it, Lauren," one of them commented. "Two months, whew."

"By any chance, does he have a brother coming out this way?" They all stopped chewing and shared a laugh. Even her mother shared a chuckle.

"No, but I do know of a nice young man who works at the newspaper." Lauren smiled.

"Enough excitement for one morning." Mrs. Campbell raised her hand.

A heavy knock sounded on the door, and all four young ladies jumped from their chairs. "It's him!"

"Sit, sit, ladies, please." Mrs. Campbell shook her head. "It's probably the milkman, collecting.

Lauren could not stay seated. Nothing in her body would cooperate. As soon as her mother stepped back from opening the door, her heart leaped to her throat. Elias peeked around the door holding a bouquet of blue and red flowers. A chorus of sighs came from the table. Her new glasses must be working. He looked so good, tangibly good. Shaved and clean, looking proud in the shirt she had made him. Hair neat and combed, his smile made her tingle from head to toe. Without an audience, she would have plowed into his arms.

"Mr. Browne, you have returned," her mother closed the door, "to my Lauren's delight. Would you care for some coffee, breakfast?"

"No, ma'am." He handed the flowers to Lauren. More sighs sang from the table, as Elias and Lauren stared at each other.

Mrs. Campbell cleared her throat. "Maybe you and Mr. Browne could catch up in the parlor while we finish?"

Lauren floated into the parlor, feeling his hand like fire on the small of her back.

They sat and she held the flowers on her lap. "These are lovely. Thank you." Why was she struggling to look him in the eye? They were not strangers by any means. Her lungs were fraught, fighting for enough air. He smelled so good.

"You look more beautiful than ever. I'm glad your time here was needed."

"Is my time here about to conclude?" She met his soft blue eyes, offering warm smiles.

"I hope so." He looked over to the dining room. "Is there anything else I have to do?"

"You still got a preacher?"

"I do." He nodded.

"Still got a ring?"

"Yes, I do." His smile rising. "And I have a church. Pews and everything."

"How about we meet there on Saturday? Maybe invite our friends and family?"

"I think I am free Saturday." He shrugged, holding back a crooked grin. "Say, maybe, one o'clock. It's the church four doors down from the," he paused dramatically, "hardware store."

"Just as long as it's not next to a funeral parlor." She coyly dropped her chin, her eyes smiling up at him.

"Fair enough, I will see you then." He stood, still grinning. "Goodbye ladies, Mrs. Campbell." He waved into the dining room. "See you all Saturday."

Lauren closed the door behind him and leaned against it. His presence still making her knees quiver.

SATURDAY AT ONE o'clock and maybe ten extra minutes, Elias stood in the front of the church building with Ida Bell. The new pine floors still smelled like a lumber yard and a small afternoon breeze floated between raised windows. Lauren's mother appeared at the front door and gave him a quick smile. Walking slowly to the front, she sat on the front pew. Elias grinned at the Coolidge family smiling back at him. Lauren's sister and her husband and the roommates were smiling on the other side of the aisle. The Reverend appeared at the back door with the most beautiful vision Elias could imagine. Except, he never could have imagined what it would do to him to see those bright round eyes and a flowing beauty in a new dress and veil. How could this gift be for him?

Rolling his lips, he shook his head but couldn't fight the emotions. This had to be the great love of God. Love that he didn't know was possible. He should be disqualified from birth, yet here he stood with a veiled dream coming toward him. He swiped his wet cheeks with his thumb. Through the soft lace, their eyes met, and he saw everything he'd ever wanted. "How good is God?" he whispered to Ida Bell reaching out to take Lauren's gloved hand.

"I WOULD HAVE been happy to be alone with you in the wagon." Lauren rubbed his back as he opened the door of the Denver City hotel room. She walked in. The soft white curtains billowed in the evening breeze and large brass bed loomed in the middle of the room. Elias struck a match and lit the lantern. "As long as we are really married. I'd be happy anywhere."

"But then, this is nice," she said, nodding to the bed, a sheepish grin covering her face.

He set their things down and looked around the room. "I've dreamed of this for months and now I feel, well, embarrassed, like we just met or something. Remember in the beginning, you would never look at me?" He chuckled. "That was forever ago."

"And now I can't stop looking at you." She winked running her hand over the large bed. "This room is vastly different from our wagon train days." She turned, pulling back the covers. "Are you okay, if tonight we don't need a blanket?" She set her glasses on the side table.

He squinted at her teasing and came up behind her, undoing the little buttons down the back of her soft white dress. "From the minute you got me off that ice table, I've never really been cold. Everything about you covers me in warmth." Placing tender kisses up her neck, he tugged the dress to the floor. She turned to him, and her little chemise strap slipped off her shoulder. Running his finger down her soft skin made him lose his bearings. "I love you so much." His lips pressed against her ear.

She reached up and removed the pins until her hair fell around her shoulders. "I love you and will always be good to you, no matter what." She ran her fingers through his soft hair.

Mind and body stilled and surged at the same time until he found her lips. Long and slow, fast and hungry, each kiss making up for weeks apart. The breeze, like the open door of freedom, entered the room as he welcomed his lovely Lauren into their future.

Epilogue

Six months later

LAUREN MOVED HER growing belly back from the heat. Her wonderful stove that Elias had waiting for her at their new home had been a challenge and a blessing. She had a new appreciation for Chrystal and her endurance to cross the country pregnant. Her letter from the sisters last month had delighted her. Little baby Cody had found a name and a large group of siblings had been waiting desperately for their mothers to arrive. She stirred the stew and peeked in the oven door to see the rolls.

"Something smells wonderful," Elias said before he had a chance to close the front door and hang his jacket. "I saw some snowflakes outside."

"Really?" Lauren stepped back and greeted him with a kiss. "Thank you for bringing my mother for the day and taking her home." Smiling, she tried not to blurt out the news that came with the mail her mother had brought.

"How's my baby?" He reached under her apron and rubbed her belly.

"Probably a bit too warm, this stove can put out the heat."

"Go sit down, I'll see to supper."

Lauren sat a few steps away at their little table and propped her feet up on another chair. "My mother brought some mail."

"Another letter from the sisters?"

"No. First Cammi wrote my mother and me. They are expecting, too."

"That's wonderful—cousins." Elias brought the spoon up to his mouth and blew on the steaming stew. "The mother who didn't want anyone rushing to the altar is awfully delighted to be a grandmother." He took a careful bite.

"She is. You should see the little things she brought today. Mother can be here with me for the delivery, and then a few months later she's already planning to travel to Pueblo to be with Cammi. Then," she waited till Elias turned to her, "she also received a letter from my father, he's hinting about making a trip out here."

"Whoa, what do you think of that?"

"I don't know, I'm a bit shocked and hopeful. His letter to me sounded like he had quit drinking." She sighed. "But I don't know. I often still feel bad for the state I left him in."

"What if your leaving was the very thing that made him take a second look at his life. I'm no Reverend Little, but he insists that God uses everything for our good." He grabbed a rag and pulled out the browned rolls. "I dropped off those cookies you made for them; they said to tell you thank you." He quickly popped the rolls into a little basket and set them on the table. Grabbing two bowls, he scooped up the stew and set it on the table with two spoons. "You're smiling like when you found out about the baby. Is this about the possibility of your father coming here?"

"No, I'm waiting until you sit down." She'd been known to easily cry these last few months, and it was starting again.

"Hey." Elias sat and touched her arm. "One minute smiling, the next minute tears."

"Did I tell you this morning I love you?" she asked, throat tight.

"I believe you did, Mrs. Browne." He dabbed a tear off her face.

"I have one more letter." She pulled it from her pocket and slid it over next to his bowl. "When we were apart those two months?" She swallowed. "I did something. I was just so moved by all that you had done for me. It didn't take me long to want to do something really special for you."

"Love, if you only knew, you already have." He leaned over the table and kissed her.

"It was such a long shot, that I didn't want to say anything." Her throat sucked in a sob. "But I wrote to the Lennhurst Asylum Hospital and School for Disabled Children in Brown Township. Pennsylvania. Right?"

He skeptically nodded his head.

"I couldn't ask you who to address it to, so I wrote about eight letters. I addressed one to the chaplain, one to the asylum secretary, one to the head nurse, one to the headmaster, and one to the back row supervisor. Maybe one to the custodian." She laughed quietly and took a deep breath, watching his confusion. "I asked them all the same question. Did they have any information on the young woman named Anna who had been a patient, but like a worker there, sometime before the war? I asked them to forward me her address."

Elias looked down to the envelope. "Are you serious, Lauren?"

"I am. And this came today. My mother brought it. I took a peek. It's Anna's address. She lives in Kentucky, Centerville. It has her married name, too."

"I-I can't believe you went to all this trouble." He opened the envelope and scanned the letter. "I'm speechless." His eyes misted. "I," his voice held sincere awe, "don't know what to say."

"Think of her joy, Elias, when she receives a letter from you. Maybe you should include the little birthday trinket."

"Joy and shock." He smiled, wiping his sleeve across his damp face. "All the goodness and love she invested in me is the only good I had growing up."

"Then, if it's okay with you, I might have to

sneak a little thank you note in your next letter."
Slipping her glasses off, she reached over and
ran her fingers through his hair. Locking eyes
on each other, a familiar blanket of love and of
gratitude covered them again.

Author's Note

For around 15 years our family took in foster kids. Thankfully, at this time in history, the displaced and crisis-stricken children ended up in a home over an asylum. Since I believe my stories for a moment of needed escape, I didn't go into too much detail of the depravity those places were really like. But here is what I do know about children. They are amazingly resilient. They could come from abuse, neglect, and trauma and still get up in the morning with a sliver of hope that something good was going to be theirs. Teachers, teacher's aides, Sunday school leaders, coaches, therapist, neighbor families . . . it's already been said, but loving a child does take a village. Anna was just being Anna, but she marked Elias with love and belonging. He could have gone up or down. Resilience and simple love won in his life.

One of my little foster girls was a nighttime hair plucker. I'd often do her hair into two pony tails, but one side was thick and one thin. I knew she laid on her pillow, probably facing the door and plucked to release anxiety at night. I asked Jesus how to help her. More counselling, maybe a reward for good behavior, but the Lord showed me some yarn. I tied a piece of fuzzy yarn to her headboard and told her she could twist, pull or finger it all night. It worked. (Along with many others things securing her life—like her adoption into our family).

The scripture says in 1st Peter, *to love deeply.* Don't let that ever get in your way. Simple is deep. A season is deep love. We can never predict how God will use us. Just that He does and it's amazing.

Blessings,
Julia

If you're considering fostering or adoption
I wrote my "helps" out on a little website:
http//:www.Adoption202.com.

Love to have you swing by.
Please visit https://www.juliadwrites.com/
Blogs, Newsletter (new book notices)/Giveaways.

Books are produced in the United States using U.S.-based materials

Books are printed using a revolutionary new process called THINKtech™ that lowers energy usage by 70% and increases overall quality

Books are durable and flexible because of Smyth-sewing

Paper is sourced using environmentally responsible foresting methods and the paper is acid-free

Center Point Large Print

600 Brooks Road / PO Box 1
Thorndike, ME 04986-0001 USA

(207) 568-3717

US & Canada:
1 800 929-9108
www.centerpointlargeprint.com